I0746393

Stories of Crime & Detection

Volume Four

They Can't Hang Me

James Ronald

Edited by Chris Verner

 Moonstone Press

This edition published in 2024 by Moonstone Press
www.moonstonepress.co.uk

Introduction and About the Author © 2023 Chris Verner

They Can't Hang Me originally published in 1938 by Rich & Cowan
The Man Who Came Back originally published in 1934 by Gramol
Accident originally published in 1932 by *20-Story Magazine*
Out of the Fog originally published in 1933 by *The Australasian*

Stories of Crime and Detection, Vol IV: They Can't Hang Me © 2024 the
Estate of James Ronald.
The right of James Ronald to be identified as author of this work has been
asserted in accordance with the Copyright, Designs and Patents Act 1988

ISBN 978-1-899000-72-2
eISBN 978-1-899000-73-9

A CIP catalogue record for this book is available from the British Library
Text designed and typeset by Moonstone Press
Cover illustration by Jason Anscomb
Printed and bound by CPI Group (UK) Ltd, Croydon CR0 4YY

Royalties from the sale of this book will be donated to MND Scotland,
who fund ground-breaking MND (motor neurone disease) research and
world-class clinical trials to combat an uncommon condition that affects
the brain and nerves, and causes weakness that gets worse over time,
eventually resulting in death.

Contents

INTRODUCTION

This fourth volume of *James Ronald Stories of Crime and Detection* contains a novel and three short stories.

The novel is *They Can't Hang Me*, another impossible crime story—in fact, it contains two impossible crimes. The phrase Locked Room Mystery, or Locked Room or Impossible Crime Mystery refers to a type of crime described in crime and detective fiction—usually murder—that on the face of it could not have happened, because there is no evidence to explain how the perpetrator could have entered or left a murder scene. Usually, a dead body is found inside a room that has been sealed somehow from the inside. The reader is normally presented with the puzzle and all of the clues, and is encouraged to solve the mystery before the solution is revealed in a dramatic climax. *Locked Room Murders* is a bibliography by the late Robert Adey containing a description of the problem and, separately, the solution to locked room and impossible crime novels and short stories with insightful comments. Adey's book lists four novels by James Ronald and *They Can't Hang Me* is one of them.

Lucius Marplay, former owner of the *Echo*, a London newspaper, escapes from the asylum where he was committed for threatening the new owners of the newspaper. One by one, three of them are murdered, with each death preceded by an advance notice in the paper, naming the hour of doom.

"I don't want to be pronounced sane. One of these days, you see, I shall escape from here and commit those murders and then not being right in the head will come in very handy. If I'm a certified lunatic they can't hang me."

During 1938 James Ronald had moved to publisher Rich & Cowan, 37 Bedford Square, London WC1. He published three books with them during that year: The first, *Hanging's Too Good*, July 1938, which contains two other novellas in addition to the title story: *Angel Face* and *Hard-Boiled* (both previously published in The Thriller Library). The third Rich & Cowan publication was a racy Chicago thriller, *Murder for Cash*, September 1938, but the second, published in March 1938, was another impossible crime story: *They Can't Hang Me!*

The text for this extended version of the story is taken from the Crime Club edition, published by Doubleday, Doran, 1938, and The Thriller Library 2-part version. The first part of the story *They Can't Hang Me!* appeared in The Thriller Library (No 492, 9 July, 1938) taking the reader to the end of Chapter 13, 'At Dead of Night':

"Marplay had made things quite clear to the four heads of the *London Evening Echo*. 'I shall kill you, one by one, and I'll get away with it,' he had said. 'They Can't Hang Me!'"

Lucius Marplay has spent the past twenty years in an asylum – with good reason, as he has been diagnosed with homicidal mania. He has made countless threats against the four men who took over The *Echo*, the London newspaper that he himself once owned—and, as there wouldn't be much of a story otherwise, he has escaped! As his daughter, having just discovered that her father is in fact alive and insane, rather than dead, as she had always been told, endeavours to track him down to talk sense into him, he begins his scheme of revenge. But as the four newspaper men begin to die one by

one, can anyone catch this clever murderer, a murderer capable
of vanishing into thin air?"

The conclusion to the story, entitled 'The Fourth Victim',
appeared in The Thriller Library (No 493, 16 July, 1938) and
begins with Chapter 14, 'Appointment in a Pub':

"I planned to kill four. The first is dead. My vengeance will be
complete only when two, three and four have died!"

The text from The Thriller Library version that had been cut
from the novel is restored in this slightly extended version.

The first short story in this volume is *The Man Who Came
Back*, published by Gramol in 1934 as one of their Mystery
Novels, number 17. The story shares the book with a James
Ronald novelette, *Diamonds of Death*.

The second short story is *Accident*. The story first appeared
in *20-Story Magazine*, number 117, March 1932. The story was
'Americanised' and published as *Death Goes A-Riding* in *The
Illustrated Detective Magazine*, August 1932. The story also
appeared 11 September 1932, in *The Sun*, Sydney, NSW, Australia.
All versions were written under the pseudonym Michael Crombie.

The third short story *Out of the Fog* is set during prohibition
in the U.S., and appeared 9 Sept 1933, in *The Australasian*,
Melbourne, Victoria, Australia, and The Falkirk Herald,
Scotland, in February 1935. The story also appeared 24 June
1939 in *The Saturday Evening Express*, Launceston, Tasmania. All
versions were written under the pseudonym Michael Crombie.

ABOUT THE AUTHOR

James Jack Ronald, to give his full name, was born 11 May 1905, in North Kelvinside, Glasgow, Scotland. He was the son of James Jack Ronald, a Chartered Public Accountant, and Katherine Hamilton Ronald. He was educated at Hillhead High School, Glasgow, established in 1885.

Until he was five, James Ronald says he was chubby, happy, and irresponsible; but in 1911, his sixth year, he was run over by an automobile causing a very real morbidity to creep in. For ten years following the accident he suffered recurrent dreams about a wheel that became larger and larger as it turned faster and faster. He was invalided over a long period during which, with his mother Catherine's encouragement, he enjoyed a prodigious amount of reading. He later claimed he owed his literary gift and resultant career to this near-fatal automobile accident, which caused him to change from a sunny little extrovert to a cloudy introvert.

When he was fourteen he wrote an account of the accident, setting down all the details in a somewhat light vein, not forgetting to note that the candy he had purchased with such delight on that foggy morning was found sticking to the wheels of the car as he was being carried off. The piece won him first prize for composition and congratulations from the masters at the school and even the headmaster wished him well, but that did not prevent corporal punishment for his appalling handwriting. He was called into the headmaster's office, but kept waiting so that everybody knew that he, James Ronald, was going to receive a beating from the headmaster. This injustice obviously affected him very deeply, because it remained with him all his life, and crops up in interview after interview:

> After all, I taught myself to read before going to school and could see no reason for accepting a beating because they failed to teach me how to write, so I bolted.

In a spirit of rebellion against repeated punishments for bad handwriting for compositions for which he invariably got an 'A', Ronald came home from school one day announcing he would never return. It was time to leave. His mother Catherine was understandably distressed, concerned her elder son leaving school at such a young age would diminish his career prospects. Aware of the scarcity of jobs just then in Glasgow, she told him he could only stay away from school if he remained active in some useful employment, making it clear she would not condone an idler in the family.

Within three days James Ronald was an errand boy for the *Glasgow Evening News*, a paper into which he had smuggled a poem some months earlier. But there was 'no writing, nothing editorial' in his set up and he thoroughly disliked it and lost the job. He found another post immediately with the *Glasgow Sunday Mail* and kept this one until he printed his own rival paper on the office mimeograph. He broke the machine and, failing to cover his tracks by leaving a sheet in the copier, he was fired. Then came a dozen jobs, including one with an art dealer for whom he gilded statues and washed windows. His mother told him, 'It is no disgrace to wash windows, James, but it is a disgrace to wash them like that.'

By the age of seventeen, James Ronald had run through all prospective employers in Glasgow, including every newspaper.

He felt the need of open space—'a lot of it'—and after various and sundry abortive departures, finally won grudging permission to seek his fortune in the New World.

For some reason, Chicago stuck in the mind of the young Ronald as a magic word. He became determined to travel to the United States of America. The main method of crossing the Atlantic Ocean in the 1920s was by steamship and ocean liner. The passengers aboard the *SS Saturnia* included seventeen-year-old James Ronald, who arrived at his destination on 6 December 1922, at the Port of Québec, an inland port located in Québec, Canada. From there he continued his journey across the Great Lakes to Chicago, Illinois, United States. He managed to survive in Chicago; the fastest-growing city in world history, with a flourishing economy approaching three million people, attracting huge numbers of new immigrants from Eastern and Central Europe. Ronald stayed in Chicago for five years, wanting to write, but unable to afford the time because he was forced to earn money to live. He was taken on and fired from a variety of jobs with monotonous regularity. Like his experiences in Glasgow, he exhausted all potential employers, dabbling in some forty jobs ranging from short-order cook and dishwasher to muslin salesman; from dance promoter and theatre manager to washing dishes again in a Greek restaurant. He edited ten trade journals at one time for a Chicago publisher; and gave new life to a women's religious magazine. A chain-smoker, he confessed slyly to have worked for the Anti-Cigarette League, his excuse being 'a man must eat don't you know'—at that time eating being the only philosophy he could afford to practise. It was in the Windy City that he learned about life.

Working in the U.S. as 'a visitor' to avoid immigration may have caught up with Ronald because, in 1927, he returned to Britain on a more permanent basis, and secured a well-paid job with an English newspaper chain, and a promise of future advancement. However, during his first holiday in the job, a car accident disrupted this promising career trajectory. Whilst driving a small open two-seater Rover 8, Ronald was struck by a two-ton truck and thrown out against the radiator of another vehicle. Left with a broken hip and temporarily crippled (and without the newly acquired job), he settled down to write.

Ronald's writing developed in three stages. First, he hammered out serializations and short stories which were syndicated in newspapers, both at home and abroad; and a number were also published in obscure pulp magazines. Some stories then became lost and forgotten and this has unfortunately contributed to a lack of recognition for an impressive body of work. These early narratives were very difficult to track down, but searching has provided me with an enjoyable and rewarding task—a treasure hunt for lost tales. This was not made any easier because many of these stories were published under pseudonyms; Peter Gale, Mark Ellison, Kenneth Streeter, Alan Napier, and even women; Cynthia Priestley and Norah Banning—in addition to known pseudonyms Michael Crombie and Kirk Wales. Those I have discovered have all been gathered together for republication in this series.

A second writing stage followed; the full-length mystery stories which have made him so popular with Golden Age of Detection aficionados. They are out-of-print, elusive to find, and first editions are very expensive.

Finally, late in life, James Ronald embarked on his Dickensian-style life drama novels. He received enthusiastic praise for his ingenuity, freshness, and sharp sense of humour by many critics and writers of the time, such as August Derleth. Orville Prescott, the main book reviewer for *The New York Times* for 24 years, called James Ronald 'a born novelist', and that he 'has in full measure the two basic drives which inspire a writer of fiction—the urge to create characters and to tell stories about them. Mr. Ronald does both naturally, directly and well.' His work received praise and has been compared to William de Morgan, H. G. Wells, Rudyard Kipling, J. M. Barrie, and Somerset Maugham.

James Ronald is a writer who has not gained the long-term recognition he deserves. His work has received high praise for his ingenuity, freshness, and sharp sense of humour by many critics and writers of the time and current enthusiasts, highlighting him as one of the leading storytellers of the day, yet barely anything has been republished since his death in 1972. I hope the reader will enjoy these imaginative and entertainingly written stories as much as I have collecting them.

Chris Verner
Berkhamsted, Buckinghamshire, UK
April 2023

THEY CAN'T HANG ME

What Happened to Marplay?

Above the treetops the spire of the village church tapered to a cloudless sky. On a lawn three centuries old, smooth as a carpet, figures in white were playing tennis, darting and leaping as though their bodies were made of fine springs. On the terrace of the rose-brick manor house two old gentlemen sat in canvas chairs watching the play with wistful eyes. One of them sighed and reached for a decanter which stood on a table between them.

"Not too much soda in mine, Sir Charles," murmured his companion sleepily. He listened for the swish of the syphon and raised a warning hand when he heard it. "That's enough. Don't drown it."

Sir Charles poured a second whiskey-and-soda and settled back in his chair to enjoy it. "That's Featherstone's boy playing on the second court. Livin' image of his father."

"Poor old Feathers! Sad end, eh?"

"Damned sad. Makes you think when you hear of old friends poppin' off right and left. Not many of us left, eh?"

"Dashed few," said the other old gentleman sadly, shaking his head. "Dashed few. Still," he mused, sipping his whisky, "there are worse fates than death."

"Lord, yes. Take what happened to Marplay, for instance."

"Poor old Lucius Marplay! His was an appalling fate. Heard anything of him lately?"

"Not for years."

"I suppose he's still——"

"Yes."

They heard a patter of feet from behind and the next moment a girl stood between them.

"I'm sorry, Sir Charles," she gasped, "but I couldn't help overhearing. You were talking about Lucius Marplay. I want to know what you meant. What happened to him?"

The old gentlemen rose and Sir Charles took off his ancient panama. He shifted his weight uncomfortably from one foot to the other.

"I'd no idea you were in the offin', Joan. Thought you were playin' tennis."

"Won't you please tell me what you meant? Why would you a thousand times rather be dead than in his shoes? Then he isn't dead?"

"My dear, this is—I don't know what to say. Hadn't you better put these questions to your guardian?"

For a moment the girl stood staring from one to the other; and then she was gone. Sir Charles dabbed at his forehead with a silk handkerchief. "That was an awkward moment."

"Pretty girl. Who is she?"

"Lucius Marplay's daughter."

"Good God!"

"Exactly," said Sir Charles. "She doesn't know. She thinks he's dead."

*

Joan Marplay cut across the garden to a gap in the hedge. She ducked her head and went through without slackening speed and darted over the neighbouring meadow into a spinney of young larches, coming out at a low stone wall bounding the garden of a thatched cottage. She put one hand on the wall, one foot on a protruding stone, and vaulted over.

The garden was tiny but there was nothing prim or finicking

about it. No neat flower beds, no trim paths. Flowers grew riotously all over the place, like children swarming in a playground. In their midst squatted the cottage, an enormous mushroom. Almost rounded, the thatched roof gave the impression of having been spread on thickly with a blunt knife. The windows were not level—they seemed to squint—and those on the upper floor were shadowed by the overhanging roof, with the appearance of a hat drawn down over the eyes.

At the open door of an outhouse Joan paused and looked in. A shaft of sunlight flecked with dancing specks of dust fell across the back of a middle-aged woman who was painting a dilapidated two-seater car. She plied the brush expertly, hissing through her teeth like a stable boy grooming a horse. In her mouth was a cigarette, which she did not remove even when the ash grew so long that it threatened the fresh paint. She leaned back, nodded her head, and the ash fell on the floor.

Her angular frame was clothed with masculine severity in an old tweed skirt, a blue shirt, heather mixture woollen stockings and heavy brown brogue shoes. On a hook behind her hung a weather-stained felt hat and a jacket to match the skirt. Facially she bore a startling resemblance to a horse. Her greying hair was parted in the middle and brushed flat, exactly like that of a man except for a tight knob at the back of her head. Her best feature was a pair of large brown eyes whose gaze was forceful and direct.

Agatha Trimm had no illusions about herself. At the age of thirty she had overheard her mother lamenting to a friend that poor dear Agatha had never been anything but plain. "Plain be damned," she had interrupted cheerfully. "I'm downright ugly!"

For a while the girl stood watching in silence and then the older woman looked up. Agatha smiled, baring an unbelievable expanse of all-the-better-to-bite-you teeth. Resting on the slim form of the girl outlined in the sunny doorway, her eyes lit up with affection. With the sun glinting on the red-gold of her hair, her cheeks flushed with running, her eyes sparkling with excitement, Joan looked breathtakingly beautiful.

"Hello, you're back early. Was the garden-party a flop?"

She guided a strip of glossy blue down the bonnet of the car and nipped it off at the bottom.

"Trimmy," said Joan in a voice that tried desperately hard to be calm, "you've brought me up since I was three years old."

"And now you're twenty," said Agatha, speaking out of the side of her mouth which was not occupied by the cigarette. "What of it? You can't be going to ask me the facts of life, for I told you those when you were fourteen."

"You took charge of me when my mother died. I never knew my father. When I was old enough to wonder about him, you told me he died abroad when I was a year old and was buried in Vienna."

Agatha stiffened. She dipped her brush and poised it for another stroke.

"Well?"

"A couple of years ago when we were holidaying on the Continent, I wanted to go to Vienna to see Father's grave. You wouldn't let me. You said the idea was sloppy and sentimental, that there was nothing to see but a few feet of earth and a head-stone. You said that when a person died his remains were no more him than the clothes he had worn, or his old boots. I forget all the things you said. Anyway, you talked me out of going."

The deft strokes of her brush seemed to absorb Agatha completely. For a time, Joan was silent and then, in desperation, she blurted out:

"Trimmy, my father is not dead."

Agatha wiped her brush and stood it in a jar containing

paraffin. With a petrol-soaked rag she cleaned a smear of blue from the running-board. Straightening her back, she fumbled in a pocket of her jacket, produced a yellow packet, and lit a fresh cigarette on the stub of the last. She ground the stub under her heal.

"You were bound to find out in time."

Joan grasped her arm and shook it.

"Trimmy, where is he? What has happened to him? Why have I never seen him?"

"You know Joan, don't you," said Agatha gravely, "that there isn't anyone in the world who cares for you as I do? You can trust me, can't you? If I tell you that you'll be happier not knowing—"

She broke off abruptly and shook her head.

"No, that won't do. You've got to know. I can see that. I've always known the day would come when you'd have to know. But I can't tell you. Not now, at least. I promised I wouldn't. I'll tell you what: I'll write to Mr. Jerome tonight and explain the position. I'm sure he'll understand that the time has come when you've got to be told—although I warn you, it'll hurt like the devil."

Joan shook her head. "That won't do, Trimmy. I've got to know now. Today. If you won't tell me, I shall go up to London and see Mr. Jerome myself."

"But, Joan, another day—"

"It's no good, Trimmy. It's got to be today."

Turning on her heel, Joan went into the cottage. Agatha stared after her for a moment, then she picked up the petrol rag and began to clean her fingers with it. Before she had finished Joan appeared again, wearing a camel-hair coat over her tennis frock and carrying a handbag.

"Give me two minutes to wash and change," said Agatha quietly, "and I'll come with you."

"Can't wait, Trimmy. If I do, I shall miss my train."

"Joan! Hold on a minute! Joan!"

But the garden gate swung to with a thud. Joan was gone.

*

The road from the cottage to the village went over a hill, the only rise in the ground for miles. From the crest of the hill, you saw the village spread at your feet like a child's playthings on a nursery hearthrug and, for an instant, Joan always felt that she could take it in her stride. The train rushing through the fields to the tiny station was surely a toy; the plume of white smoke that rolled behind it to flatten across the meadows could be nothing but cotton wool.

The illusion only lasted a moment, and then Joan was running helter-skelter down the hill in a frantic effort to reach the station before the train fussed into it and grumbled out again. She sprinted down the narrow main street and made a beeline across it to a lane which led to the station.

A frantic shout. A screaming of brakes. An idler leaning against a wall straightened up and gaped at Joan with a frightened face. Joan faltered and turned her head. A long black sports car slithered past her at an angle, missing her by less than an inch. It came to rest broadside on across the street. The young man at the steering wheel took off his green felt hat and fanned himself with it.

Joan ran up the lane into the station in time to see the rear of the train disappearing round a bend at the far end of the platform. She looked after it, her breath coming in gulps. That was that! The next London train did not pass through for hours, and it reached Victoria at one in the morning, too late an hour at which to rouse an elderly solicitor from his bed. She would have to wait until morning after all.

Coming out of the station she walked into the driver of the sports car. Long and lean, clad in grey flannels, he towered over her, looking down at her with the exasperated expression of a parent rebuking a naughty child.

He had a pale, bored face with sleepy blue eyes. His nose barely escaped being a beak. It suggested a strength of character denied by the sleepy eyes and a self-indulgent mouth. His blond hair was brushed flat and was thinning at the temples, although he did not look more than thirty.

"Missed it after all? Serves you right. You made me do everything but stand my car on its head. Next time you attempt suicide, remember the ads say you can do it better with gas."

He looked so indignant that Joan could not help laughing. The young man looked at her appreciatively and grinned.

"All right. I give in. I'm not going to quarrel with a girl with a laugh like that. Was catching the train so very important?"

"Very. I wanted to be in London this evening."

"I'm on my way to London. Give you a lift, if you like. You needn't look at me like that," he added. "I'm all right. My name is—"

"You're Lord Noel Stretton. I saw you at the garden party. You do the society gossip in the *London Evening Echo*."

"I don't like the way you say that. However. About this lift, Miss—Miss—" He paused, but Joan did not take the hint. "I saw you at the garden-party too. In fact, I asked Lady Harriet to present me but when we looked for you, you'd gone. About this lift, Miss—"

"Trimm," said Joan. After she had said it, she wondered what had prompted her to lie. "It's very kind of you."

"Not at all. You did things to my nerves and I'm simply itching to return the compliment."

He made good his threat by keeping the speedometer needle

quivering between sixty and seventy, but Joan sat placidly by his side. There was something about the grip of his long fingers on the steering wheel that inspired confidence. He did not bother to make conversation but there was nothing uneasy about the silence in which they sped through the waning afternoon sunshine.

Joan loosened the collar of her coat and let the rushing air play on her throat. She closed her eyes and leaned back. There was something very soothing about this smooth, effortless speed.

But at the back of her mind was a nightmare picture which sprang to life as soon as she closed her eyes. She imagined herself running down a long corridor in pursuit of a man who never looked back, never slackened or quickened speed except when she did, who ran in step with her so that he was always the same distance in front. Somehow, she knew that the man was her father. She must catch up with him, grasp his shoulder, look into his face. It was frightening to think of what she would see there, but she must do it. She ran faster, faster, but did not gain on him by so much as an inch....

"Penny for 'em," said Lord Noel casually.

Joan shivered and came out of her trance. "They weren't the sort of thoughts one tells."

For a time, there was only the purring of the engine, the play of the wind on her face, the long blur of hedges that flew past the car; and then Joan said:

"You know a great many people?"

"Quite a few."

"Have you ever heard of a man named Marplay?"

"Marplay? Uncommon name. There was a Marplay who owned the *Echo* a dickens of a long time ago. Julius—Lucien—"

"Lucius?"

"That's it."

Then, unless there were two Lucius Marplays, her father had once owned a newspaper. Odd, but this was the first concrete thing Joan had ever known about him. In a studiedly casual tone she said:

"What happened to him?"

"Don't know. Before my time. Now I come to think of it, I have heard a suggestion of some scandal or other connected with the old boy. Don't think he murdered anyone but I've an idea it was something rather bad. Why? Interested?"

"No," said Joan hastily. "Not particularly. I heard the name mentioned today, that's all."

It was barely seven when Lord Noel dropped her in Bedford Square. He delayed her at the curb for a few moments, trying unsuccessfully to persuade her to lunch with him the following day. "But I shall see you again?"

"Perhaps. I don't know." Joan held out a small hand. "Goodbye. And thanks again."

"Au revoir," he said firmly.

Joan ran up the steps of her guardian's house and rang the bell. It was with a feeling of inward emptiness that she waited for the door to be opened. She had passed through it before, many times, but this was different. This time was going to change everything. She wondered, a little fearfully, what the change was going to mean to her.

The butler did not precisely smile—Joan could not imagine a smile on that bleak, austere countenance—but at sight of her his severity perceptibly relaxed.

"Mr. Jerome is awaiting you in the library, Miss Joan."

He ushered her into a long room, rosewood panelled, lined with books, in which everything was old and polished except the flowers which stood here and there in tall vases. Although it was a warm evening, a fire was burning in the grate.

Humphrey Jerome, a handsome old man with the figure and manners of a Regency beau and the high forehead and prominent nose of a lawyer, clad in evening clothes of old-fashioned cut, with a high collar like a rampart round his wrinkled throat, rose from a chair beside the fire and held out two shapely hands the colour of the keys of a very old piano.

"My dear, I'm delighted to see you. How well you look. But your hands are quite cold. Sims, a chair for Miss Joan. Not too near the fire—her blood isn't as thin as mine. A glass of sherry, my dear?"

To her inward annoyance, for she hated to give way to weakness, Joan burst into tears. The butler discreetly withdrew.

"Now, now," said Humphrey Jerome, greatly concerned, "you mustn't cry. Here—use this."

"This" was a white linen handkerchief only slightly smaller than a teacloth.

"Powder your nose," said the solicitor gruffly. "It's shiny—and if there's one thing I can't stand it's a pretty girl with a shiny nose."

"I'm sorry I made a fool of myself but I heard something this afternoon—"

"I know. Miss Trimm telephoned me after you left the cottage."

"Uncle Humphrey, you've got to tell me about my father. Where is he? Why have I always been told that he's dead?"

"Let me do the talking, my dear. It will be easier that way."

He walked stiffly across the room. When he came back, he handed Joan a crystal glass of wine that glowed golden in the firelight.

"You'll like this. Isn't the colour exquisite? Sip it, my dear. There. What did I tell you?"

"It's delicious."

"Not too dry for your palate?"

"I like dry wines."

"And so you should, my dear, so you should."

A little nervously, Humphrey Jerome stroked his thinning white hair with ivory-yellow fingers.

"Joan, this isn't going to be easy for either of us. What I am going to tell you will come as a shock but I want you to meet it bravely."

"I—I'll try."

"I know you will, my dear. I know you will."

The lawyer leaned back in his chair, crossed one thin leg over the other, placed the tips of his fingers together and shut his eyes. For a time he was silent, and when he spoke his weary voice seemed to be coming from a great distance.

"About thirty years ago I met your father for the first time at a musical evening at the house of some mutual friends. He was then thirty-five and I was a few years older. He had recently acquired the *London Evening Echo*, which had been losing ground until it almost passed out of existence, and he was building it up to the flourishing enterprise it afterwards became. He was full of this new venture of his; and on his arm was his young wife, the most beautiful girl I have ever seen." The old man sighed. "Ah, but she was lovely! Very, very lovely. I think I shall die adoring her memory.

"Later your father came to me for advice and shortly all his legal affairs were in my hands. I spent many pleasant evenings at his house, listening to your mother playing the piano—she had great feeling and a delicate touch—and envying your father, whom I thought the luckiest man on earth. During the ensuing ten years the *Echo* became one of London's foremost evening newspapers. Your father was something of a genius in his own way. Like many brilliant men, he had his little eccentricities. When he had something on his mind, he would hide himself away for days on end. No one knew where to find him.

"Having made a remarkable success at an early age, he had an almost fanatical faith in young men. His editor, his business manager, all his department heads, in fact, were in their early thirties; some of them were even younger.

"When he was forty-five you were born. I thought he would go mad with delight. He took you and your mother away to a house he had bought in Devon and spent most of his time there with you, seldom tearing himself away even to attend to the affairs of his beloved newspaper. He had built up an efficient staff, he said: let them run it for a while. In this he was not altogether wise.

"Things began to go badly with the *Echo*. Your father came up to town and plunged himself back into the business. But the strain was too much for him. He had a nervous breakdown.

"Before he had fully recovered, ignoring the warnings of his physicians, he returned to his office. He put up a hard fight but it only resulted in a worse muddle than before. His brain could not stand it. After a long illness it—it was found necessary to place him under restraint. He—he was—certified insane."

Joan gasped and her hand flew to her throat. There was an aching dryness at the back of her throat.

"Go on," she whispered.

"It was a terrible blow to your mother. From the day they took him away she was a dying woman. Two years later she died. You had no near relatives and I found myself your legal guardian. I thought it best to keep you in ignorance of your father's fate as long as possible. I engaged Miss Trimm, a lady with excellent recommendations, to look after you. The *Echo* went into liquidation and was sold for a song. Out of the wreckage I salvaged a sum sufficient to bring in income of twelve hundred pounds a year. Slightly more than half of the income is placed at Miss Trimm's disposal to use on your behalf and the balance supports your father in an—er—a private mental home where he receives every comfort and attention. He is—not unhappy, Joan. I get to see him twice a year and I assure you he is not unhappy."

"Not unhappy! Oh God!"

Joan buried her face in her hands.

His lined face quivering, Humphrey Jerome hovered about her. He put an arm about her shoulders, a trembling hand on her knee.

"Joan. My dear. Please—"

Slowly, Joan raised her head. With a tremulous smile she patted his hand. Tears glistened in her grey eyes.

"I'm all right, Uncle Humphrey. I think I'd like a cigarette."

"By all means, my dear."

He crossed the room to a walnut table and picked up a silver box. While his back was toward Joan he heard a sob and his face twitched with pain. When he turned Joan was composed but very pale.

"You'll find these rather good, I think," he said in a low voice, fumbling with the lid of the box. "Never smoke 'em myself—I prefer a cigar—but my friends are kind enough to approve of 'em."

Joan lit a cigarette and for a time sat smoking it and gazing into the fire. Her guardian lowered himself gingerly into his chair watching her face with pathetic anxiety

"He isn't— they don't—bully him—and keep him—shut up?"

"Oh dear, no. He has the run of the place and is very friendly with everyone. Does quite a lot of gardening, they tell me. And reads; he was always a great reader."

"What is he like, Uncle Humphrey?"

"Well, now, let me see. I'm not very good at describing people. He's very charming, you know—always was. Young for his years, although his hair has turned white. His cheeks are as rosy and round as an apple. Rather on the short side and beginning to be stout. Dear me, yes, definitely stout. In fact, I told him so when I last saw him. 'Lucius,' I said, 'if you don't look out you'll be a barrel before you're much older.' That made him smile. He chuckled like a schoolboy. 'My dear Humphrey,' he replied, eyeing me from head to foot, 'I'd much rather be a barrel than a beanpole!'"

"He sounds nice," said Joan, with a faint smile.

"He is, my dear."

"Do you think he'd like me?"

"Who could help liking you?"

"I hope he will because from now on he's going to live with me."

Her guardian stared at her, shaking his head slowly. "Oh, but he can't."

"Why not? I could have a trained nurse for him. I'd devote myself to him. Surely, he'd be happier with me than in that place?"

"It's sweet of you, Joan, but—you see—he—"

"What are you trying to tell me, Uncle Humphrey?"

"You can't have him to live with you, Joan, because he isn't safe. He has homicidal tendencies."

"Oh," said Joan, in a small, still voice.

"I hadn't meant to tell you that."

"I shall go to see him."

"It would be better if you didn't. He has forgotten that he ever had a daughter. There is no saying how he would be affected by your appearance after all these years."

"He's my father. I must see him."

"Then let me prepare him first. Sir John Digby, the brain specialist, is one of your father's oldest friends. Let me send him to ascertain whether your father can stand the surprise. If it is Sir John's opinion that a visit from you will do no harm, I shall raise no objection."

"You'll send him at once, Uncle Humphrey?"

"Immediately, my dear."

The door opened and the butler entered. "Miss Trimm," he said, in a sepulchral tone.

Agatha came in with a rush. She was still wearing the shabby tweeds and—from the angle at which it rode on her head—she had put on her battered hat without looking in a mirror.

"Joan. You're alright?"

"I'm all right, Trimmy," said Joan, her eyes moist with tears. "Still keeping my chin up. But how did you get here so soon?"

"Came up in the car," replied Agatha grimly. "There are about two inches of dust on the fresh paint. Lord knows how long it'll take me to scrape it off before I can start painting the damned thing all over again!"

After dinner Humphrey Jerome told Joan more about her father—and about the plans Lucius Marplay had been making for years, plans to murder the four men who now owned the *London Evening Echo*.

Mr. Marplay at Large

Sir John Digby closed his eyes and leaned back against the cushions of his Rolls-Royce as the elderly car—dignified and stately as a dowager on wheels—rolled down Harley Street and turned west. It was three o'clock in the afternoon of the day following that of Joan's visit to her guardian. Sir John had been through a trying morning, forced to listen while one middle-aged woman after another gabbled in his ear a lot of confidential twaddle about her repressions and inhibitions. Some of the things they told him about their inner thoughts would have shocked the habitués of a four-ale bar; but Sir John was weary of pornography. He had a suspicion that they delved into Freud and Jung for juicy bits before they came to see him.

The devil of it was that he had to pretend to take them seriously, for their fat cheques were necessary if Lady Digby was to be maintained in the manner to which she had become accustomed. He longed to say to them: "What you want is more fat there"—slapping them where a woman should be comfortably rounded— "and then you'd have less fat here"—smacking them on the head; but that wouldn't do, it wouldn't do at all.

While the car purred along Oxford Street, past Marble Arch, into Hyde Park, Sir John tried to forget his garrulous patients. His eyes tightly shut, he counted society women jumping over a stile—a device which had never failed him—and, when he reached three hundred and twenty-nine, fell fast asleep. He woke with a start when the car was passing through the gates of a mental home on the outskirts of Kingston.

Gliding up the drive, Sir John looked appreciatively at the flower beds, green lawns and shady trees that slid past on either side. In a garden like this, remote from the confusion of modern life, one could find forgetfulness and peace. Here and there he glimpsed men and women sitting in canvas chairs with books, or playing croquet on the lawn. Lucky beggars, he mused. There was something to be said for having a bee in one's bonnet. It gave one an interest in life, at the same time relieving one of all cares and responsibilities.

The pretty maid who admitted him moved warily, as though she were accustomed to being pinched in the rear. Probably she was, he reflected with a start. She relieved him of his coat and silk hat and laid them on a chair in the hall.

"You needn't take them away. I shan't stop long."

"Very good, Sir John. This way, sir."

Dr Hepburn, the proprietor of the home, awaited him in a sunny room on the ground floor.

"Your secretary 'phoned me, Sir John. You wish to see Marplay."

"How is he?"

"Physically, very fit. As to his mental state, I haven't had a talk with him for some time, but—"

"Do you think that is wise? In my experience, personal contact is essential in treating mental cases."

"Oh, quite," agreed Dr. Hepburn nervously, playing with the cord of his pince-nez. "But, you see—well, he's rather a disconcerting patient. Hang it, he always gives me the feeling that he's humouring me."

"Ah," said Sir John, with a dry smile. "Disconcerting, I agree."

"Besides, on every point but one he is as sane as you or me."

"And that point is?"

"Murder. He thinks of little else. When he first came here his mind was quite clouded and for a long time he took no interest in anything. Later there was a distinct improvement in his mental condition but hand in hand with it came this strong impulse to kill. Don't misunderstand me, it isn't an uncontrolled impulse by any means. With most people he is quite safe. The desire to kill is directed at four of his former employees. He imagines, you know, that they stole his newspaper. He has filled dozens of thick notebooks with ingenious schemes to end their lives."

"As long as the impulse finds an outlet in scribbling wild plans you have little to fear."

"Oh, but they aren't wild plans. They're amazingly shrewd."

"He'll work it out of his system in time."

"Ah, that's just it. He has destroyed his notebooks."

"A sign, probably, that the desire to kill is weakening."

"I don't think so, Sir John," said Dr Hepburn earnestly. "I really don't think so. I am afraid it means that his plans are completed. Recently he contrived to smuggle out letters warning these former employees that they have not much longer to live. Frankly, I'm worried. He is clever—devilishly clever. So far, he has made no attempt to escape but I have a feeling that he soon will. I have taken the precaution of assigning one of my men to keep a close watch on him."

"My dear Hepburn, you're causing yourself needless anxiety. The patient who makes these elaborate plans seldom carries them out."

"I hope you're right. I hope so indeed. After you have seen him, I shall be interested to hear your opinion. Perhaps you would prefer to interview him in private?"

"Most certainly."

"Very good, Sir John. I shall send him to you." When Dr Hepburn had gone, Sir John paced the room.

"Idiot!" he grunted. "Making a mountain out of a molehill."

"My dear Digby," said a mellow voice behind him. "How nice to see you again!"

Turning, Sir John gazed into a smiling face with rosy cheeks and a shock of white hair.

"Hello, Lucius. You're looking well."

"Never felt better in my life."

Shaking hands, they took stock of each other. They were almost of an age, but Sir John looked the older by quite ten years. They were about the same height and both had white hair, but there the resemblance ended. The specialist was thin, the patient plump; the specialist's eyes were tired and pouchy, the patient's youthful and bright; the specialist's forehead was deeply lined, the patient's smooth and serene. They looked, in fact, like the drawings in the nerve tonic advertisements 'before' and 'after'.

"My dear Digby," said Lucius Marplay anxiously, "you're looking quite rundown. Overwork, I expect. What you need is a month or two out here. It'd make a new man of you."

Sir John fancied there was a mischievous twinkle in Mr. Marplay's eyes. Could it be that he was having his leg pulled?

"Sit down, my dear fellow, sit down," said Mr Marplay hospitably. "You must tell me all you've been doing since last we—" He broke off and stared out of the window. "Ah, there he is again!"

The specialist twisted in his chair and saw a burly man standing outside the open window in a suspiciously casual attitude.

"My personal attendant," confided Mr. Marplay pleasantly. "Keeps popping up wherever I go. I do hope he doesn't make you nervous? He never bothers me, but some people have a horror of being watched."

"I don't intend to have him standing there throughout our conversation," said Sir John. "Here, you!"— he snapped his fingers— "You may go away. I shall let you know when you are required."

The attendant looked at them morosely. Recognizing the alienist, he tugged at a lock of hair and walked gloomily away. Sir John turned back to his patient with the reassuring smile which was part of his professional equipment. In a suave, man-to-man tone he began the familiar business of drawing the patient out. To his tactful questions Mr. Marplay returned disingenuous replies—but the disconcerting twinkle lingered in his eyes.

"My dear fellow," said Mr. Marplay at last, "you're barking up all the wrong trees. I have no delusions of grandeur, no persecution complex. I don't for a moment think I'm Napoleon, nor do I imagine myself to be followed about by black dogs. If you must catalogue me, mine is a straightforward case of homicidal tendencies."

He chuckled at the crestfallen look on his old friend's face.

"Confidentially," he went on, "I'm not crackers at all. I'm sure I could persuade you to believe that, if I wanted to. But it would be a dirty trick to play on you, for what a fool you'd look if you pronounced me sane and I went straight off and committed four murders. That would put you in a nice hole, wouldn't it? But I don't want to be pronounced sane. One of these days, you see, I shall escape from here and commit those murders and then not being right in the head will come in very handy. If I'm a certified lunatic they can't hang me."

I must certainly warn Hepburn, thought Sir John, never to let him alone for a moment. He opened his mouth to speak but could find nothing to say. Mr. Marplay smiled charmingly at him.

"Now that the position's clear, let's not discuss it any further. I punched your head so often when we were fags at Winchester that I find the patient-and-doctor pose difficult to sustain. Let me show you my card tricks. I'm rather good at them."

He took a pack from his pocket and shuffled them expertly.

"Take a card. Any card."

With a feeling of unreality, Sir John obeyed. For once in his career the situation was beyond him.

"Now, watch closely."

Marplay was right. He was clever with the cards. Really, one or two of the tricks would have done credit to a professional.

"Dashed good," said Sir John heartily. "Dashed good."

"Oh, that's nothing," replied Mr. Marplay, with the self-conscious air of a schoolboy who knows he is showing off. "I can do a much better trick with a glass of water and three coins. Let me show you. You'll have to lend me the coins."

Sir John eyed Mr. Marplay suspiciously but the patient looked void of guile. An innocent delight at his own cleverness was written largely across Mr. Marplay's beaming countenance.

"Help yourself," said the specialist, holding out a handful of silver.

Mr. Marplay selected three half crowns. He placed them in a row on a table and filled a glass with water from a carafe on the window ledge.

"Now, watch carefully. Come a little closer. That's better. I take the coins in my right hand, the glass of water in my left— Oh dear, I am so sorry! How incredibly clumsy of me!"

In picking up the glass he had tilted it and the contents had slopped over, splashing the specialist's white linen spats. Murmuring apologies, Mr. Marplay produced a snowy handkerchief and dabbed at the spats but the water had soaked into the thin fabric.

"I'm afraid they're sopping wet. How I could have been so careless I really don't know. Do forgive me, my dear Digby."

"Say no more about it, Lucius," replied Sir John magnanimously, fumbling with the buttons of his spats. "Accidents will happen."

Laying the spats on the fender, he felt his socks anxiously and was relieved to find that they were quite dry. Raising his head, he found Mr. Marplay looking at him rather oddly. Mr.

Marplay put a finger to his lips and glanced over his shoulder at the door leading to the hall.

"Have you seen Doctor Hepburn's wife?" he asked, with an air of mystery.

"Charming woman," said Sir John, a trifle bewildered.

"Oh, her. I don't mean that one. I mean the other. The one he keeps in that room." Mr. Marplay pointed to a door to the left of the fireplace.

Aha! thought Sir John. Oho! Now I shall learn something. At last, he is displaying some tangible symptoms.

"Dear me," he murmured. "Can you be serious, my dear fellow?"

"It's perfectly true. Come and see for yourself."

To humour his patient, Sir John walked to the door Mr. Marplay had indicated. Mr. Marplay opened the door and Sir John peered in. Before he could make a move to prevent it the specialist was bundled into a cupboard, the door was slammed behind him and the key turned in the lock. He opened his mouth to shout but the shout was stillborn, for it occurred to him that if he were discovered in this plight he would never be able to live it down. His colleagues would hear the story and split their sides with laughter. Such ignominy was not to be faced. Better to reason with this lunatic and persuade him to open the door before anyone came.

"That was very clever of you, Lucius," he said in a wheedling tone. "But aren't we a little old for practical joking? Open the door, like a good fellow."

"In a moment, old chap. Keep your hair on. I'll let you out directly."

While speaking so reassuringly, Mr. Marplay was moving quietly about the room. He pocketed the three half-crowns. He put on the white spats over his house slippers. Stealthily, he opened the door leading to the hall and looked out. There was no one in sight. He snatched Sir John's silk hat and fur-lined coat from the chair on which they lay and ducked back into the room with them.

"Marplay! Let me out at once, do you hear? This is going beyond a joke!"

"All in good time, my dear Digby," replied Mr. Marplay soothingly, slipping his arms into the coat.

He put on the silk hat at a dignified angle, tiptoed out to the hall, opened the front door and sauntered down the steps to the waiting limousine.

The chauffeur had brought to the mental home a short elderly man in white spats, silk hat and fur-lined coat; and when, out of the corner of his eye, he saw just such an elderly gentleman climbing into the car, he started his engine and drove off. When the car approached him with apparently the same occupants as when it arrived, the gatekeeper swung open the gates without giving it a second glance. The Rolls-Royce glided through and went off toward London, gaining speed rapidly.

At Hammersmith the car was held up by traffic and Mr. Marplay opened the door and slipped out without attracting the chauffeur's attention. From the pavement he watched the stream of cars moving on and rubbed his hands with glee. Free, after almost twenty years! The only rub was that his cash capital was precisely seven shillings and sixpence; hardly an adequate reserve on which to start a campaign against his enemies.

Three brass balls projecting from the wall of a building gave him an inspiration. He followed his nose into one of a row of wooden booths which opened to a counter. The pawnbroker came forward, his eyes narrowing as they took in the distinguished appearance and affluent bearing of his new client.

"What can I do for you, sir?"

"This is really rather amusing," replied Mr. Marplay, with

a smile of good-natured embarrassment, "if the reason for it weren't so sad. I've just run into a young friend of mine; the son, in fact, of one of my late colleagues. Until today I hadn't seen him for years and he has fallen on hard times. Indeed, he tells me that he is to be evicted from his home within the hour for failing to pay his rent. Think of it! —and the poor boy has a wife and three children to support! Naturally, I am anxious to help him but he requires funds without delay and I came out with no more than a little loose change. The banks are closed, so I can't cash a cheque. While I was wondering what to do I saw your sign and it occurred to me that you might be prepared to advance the small sum which is required if I left my coat as security."

Mr. Marplay chuckled as though it were the best joke in the world. In sympathy, the pawnbroker's sharp features relaxed.

"But won't you be cold without it, sir? Perhaps your watch—"

"Oh no, it is a warm afternoon," said Mr. Marplay peeling off the coat and placing it on the counter.

"And how much do you wish me to advance, sir?"

"The poor boy tells me he will need twenty pounds."

"Twenty pounds?" The pawnbroker fondled the rich skins with which the coat was lined. He glanced inside the breast pocket and noted, with a lift of his brows the name that was written on the tailor's label. "Certainly, Sir John."

Waiting to receive the money, Mr. Marplay inspected his surroundings with a genial eye. Hanging on the wall at the rear of the place he noticed a short weapon made of rubber with a leather thong attached to the handle.

"What on earth is that?" he asked, pointing to it.

"That's a rubber truncheon, sir. Would you care to examine it more closely? No trouble at all, sir, here you are. I took it in pledge with a number of other articles and it has never been redeemed. You'd hardly credit it, sir, but one blow from that will knock a man out and scarcely leave a mark on him."

"How very interesting," said Mr. Marplay, toying with the weapon. "Useful in case of burglars, eh? Is it for sale?"

"Well, sir, I'm not supposed to sell that sort of thing, but in the case of a gentleman like yourself— Shall we say five shillings?"

"By all means," replied Mr. Marplay, placing two of his coins on the counter and pocketing the truncheon. The pawnbroker handed him four crisp five-pound notes, which he stowed away carefully. "Good afternoon!"

"You're forgetting something, sir."

Mr. Marplay turned back with a look of enquiry on his rosy face.

"The ticket, Sir John," said the pawnbroker, holding out a slip of paper.

"The ticket? Of course, how stupid of me."

Mr. Marplay glanced at it before slipping it into a waistcoat pocket. It was made out to: 'Sir John Digby, Harley Street, W.1.' A smile of pure mirth crossed his features.

He strolled out into the sunshine and hailed a crawling taxi.

"Fleet Street," he said, climbing in.

Four Murderers in Conference

At five o'clock that afternoon a pigeon was strutting about on the window sill of Ambrose Craven's room on the top floor of the large concrete structure which had lately been erected to house the staff and equipment of the *London Evening Echo*. Mr. Craven's secretary tried to concentrate on the pigeon and ignore the bloated pink face on the other side of the desk but she could not help being conscious of the piggy little eyes which were fixed gloatingly on her silk-clad legs. That they were nice legs she was well aware and she did not resent the measure of masculine approval which was their due, but there was something about her employer's gaze that revolted her.

She tucked the legs under her chair and meaningfully poised a pencil above her notebook.

"Shall I repeat the last paragraph, Mr. Craven?"

"Hang the last paragraph. The letters can wait. I was saying that you are much too attractive to be wasted in an office."

Ambrose Craven stood up, shaking his trousers to restore the crease. A middle-aged male flapper, trying hard to look youthful and only succeeding in looking ridiculous, he resembled nothing so much as one of those stout elderly women whose lives are one long wrestle with wrinkles and sagging chins. Beneath a snugly fitting jacket and waistcoat an abdominal belt held in his fat stomach so tightly that he seemed to be all chest and posterior. Two shaves and one facial massage every day kept his plump cheeks smooth and pink, and a mask of powder disguised the blueness of his chin.

"I've asked you to dine with me three times this week," he said peevishly, "and you've always had an excuse."

"Well, you see, Mr Craven, I live rather far out and unless

I get to bed early, I simply can't rise in time to be at the office at nine."

"If you'd be nice to me, you could sleep all day. Why won't you be nice to me?"

The girl did not reply. She kept her eyes on the notebook. The pigeon had flown away, apparently despairing of strutting in competition with the elegant Mr. Craven.

"Use your head, my dear. In return for slaving in this office five and a half days a week we pay you fifteen pounds a month. Some girls spend more than that on their stockings. You could, if you were clever. I'm generous, you know, with those I like. I like you. Why won't you let me do things for you? A girl like you should have clothes, jewels, furs. Wouldn't you like to travel and see Paris, the Riviera, the Lido?"

Why doesn't he bring in Brighton? she thought, trying to make a joke of it, trying to keep in check her smouldering anger. His technique creaks with age. Oh, why are jobs so scarce? Why don't I tell him what I think of him, even if it would mean the sack? Why don't I pick up the wastepaper basket and bang it on his silly fat head?

"There isn't anything I wouldn't do for you, if you'd only be nice to me."

His podgy fingers were stroking her neck. She sprang up but he was between her and the door. He put his arms about her stiffening shoulders, his moist mouth came near her face. Gritting her teeth, she kicked him on the shin as hard as she could. It was the most satisfying action of her life. With a pained yelp Mr. Craven hopped back, holding his ankle and cursing.

"You dirty little—"

"This means the sack, I suppose. Well, before I go there are one or two things I'd like to say to you—you—"

The door opened and three men stood on the threshold. The

foremost was a very small man but he carried himself with the assurance of a born dictator. He had a pale thin face with prominent cheekbones, a long nose, a high forehead and dark, heavily lidded eyes etched with deep lines at the corners. Although he was over fifty, he had the slim, compact figure of a youth. He took in the situation at a glance and his eyes hardened.

"Don't go, Miss Phillips. I have something to say to you. You have applied for a transfer to the circulation department?"

"Y-yes sir."

"It is granted. Report to Mr. Nathan tomorrow morning."

"Oh, thank you, Mr. Peters."

He made a gesture of dismissal and the girl hurried out of the room. The men who had entered with Mark Peters stood aside to let her pass, then they came in and sat down. One of them looked at the other and closed an eye.

Mark Peters went to Craven's desk and lifted the telephone.

"Connect me with the staff manager. Nathan? Mr. Peters speaking. Miss Phillips is to start work in the circulation department tomorrow morning. Miss Withers will take her place as Mr. Craven's secretary."

Replacing the receiver, he took a leather case from an inside pocket and selected a cigar.

"Confound you, Peters!" stormed Ambrose Craven. "Why the devil don't you mind your own business?"

Peters rolled the cigar between his fingers. He pierced the end with precious care.

"Anything which affects the discipline of the staff," he said, striking a match, "automatically becomes my business."

"I won't have this Withers woman in my office. She's over fifty. She's as wrinkled as a crocodile."

"That, my dear Ambrose, is precisely why she is going to be your secretary!"

"You seem to think you've only got to crack your whip like a lion tamer and the rest of us will jump through hoops," sneered Craven.

Mark Peters' voice was usually suave and pleasant, but it could sting like a barbed whip. It stung now.

"It is no affair of mine what you do with your spare time, Craven. Outside this office you can paddle muddy pools to your heart's content—but your dealings with the employees of this newspaper must be strictly business. You've made yourself the laughingstock of the office. Do you know the nickname the girls have for you? They call you Elegant Ambrose, the Cardboard Casanova!" He laughed scathingly. "Don't stand there goggling at me. Sit down. I have something to say."

"We'll dispose of this first!"

"I have disposed of it," said Peters calmly.

With the casual air of one accustomed to the place of importance, he dropped into the chair behind Craven's desk. He studied the faces of the other men in turn, appraisingly, dispassionately. His eyes rested longest on the face of Nigel Partridge, business manager of the *Echo,* who had seated himself on a blue leather couch against the far wall. A tall muscular man in his early fifties, with a clipped brown moustache above a large mouth, Partridge had a brain which could probe to the heart of a problem almost as quickly as the agile intellect of Mark Peters.

The fourth man, Sinclair Ellis, titular editor-in-chief, was almost a complete nonentity. His editorial duties consisted of sitting in an elaborate office looking important. A large head with bulging brows helped him to sustain the 'great editor' pose. He had a shaggy mane of iron-grey hair of which he was very proud. When he was being emphatic, he had a trick of pushing out his chin. On a dominant nose he wore a large pair of horn-rimmed eyeglasses from which dangled a thick black ribbon. His mouth, weak and petulant, gave him away.

After a pause Peters said quietly: "Marplay has escaped."

In the sudden hush that fell upon the room the roar of traffic from Fleet Street, a hundred feet below, swelled up to them like the growling of an angry beast. Ambrose Craven collapsed against the window like a pricked balloon, all the bluster whistling out of him in a horrified gasp.

"Marplay escaped! Mark, you don't mean it! My God, it can't be true!"

"The proprietor of the place 'phoned me a few minutes ago."

Craven's eyes were like goldfish darting about in a bowl.

"Marplay escaped!" he wailed. "Do you realize what that means?"

"Pull yourself together, man!" snapped Peters, his lips curling with distaste. "What can Marplay do to us?"

"He's threatened to kill us! He will, too, if he gets the chance. My God, it's awful! Marplay at large, after all these years"

"This is serious, Mark," mumbled Ellis, his face grey.

"'This is serious!' 'He's threatened to kill us!'" said Peters, perfectly mimicking the voices of his partners. "Have you no guts? What are you afraid of? A demented old man? The authorities will have him in a padded cell within twenty-four hours. He's over sixty, any one of us could handle him with ease"—his eyes twinkled with malicious amusement— "with the possible exception of Craven."

"If he tells his story to the authorities—" began Sinclair Ellis uneasily.

"Do you think they'll listen to the ravings of a madman?"

"But he isn't mad," whispered Craven.

"He's had twenty years in a lunatic asylum."

Nigel Partridge shivered. He saw the meaning behind Peters'

brutal retort. Twenty years in a lunatic asylum should be enough to unhinge the strongest mind.

"He'll attempt to carry out his threats, Mark," he said soberly. "We can't simply fold our arms and wait for it."

"If you care to make yourself ridiculous by employing a bodyguard to protect you from a feeble old man, by all means do so," said Mark curtly. "I prefer to take whatever slight risk there is."

"I want two bodyguards," said Craven shakily. "And they must be armed. Marplay's clever, clever as hell."

"I'll get you a machine-gun squad and a bulletproof waistcoat, if that will make you happy," snapped Peters. "And now, let's forget Marplay. There's something else on my mind. I hear the *Morning Courier* is about to come on the market again."

"I thought we settled that question six months ago," said Partridge bluntly.

"You three outvoted me. I was in favour of the purchase. I still am."

"The *Courier's* been going down steadily for years."

"So much the better. We'll get it cheaply. I understand the owners will take three quarters of a million."

"Reasonable enough—but we haven't got it. The new building and machinery cost us a fortune."

"We can raise it. The banks have faith in us. In a few months I guarantee to put the *Courier* on its feet. I've always wanted a morning paper to run in double harness with the *Echo*."

"We've made a fortune out of the *Echo*," grumbled Ellis. "I think we should be satisfied. We might lose it all on the *Courier*."

"I agree," said Partridge. "I don't say we couldn't make a good thing of the *Courier* in time but it would mean a stiff fight and at our time of life we ought not to embark on speculative ventures. It's all very well for you, Mark, you're a bachelor. Ellis and I have wives and children to think of."

"And Craven has two ex-wives to support," retorted Peters, with a grim twist to his mouth. "Perhaps you're right. If this is your attitude, we'd be beaten before we started. But if we let the *Courier* go, we're turning our backs on a gold mine. Oh, I'm not thinking only of the money. I'm thinking of the prestige and power vested in the ownership of a national daily."

"You're a megalomaniac, Mark," said Sinclair Ellis with an uncomfortable laugh.

"So is Mussolini. So was Napoleon. So was Julius Caesar. To get things done on a big scale you've got to be something of a megalomaniac."

His partners looked at each other uneasily, the same thought in the mind of each: Mark had a habit of getting his own way over their heads and this time he seemed doubly determined.

"We'd better think it over," said Partridge at last. "A question of this magnitude can't be decided in hurry."

"If I were only in a position to make the decision myself," snapped Peters, "I shouldn't hesitate for moment."

"Ah, but you see, Mark, you're not," sneered Craven. "You can crack the whip and hold up the hoop, but you can't always make us jump through!"

*

When the others had gone Ambrose Craven sat down at his desk and opened a drawer. With shaking hands he brought out a crumpled piece of paper and flattened it on the desk. His lips trembled as he read for the hundredth time a quietly worded but ominous letter which Lucius Marplay had smuggled out of the mental home to him. In a flurry of fear he tore it into tiny pieces and let them flutter through his fingers into the wastepaper basket.

"I don't want to die," he whimpered, mentally wringing his hands. "Oh, my God, I don't want to die!

*

A pleasing old gentleman in a silk hat and white spats walked up the lane which led from Fleet Street along the side of the *Evening Echo's* imposing new building. He carried a brand-new suitcase and his plump body was inclined to one side with the weight of it, but he hastened along with the eagerness of one who is going home after a long absence.

Against the rear wall of the new building huddled the ramshackle old one, shortly to be demolished, which had formerly housed the newspaper. Dark, deserted, it looked like a beggar importuning an opulent acquaintance. With a swift glance to right and left the old gentleman stepped into the entrance and tried the door. It was not locked. There was no key. Thirty years before Lucius Marplay had thrown away the key with the remark that a newspaper's door should never shut. He pushed the door open and walked in. The dismantled entrance hall was cluttered with debris. Fastened to the gates of the disused lift shaft was a pencilled notice:

HAVING MY TEA. IF WANTED, HOLLER DOWN BASEMENT STARES. THE CARETAKER.

The old gentleman did not 'holler.' He picked his way over the debris and climbed the dusty stairs to the fourth floor, his footsteps echoing from one bare landing to another. Pushing open a door, he entered a large room which was completely empty. Putting down the suitcase, he crossed the floor and did something to a panel in the wall beside the fireplace. The panel swung back, revealing another room within. It had evidently been overlooked by the furniture removers for it contained a table, a padded chair, a well-filled bookcase and a long couch. Dust lay thickly over everything, like a covering of grey felt. The old gentleman lugged his suitcase into the secret room and closed the panel.

Rubbing his hands, he opened the suitcase and emptied on to the table a jumble of articles which included tins of food, bottles of beer, and blankets. From an inside pocket he took a rubber truncheon with which he playfully whacked the couch, causing a cloud of dust to rise.

He smiled, a slow, lingering, reflective smile...

Miss Trimm Puts Her Foot Down

When the following day was young, Joan rose and put on an old skirt and jersey. Bareheaded, barelegged, with a basket on her arm and a wire-haired terrier romping at her heels, she let herself out of the cottage, crossed the road and climbed a stile into a field where dull-eyed cattle were browsing. As far as she could see stretched more fields, divided by rough stone dykes. To the sun, lending a smiling face to a new day, a cock shrilled a challenge from his dunghill in the cobbled yard of a farmhouse which drowsed in a hollow. A wisp of smoke curled lazily from the tall farmhouse chimneys.

Barking insults, the terrier ran at the moping cattle, but they only stared with stolid brown eyes and he turned his back on them in disgust and raced across two fields after an imaginary rabbit. Joan had an almost irresistible impulse to take off her shoes and run barefoot on the dewy grass. Fine mornings always made her spirits soar as high as a kite. Her eyes roved ahead, distinguishing the round white shapes of mushrooms from the round white shapes of pebbles. Now and then she stooped, gathered a mushroom and dropped it into her basket. She moved backward and forward until the basket was full, then she left it on the grass and joined the terrier on the bank of a chalk stream where he was scrambling about, searching for rabbit holes. The flowing water was dimpled by rising trout.

On the way back an hour later she passed the farm cart, drawn by a briskly trotting pony, clattering down a rutted lane, returning from the morning milk delivery. She exchanged greetings with the apple-cheeked boy who was holding the reins. Collecting the morning paper from the doorstep of the cottage, she went in, her cheeks rosy with health, her eyes sparkling. The tempting odours of sizzling bacon and brewing coffee greeted her. She went to the kitchen and gave the mushrooms to a brawny country wench, with her sleeves rolled to the elbows, who was bending over the range.

In a small room with leaded windows, creamy walls and a low ceiling, supported by thick uneven beams, Agatha was laying the table for breakfast and scattering ash from a cigarette pasted to her underlip on the orange checked cloth. Joan dropped the newspaper beside the marmalade dish.

"Morning, Trimmy! Isn't it a lovely day? Why do we take the *Courier*? It's such a dull—"

The last word was never uttered. As it fell, the paper unfolded and Joan glimpsed a headline at the top of the front page:

MADMAN TRICKS ALIENIST

ESCAPES FROM ASYLUM

IN SPECIALIST'S CAR

With a gasp she picked up the paper and read the paragraph below the headline. She dropped into a chair and let the paper slip through her trembling fingers. Agatha stared at her.

"Something wrong? Joan! What is it?"

The girl rose and stumbled out of the room. She went to the telephone in the hall and asked for her guardian's Holborn number. In a few minutes the detached voice of Sims, the lawyer's butler, came to her over the wire:

"This is the residence of Mr. Humphrey Jerome."

"Miss Marplay speaking, Sims. I must talk to Mr. Jerome at once."

"Mr. Jerome has not yet risen," said the butler reprovingly, "but I shall tell him that you are on the wire, miss. Hold on, please."

Joan fumed with impatience while she waited, although the wait was quite short.

"Joan, my dear! I didn't expect to hear your voice so early in the morning."

"Uncle Humphrey, I've just seen the morning paper. Why didn't you let me know at once that father had escaped?"

"I didn't wish to alarm you, my dear. I thought he would probably be found within a few hours."

"He hasn't been found yet?"

"Not so far as I know—and I am in constant touch with the authorities. The police, have, of course, been informed and they are—er—taking steps. I have an old photograph of your father which is being touched up to resemble him as he is today and within a few hours a copy will be sent to every police station in London and the Home Counties."

"I should like one, Uncle Humphrey."

"You may have it with pleasure, my dear."

"What does Sir John say about him?"

Mr Jerome coughed.

"Sir John is very annoyed. Furious, indeed. He says that—er—"

"Don't try to break it gently, Uncle Humphrey."

"Well, my dear, he seems to think that your father is incurably insane—a dangerous homicidal lunatic, in fact."

"Then he really may make an attempt to kill these men?"

"There seems to be no doubt of that."

Joan thought for a moment.

"Send the photograph, please, to Miss Joan Trimm, Malbrouk Court, Marble Arch."

The lawyer was startled. "What did you say, my dear? I didn't quite catch it."

"I asked you to send the photograph to Miss Joan Trimm,

Malbrouk Court, Marble Arch. Goodbye, Uncle Humphrey. I'll get in touch with you again in a day or two."

"But—Joan!"

Joan hung up. She went back to the breakfast room. Agatha saw at a glance that a scene was brewing and if there was one thing Agatha abhorred it was an emotional display. Playing for time, she rang for the maid, who for the next few minutes was in and out of the room with trays, giving Joan no chance to unburden herself.

"You've seen the paper?" Joan exploded when they were left alone at last.

"I have. Toast?"

Joan dismissed the subject of food with an impatient gesture.

"Trimmy, my father has escaped."

"My good girl, that's no reason why you should go without your breakfast. It's no good worrying on an empty stomach. The doctors say that only leads to stomach ulcers. Will you have an egg with your mushrooms and bacon?"

"I don't want anything."

"I thought the time had passed when I had to make you eat. When you have had some breakfast, I shall willingly discuss the situation—but not before."

Joan snatched up a piece of dry toast and broke it savagely.

"Trimmy, you can be the most exasperating person in the world."

"You try playing nursemaid to a girl of twenty, then you'll be qualified to talk about exasperating people. Pass the marmalade." But Agatha's curiosity got the better of her:

"Why did you tell Mr. Jerome to send something or other to Miss Joan Trimm? She doesn't exist."

"Yes, she does," replied Joan, through a mouthful of toast. "I'm Joan Trimm. It's an alias I'm adopting for my job."

Agatha's eyebrows rose almost to the roots of her hair. "What job? No, don't tell me now. Breakfast is no time to explode bombshells. I can see you're on the verge of spontaneous combustion." She sighed. "Has all my training in ladylike repose and decorum gone for nothing?"

"Not quite nothing," replied Joan pointedly, picking up Agatha's cigarette which had rolled off the edge of her saucer and burned a hole in the tablecloth. "I seem to have heard of ashtrays, for instance—although probably not from you."

In spite of herself Joan made a hearty meal. Although she was boyishly slim she had an excellent appetite.

"We're going to London today, Trimmy," she said, over her second cup of coffee.

"We can't," replied Agatha, lighting a cigarette. "I've started to paint the car again."

"We'll go by train. Trimmy, I've got to be on the spot."

"There's nothing you can do. You can't find your father. You've never even seen him."

"I want to be there when he's found."

"But he may remain at large for weeks."

"We'll stay in London until he's found."

"My sweet but brainless infant, have you thought what our hotel bills would amount to?"

"We shan't stop at a hotel. There's a place at Marble Arch which advertises furnished flats by the day, week or month at modest rentals. We'll go there."

"And sit twiddling our thumbs in a two-by-four flatlet, waiting for news? We'll be much better off waiting here, where at least we have things to do."

"I shan't be twiddling my thumbs, Trimmy. I'm going to get a job."

"Are you quite mad? What kind of job?"

"I don't know. A job on the *Echo*."

Agatha eyed her sternly. "Joan, what wild scheme is at the back of all this?"

"Trimmy, my father is out to kill the four men who own the *Echo*. He'll make straight for Fleet Street and the best place to look for him will be in the *Echo* offices. There's something else on my mind. Father thinks he was robbed of the newspaper. I'm going to have a shot at finding out the truth about that."

"My dear Joan, if it happened, it happened twenty years ago. What earthly chance would you have to find out anything about it now? And if, by a miracle, you did find proof that the paper was stolen from your father, what good would that do him?"

"If father stays at large long enough he may kill one of these men. If I can prove that he had a genuine motive for doing so, people will view his crime in a different light. Oh, I know he'll still be mad. He'll still be a murderer. But if I can only justify him a little, I shan't mind so much."

"In my forty-odd years of life, young woman, I have never heard of anything so completely absurd. In the first place, you haven't a chance of obtaining this job."

"Then why not let me try for it?"

"In the second place, if you did find work with the *Echo* you would be in no position to pry into the affairs of the heads of the firm."

"One of them might have a weakness for pretty girls, Trimmy."

"And if they found out what you were trying to do, there's no saying what they might do to you."

"Have you ever been afraid of a man, Trimmy?"

"God forbid!" said Agatha grimly.

"Then why should I be?"

"That's different. You're young and silly and passably good looking."

"Passably good looking. I like that, Trimmy. I'm beautiful and you know it!"

"Worst of all, you're vain. When a girl's vain, heaven help her. A little flattery, and a man can do anything with her."

"I thought you feared these men would use clubs, not flattery. In any case, I'm ready to face either method of approach."

"Joan, if you think I'm going to let you—"

"We'd better start packing, Trimmy."

"Joan, for the last time, definitely and irrevocably, I will not hear of it!"

*

Two hours later Agatha sat rigidly erect in the London train, staring out of the window at the flying countryside, disapproval expressed by every taut line of her angular body.

The Spectre of Fleet Street

Keep the corpse of a tall man in cold storage until its flesh is the unwholesome white of the underside of a fish, cake the fingernails with dirt, bristle the chin with stubble, give it matted black hair, clothe it in the cast-offs of a scarecrow, set it on its feet, endow it with the jerky stalk of a robot: and you have the twin of the man who walked along Fleet Street a minutes before three that afternoon.

He was talking to himself, his grey lips writhing like sliced worms, revealing teeth broken and decayed and stained brown by tobacco tar. His eyes, bleary blue with mottled yellow irises, stared out of his head like those of an epileptic. In his shaking hand a walking stick rattled a broken tattoo on the pavement.

Passers-by gave him a wide berth. Those who had once been his friends ducked into doorways or crossed the road to avoid him, for an encounter with Flinders meant parting with a few shillings. Flinders—the living dead, an animated corpse pickled in alcohol, haunting Fleet Street by day and night, cadging the price of a drink, the price of a bed, his manhood lost in the fog of a thousand alcoholic yesterdays.

In his day there had been no greater newspaperman than Flinders. He had once had a leg broken in a railway smash and before he would let a doctor attend to it he wrote for his newspaper an account of the collision so vivid that a million readers saw it as clearly the following morning as though it were happening before their eyes. When King Edward VII died Flinders composed a memorial ode that was reprinted all over the world. He wrote it in eight minutes flat with a copy boy breathing on his neck, snatching for the printer each line as it was written. On the day the Armistice was signed, Flinders was assigned to prepare a concise history of the Great War for the following morning's paper and, by dictating solidly for twelve hours, turned out thirty thousand words of copy before the country edition went to press at midnight.

In those days he was the most inspired talker in Fleet Street, then the street of inspired talkers. Hour after hour he would stand at a bar with a glass in his hand, holding a case-hardened audience spellbound while he blended airy nonsense with profound truth, paradox with poetry, fun with fantasy, myth with mimicry. When he set down his empty glass one of the audience would silently place a coin on the bar and the barmaid would fill it up again, the measure running over while she craned her neck to catch every word.

It was his boast that he could drink three men under the table before starting a hard day's work. No idle boast, for a time; but when he did slip, he went downhill like a toboggan on the Cresta Run and wound up in the gutter with nothing left of the old Flinders but an insatiable thirst.

Looking neither to left nor to right, he steered a wavering course through the plate-glass door of the *London Evening Echo* building. The commissionaire came forward and jerked an emphatic thumb toward the street.

"Out!" he said flatly.

"L-listen, man, l-listen," gasped Flinders, his teeth grinding, "I've g-got to see Lord Noel Stretton. It's important."

"'E don't want to see you."

"But I've g-got something for him. C-copy."

"You worked that one on me before and when I let you upstairs you 'adn't no more copy than my aunt Fanny. All you wanted was to scrounge five bob off of 'im."

"I've g-got some paragraphs for him. Look."

With trembling eagerness Flinders fumbled in a torn

pocket and produced some grubby scraps of paper covered with dipsomaniacal hieroglyphics in pencil. The commissionaire regarded them—and the shaking grimy hand that held them—with distaste. Shrugging his shoulders, he lifted a telephone which stood on his desk.

"Put me through to Lord Noel. This is Parker, my lord. Flinders is down 'ere. Says 'e's got some pars for you."

"I've heard that one before," drawled the gossip writer lazily. "Chuck him out."

"That's what I meant to do, my lord. I shouldn't 'ave troubled you, only 'e's got some bits of paper with 'im—"

"Hold on a moment."

Lord Noel cocked an eye at his writing pad, on which a solitary paragraph was scribbled. His brain had gone stale and nothing worth printing had come in the post. He was desperately short of material for 'Other People's Washing,' his daily column of society gossip. If Flinders had a paragraph for him, it was sure to be pure fiction—unless he had cribbed it—but that would not matter unless it was too delirious a piece of imaginative art. After all, if Lord Noel printed the bald truth about society people his column would make dull reading.

"Read his stuff to me over the phone."

"I can't, my lord. They didn't teach Greek at the school I went to."

"Oh, all right. Send him up. If he's wasting my time, I'll give him hell."

"Very good, my lord."

The commissionaire looked severely at Flinders.

"You can go up—but 'e'll scrag you if you're trying it on again."

In desperate haste, his legs stuttering wildly, Flinders blundered into one of the lifts. The commissionaire turned and inclined his head toward a pretty girl who had just come in.

"Yes, miss?"

"I wish to see Lord Noel Stretton."

"'Ave you an appointment, miss?"

"No, but he knows me. At least we've met. My name is Trimm, Miss Joan Trimm."

"I'll tell 'im you're 'ere, miss."

Joan thanked him and let her eyes rove over the huge marble entrance hall with its wide staircase impressive battery of lifts. In a few moments the commissionaire returned to her side.

"You're to go right up, miss. Fourth floor."

Lord Noel was waiting for her at the door of glass-walled cubicle, his normally bored-looking face lit up with pleasure.

"This is a delightful surprise."

"I'm afraid it's rather an intrusion. I've come ask you to help me."

"I shall be delighted. What can I do?"

"I'm looking for a job."

He made a clicking sound with his tongue and teeth. "It would be that. What kind of job?"

"Any job at all as long as it's on the *Echo*."

"That's a tall order." Lord Noel rubbed his chin and looked down his long nose at her. "Come in and we'll talk it over."

At sight of the cadaverous figure sprawling in chair in a corner of the room Joan started back and drew in her breath sharply.

"It's all right. That's only Flinders. He's quite harmless. I'll get rid of him in a minute and we'll be free to talk. Do sit down. Cigarette?"

Joan took one and Lord Noel leaned toward her with a match.

"You know, Miss Trimm, this is one of the things that happen in dreams. I've been wishing I could see you again and—lo! Out of a clear sky, here you are."

"Looking for a job," Joan reminded him.

"H'm. Yes. Now you've said something. Jobs on the *Echo*—in Fleet Street generally—are scarce. I'm besieged by debutantes who want to be newspaperwomen. The talkies have a lot to answer for. I'll do my best, but it may not be good enough. You've had the usual experience, I suppose?"

"None whatever."

"Yes, that's the usual. But you feel sure your fresh outlook would be invaluable to us?"

"Not very sure."

"Well, you're original in that, at least. Most of 'em are certain." He leaned back and crossed one long leg over the other. "Given a free hand, you think you could make something of our Woman's Page?"

"I'm sure I couldn't."

"Then it's the Dramatic Critic's job you're after?"

"Not that either. It isn't going to be easy for you to help me, Lord Noel. I can't pretend to have a flair for writing. I don't think I should be any good in an editorial job. I can type passably well and take dictation in shorthand, if it isn't given too quickly, and—and—well, that's about all. It sounds rather hopeless, but do help me if you can. I have a strong personal reason for wanting a job on the *Echo*."

Lord Noel's eyes searched her face. He smiled.

"I'll see what can be done. Let me get rid of Flinders and we'll start again from scratch." He held out his hand to the derelict in the corner. "Let's see what you've got."

Flinders handed him the soiled scraps of paper. Wrinkling his brows, Lord Noel deciphered the wandering scrawl of the topmost:

"Society is amused by the story, which has just leaked out, of Lady Maudesleigh's orange kitten. Her ladyship's pet is actually two years old and began life white. Lady Maudesleigh had always wanted an orange kitten but could not find one for love nor money, so she bought a white one, dyed it orange, and gives it brandy every day to keep it small."

Lord Noel dropped the scrap of paper into a wire basket on his desk.

"I can use that," he said, "but I shall have to substitute the Countess of Boaz for Lady Maudesleigh. Lady Maudesleigh would sue for damages, but the countess doesn't mind what one says about her as long as her name appears in print."

He glanced at the next scrawled paragraph.

"You cribbed that from 'Mayfair Through the Keyhole' in the *Courier*," he said, dropping it in the wastepaper basket. "What's this? 'In anticipation of her death which, since she is not yet thirty, is not likely to occur for many years, Susette, the famous dancer, has had a silver coffin made to measure, which stands in a corner of her bedroom.' I bought that paragraph from you two years ago, Flinders, and you've tried it on me four times since. Next time I'll make you eat it."

The door opened and an unhealthily pink face with a bald head looked in.

"I say, Stretton— Oh, I didn't know you had visitors." A bulgy, too smartly tailored male form came into the room. Two piggy eyes stared at Joan so long and so intently that she flushed to the tips of her ears, then they looked at Lord Noel, demanding to be introduced as plainly as words should have expressed it.

Lord Noel said coldly:

"I'm busy at present, Mr Craven."

Ambrose Craven looked annoyed. He went out of the room and slammed the door.

"You haven't anything more, Flinders?" asked Lord Noel calmly.

The corpse shook his head.

"All right. You can have five bob for the orange kitten par. I'll give you a chit to the cashier."

The corpse brightened and his hands shook with eagerness, but before the slip for the cashier was made out the telephone bell rang. Lord Noel lifted the receiver.

"Stretton speaking." He listened, then scowled. "I'm still busy, Mr. Craven. Oh, if you put it that way, I'll come along to your room directly."

His brow thunderous, he banged down the receiver and stood up.

"I'll be back presently, Miss Trimm." On the point of leaving the room, he shot a hard glance over his shoulder at Flinders. "Don't try to touch Miss Trimm for money while I'm gone, or there'll be hell to pay!"

When the door closed behind Lord Noel, Joan shot an uneasy glance at Flinders, her flesh crawling with repugnance. She was reassured by his hunched, lifeless pose. He seemed to have gone into a trance.

Suddenly, without stirring, he spoke; and his graveyard croak made her jump.

"I wouldn't borrow money from you. I only borrow from my friends. I have so many friends, they're all so eager to help me. They know they'll get it back one day, every penny. I've only got to pull myself together and every editor in London will be falling over himself to secure my services. Yes, every editor in London. They know what Flinders can do when he likes. They know. Yes, they know."

"You've been in Fleet Street a long time?" Joan ventured.

It was so long before he answered that she decided he had fallen into his trance again; and it was with surprise that she eventually heard the hollow voice muttering:

"A long time? A long time? All eternity. I worked for this

paper before Stretton was born. I didn't write gossip. You don't send a man on a boy's errand. When they wanted a story to stand Fleet Street on its head, that was when they sent for Flinders."

"Then you knew the former proprietor, Lucius Marplay?"

Another lengthy pause, and then:

"Marplay! The Chief, we used to call him. I was one of his bright young men. The brightest. Mark Peters was another. Peters!" He spat suddenly and the spittle trickled down his greasy waistcoat.

Joan averted her eyes.

"What was Marplay like?" she asked eagerly.

"Marplay?" Flinders narrowed his eyes to thin slits and squinted cunningly at Joan. "Why do you want to know about him? He's mad. Crazy as a coot. Why are you asking me all these questions? What do you care about Marplay?"

"Nothing," Joan lied, in a casual tone. "I've heard stories about him and they made me curious, that's all."

Flinders regarded her suspiciously for a long time and then his head dropped on his chest and he seemed to fall asleep.

Shortly Lord Noel came back.

"Silly old fool!" he said viciously, slamming the door.

"Who?" asked Joan.

"Craven—the bald-headed old ass who looked in a few minutes ago. One of the big noises in this office. He got me up in his room and tried to pump me about you. Who were you? What did you do? Did I know you well? Were you looking for a job?"

"What did you tell him?"

"The polite equivalent of: 'Go to hell!'"

"Didn't you promise to help me find a job on the *Echo*?"

"I did, but not under Craven's wing. He's an unsavoury hound. No girl is safe with him."

"I should like to meet him," said Joan quietly.

Lord Noel stared. "After what I've told you about him?"

Reddening, Joan nodded.

"Oh," said Lord Noel. He looked stern. "I see."

He sat down at his desk and pulled the writing pad toward him. Without looking at Joan he added: "Mr Craven's room is on the top floor. You can't miss it; his name's on the door."

Joan hesitated, but there was nothing she could say unless she told him the whole truth, which was out of the question.

She held out her hand. "Thanks for seeing me."

Lord Noel did not look up. "Good day," he replied stiffly.

Almost two hours later Joan came out of the *Echo* building, her spirits seesawing between elation and gloom. Elation because Ambrose Craven had offered her a job and she had accepted it; gloom because she rather liked Lord Noel and could imagine what he must be thinking of her.

The interview with Mr. Craven had been long and intimate. Joan was to report for duty the following morning. She was not to be employed by the *Echo* but by Mr. Craven personally— Mr. Craven had made quite a point of that. There might be occasions, he had said, his eyes fixed on the ceiling, when he would require her to take dictation after hours at his flat. Would she mind that? No, Joan had said, she would not mind that. Mr Craven had rubbed his hands and said he was sure she would prove satisfactory.

Joan turned right and walked along Fleet Street toward the Strand. She had not gone far when a voice behind her said:

"Miss Marplay!"

Turning, she stared into the haggard face of Flinders.

There was a subtle difference in his appearance since she had seen him two hours ago. He looked no less dead, but somehow more alive. That was absurd but it was the nearest she could come to putting the difference into words. He smelt of whiskey.

That, if she had only known it, was the reason for the change in him. Two large whiskeys had stilled for the moment the craving that was eating him alive and stirred to fleeting life his moribund brain.

"Miss Marplay?" he repeated.

"Why do you call me that?"

"Because it's your name. Isn't it?"

"How do you know?"

"Deduction, my dear lady," he leered. "Elementary, I assure you. In Stretton's office you called yourself 'Trimm', but the initials 'J.M.' are inscribed in large letters on your handbag. You plied me with questions about Marplay. At the time I was fogged but after-wards I began to think. I remembered that twenty years ago Marplay's only child was born, a baby daughter named Joan. Two and two, my dear Miss Marplay, two and two."

Again, that narrowing of his eyes, that cunning squint.

"What do you want with a job on the *Echo*? Why did you wish to meet Craven? You're up to something, Miss Joan Marplay. You're trying to find out something."

"Supposing I am?" replied Joan steadily, watching his face.

Eyeing her furtively, he wiped his nose on his sleeve.

"I might be able to help you. I know something. Something Mark Peters once paid me a lot of money to forget."

"What?" asked Joan eagerly.

"Not so fast, not so fast. I haven't forgotten it. It's here"—he tapped his forehead— "yes, it's here—but—but—I can't always find it when I want it."

"Try to remember. If it is of importance to me, I'll pay you well."

"That's not the way one remembers," croaked Flinders, shaking his head. He went on shaking it until Joan almost screamed. "No, the way to remember is to sit in a corner by a fire with a glass in one's hand and a bottle in reach. Then the memories come, tripping over one another, a long parade of them. They come so quickly that you can hardly grasp one before the others shoulder it on."

Joan saw the hint. She took a pound note from her bag and pressed it into his grimy fingers, which closed on it eagerly.

"You'll try to think, won't you?" she said urgently. "When you remember what it was Mr. Peters paid you to forget, write it down. Where can I find you again? Where do you live?"

"I live in a dosshouse. They don't allow lady visitors. It wouldn't be proper. Give me your address. I'll get in touch with you."

Scribbling her address on a page of her notebook, Joan tore out the page and handed it to him.

"You won't forget? I shall hear from you?"

"You will hear from me."

Giving her a long look, Flinders turned and stalked off the pavement into the twin streams of traffic. Heedless of screaming brakes, shrieking horns, the curses of drivers who had to pull up sharply to avoid running him down, he headed straight across the street for the door of a public house. On the other side he stooped and salvaged a cigarette end from the gutter.

Joan stared after him. Did he really know something? Had Mark Peters really paid him to forget it? Or was it all a lie concocted for the purpose of coaxing money out of her?

The Late Sinclair Ellis

Eight fifty-five a.m. The cloakroom devoted to the feminine office staff of the *Echo* rang with eager voices like a nest of starlings in the eaves of an old house. By closing her eyes Joan could have imagined herself back at school, except that some of the snatches of conversation she overheard were a little sophisticated even for schoolgirls. A dark, serious-looking girl in spectacles, soaping her hands at a neighbouring washbasin, gave Joan a friendly smile.

"You're new, aren't you?"

"Yes, this is my first day."

"I noticed you didn't punch your card at the time clock in the employees' entrance. We're supposed to, you know."

"I haven't a card. You see, I'm not exactly employed by the paper. I'm to be a sort of personal secretary to Mr Craven."

The other girl glanced sharply at Joan, her eyes round behind her thick lenses.

"Oh," she said, putting a wealth of meaning into that one word.

Joan was aware that in her immediate vicinity the flow of airy chatter had abruptly ceased, that several girls were looking at her oddly. One of them laughed and started humming:

She Was Poor but she was Honest..."

"Shut up!" snapped the dark, spectacled girl. She turned away and dried her hands at a hot-air machine. Picking up her handbag, she started for the door but halfway she paused and looked back at Joan, beside the row of washbasins.

"I've found it pays to mind my own business but you look a decent sort, so I'll give you a word of advice. Watch your step with Elegant Ambrose."

"Elegant Ambrose?"

"Yes, the Cardboard Casanova... Mr. Craven...your new boss. He's a nasty bit of work but heaps of girls are silly enough to fall for his line and they all live to regret it. Don't be a fool like Rita."

"Who's Rita?"

"Rita was once his very private and personal secretary. She thought she knew men. She knows better now. I saw her in Shaftesbury Avenue the other day and she looked ghastly."

"Oh," said Joan soberly. "I see. Thanks for the warning."

"I hope you've enough sense to take it. Rita hadn't. I warned her, too, but she was too clever to pay attention. I've got to go now. See you later."

Joan went upstairs to her new employer's office on the top floor. A sour-faced middle-aged woman with a stiff back, clad in severe coat and skirt, was seated at a desk in the outer room. She sniffed audibly when Joan came in.

"Miss Trimm?" she said, in the chilling voice of a prison matron. "I am Miss Withers."

"Good morning, Miss Withers," replied Joan meekly, but with an impish glint in her eyes.

"Good morning. That is your desk—in the corner."

Miss Withers sniffed again and became very busy with some papers but Joan had a feeling that the older woman was studying her out of the corners of her eyes. To test her suspicion she took powder and lipstick from her bag and began to apply an elaborate make-up. Another sniff told her that she had not been mistaken.

In a few minutes a bell rang twice.

"That's for you," said Miss Withers icily.

Gathering up notebook and pencil, Joan sailed into the inner room. Ambrose Craven was seated at his desk, wearing a new tie and smelling strongly of Jockey Club.

"Ah, good morning, Miss Trimm," he said, with a glucose smile. "Sit down."

Joan took the chair he indicated, crossed one neat leg over the other, flipped open her notebook and poised a freshly sharpened pencil. For some moments Mr. Craven eyed her legs with the coy smile of a cat which has cornered a plump mouse, then he rose and walked to the window. He stood there looking out, teeter-tottering on toes and heels, his podgy hands clasped behind him. In the morning sunlight his bald head shone like a billiard ball.

"You know, Miss Trimm," he said reflectively, staring at a patch of blue above the roof tops, "you're much too attractive to be wasted in an office."

*

Two mornings later Joan encountered Lord Noel Stretton in one of the corridors of the building. He said: "Good morning!" curtly and passed on. A moment later he turned on his heel and came back to her.

"Miss Trimm."

"Yes?" said Joan, over her shoulder.

"I hear you dined with Craven last night."

"Your information is correct. If it interests you, I have another date with him tonight."

"I can't understand you. A fat pig like Craven can't possibly attract you—and you don't look the gold-digger type. Fun and games with Ambrose will only land you up to your neck in trouble."

"You said all that before."

"So I did. And you haven't taken a blind bit of notice."

"That being the case," retorted Joan icily, "mightn't it be a good idea to mind your own business?"

"It probably would," agreed Lord Noel, staring at her, "since I can't give you the damned good spanking you obviously need!"

*

Seven days passed. Lucius Marplay was still at large.

On the afternoon of the seventh day Mark Peters sat at his desk, frowning over a communication from Scotland Yard, which reported in effect that there was nothing to report. During the twenty-four hours immediately following Marplay's escape the police had made rapid strides but it now appeared that the strides had been made up a blind alley. The more they investigated the less the police knew of the madman's whereabouts.

On the morning after the escape Sir John Digby had received an envelope with an 'E.C.' postmark, addressed in Marplay's scholarly handwriting, containing the pawnticket for his fur-lined overcoat. At sight of the enclosure the specialist had almost had an apoplectic stroke. When the blood stopped rushing to his head and he was able to speak—although not very coherently—he had rung up Scotland Yard and reported the matter.

The pawnbroker was questioned and remembered having seen his unusual client stepping into a taxi outside the pawnshop (he considered it wise not to mention the rubber truncheon he had sold to Mr. Marplay). The taxi driver was found and reported having stopped at Harrods, where the old gentleman had made various purchases, including a suitcase, food and drink and other material comforts. The taxi driver had dropped him at the corner of Fleet Street and Fetter Lane; and there ended the trail that had begun so promisingly. No one could be found who had seen Mr. Marplay from the moment he dismissed the taxi and walked away.

Two plainclothes men had done nothing for a week except parade Fleet Street, looking for the elderly lunatic. They had gained useful knowledge of the varying merits of the bitter beer on draught at Fleet Street pubs, but had learned precisely nothing about their quarry.

It had seemed likely that the old gentleman had made for the disused *Echo* building and that dusty haunt of rats and mice was tramped through from basement to attic by a squad of policemen who raked over piles of rubbish and wrestled with fallen beams and broken partitions but failed to find the smallest trace of the man they were seeking, which—since they did not discover the secret room—is hardly surprising.

Mr. Marplay's photograph, skilfully brought up to date, beamed down from the walls of every police station in the country on posters offering a hundred pounds reward for information leading to his capture. The reward went unclaimed although from Land's End to John O' Groats old gentlemen out for their morning strolls were driven to profane fury by strangers peering searchingly into their faces.

Brr-rring… Brr-rring...

A small hand, white and shapely as that of a cultured woman, reached for the telephone.

"Mark Peters speaking."

"Mr. Grainger of the *Courier* wishes to talk to you, Mr. Peters."

"Put him through."

After a pause the voice of the managing director of the *London Morning Courier* came over the wire.

"Peters? This is Grainger. I've been expecting to hear from you."

"My partners and I have not yet reached a decision."

"Oh. Well…" Grainger coughed. "As a matter of fact, I've had a tentative offer from the Harmer Group."

"Yes?" Peters' voice was cold. "You haven't forgotten that you gave me a thirty-day option on the *Courier?*"

"Oh, quite…but, you see, this offer from Harmer may not remain open."

"That," said Peters curtly, "is your affair. I intend to hold you to your agreement. Good afternoon."

Replacing the receiver, Peters opened a cabinet which stood on his desk and selected a cigar. He pierced and lit it with exquisite care, holding the match so that the flame barely made contact with the tobacco.

Apart from the cigar cabinet, a blotting pad, a silver cigarette box, and a telephone, were the only articles on the desk. Mark Peters contrived to do a maximum of work with a minimum of gadgets. Except for the desk, a few chairs and a thick carpet, the room was bare. Unlike Sinclair Ellis, the dummy editor-in-chief, whose bookcase was ornamented with busts of Napoleon and Lord Northcliffe, Peters struck no attitudes to emphasize his importance.

He dressed more quietly than any of his staff, in double-breasted suits of black saxony with white pencil stripes, white linen shirts with soft collars, grey ties and black shoes. A pearl tiepin was the only article of jewellery he ever wore.

As short and slight as an office boy, he yet seemed to tower head and shoulders over much larger men. There was something electric about Peters, a magnetism he made no conscious effort to exert.

A soft-footed secretary came into the room, placed a copy of the latest edition of the *Echo* at Peters' elbow and as silently withdrew. Peters thrust the police report into a drawer and turned his attention to the newspaper. The *Echo* was Mark Peters' God. Every printed line of it was important to him. He read it in detail every afternoon, missing nothing, not even the classified advertisements. While he read, he made marginal notes in blue pencil for the benefit of the managing editor, to whom the pencilled paper was afterwards sent.

He drew a ring round a three-line paragraph at the foot of the front page and wrote in the margin: "This was worth half a column!" A long interview with a cabinet minister earned the comment: "Never waste space on Lord Halperin! All he has to say was said before the war."

Below a fatuous report of a dog show he scribbled: "Fire the man who wrote this!" The serial was tersely dismissed with: "Rubbish!" and across the Woman's Page he scrawled: "This won't do. Must be brighter. Our appeal is to housewives, shopgirls, not dowager duchesses." The political cartoon he left severely alone—the cartoonist, best in his line in England, had a contract which permitted him to draw what he pleased, whether it pleased the proprietors or not—but the comic strip was scathingly labelled: "This is not funny!"

Suddenly he dropped the pencil with a startled exclamation. He was staring angrily, incredulously, at an item among the Death Notices:

ELLIS—On the 17th of June, at his office in Fleet Street, Sinclair Ellis, aged fifty-three, of severe head injuries.

Ellis dead? This was absurd. Peters had lunched with Ellis an hour ago. The item was a stupid blunder, or an idiotic practical joke. In either case, the man responsible for it would be fired on the spot.

He read the bald lines again and his eyes narrowed to pin

points. "On the 17th of June…" That was today's date. "…of severe head injuries…" Good God! Could it be that Marplay— No, that was impossible. For an unauthorized person to pass the hall porter of a newspaper office is almost as hard as for a rich man to enter heaven.

Peters reached for his telephone, but his hand halted in mid-air. He stared out of the window for a moment in silent thought. His brows dark with anger, his mouth tightening to a thin line, he rose and left the room, carrying the newspaper under his arm. As he swept past his secretary's desk in the outer room that efficient young woman glimpsed his face and realized instantly that there was trouble in store for someone. From the bottom of her heart, she was fervently thankful that that someone was not her. When he went on the warpath Mark Peters was a holy terror.

The room occupied by Ellis was only fifty feet away down a carpeted corridor. Peters reached it in a few swift strides, threw open the door and walked in.

"Ellis, have you seen this—"

Peters drew in his breath with a hiss. The newspaper dropped from under his arm, which had suddenly become limp. He put out a shaking hand and closed the door.

Sinclair Ellis was slumped over his desk, his leonine head resting on the blotter, his arms sprawling lifelessly.

His eyeglasses dangled over the edge of the desk, swinging pendulum-wise at the end of their thick black ribbon.

On the floor lay a rubber truncheon.

The divisional surgeon's face was pale when he straightened up from examining the body of Sinclair Ellis and turned to the group of men standing behind him.

"It looks like the work of a madman. At least half-a-dozen savage blows were struck. The first or second cracked his skull like a nut. There was no need for the others. The murderer must have gone on pounding viciously at a dead man."

"He was still warm when I found him," said Mark Peters.

"He's warm now. That's your central heating system. The body won't grow cold for an hour or so."

Peters put out a hand and touched the dangling wrist of his dead partner.

"He was warmer than that. As warm as a living being."

"Then he couldn't have been dead longer than a few minutes." The divisional surgeon gathered up hat, gloves, umbrella and bag. "There's nothing more I can do here. I'll let you have my report later this afternoon, Superintendent."

"Very good, Doctor."

Tall and muscular, in the early fifties, with a clipped grey moustache, a high-bridged nose, dominant and penetrating blue eyes, Superintendent Wrenn looked more like the colonel of a crack cavalry regiment in mufti than the efficient C.I.D. official which he was. He wore a grey tweed raglan, a dark grey suit, immaculate white linen, a black tie and handmade black calf shoes, and carried a pearl-grey fedora.

Standing near the door, he watched his subordinates carrying out their routine tasks. A plainclothes man with a powerful camera and a flashgun was photographing the corpse from a dozen different angles. Another was testing the rubber truncheon for fingerprints (this man had in his possession a set of Lucius Marplay's fingerprints, taken from some of Marplay's personal belongings at the time of the escape from the mental home); a third detective was dusting every polished surface with white powder, to bring out latent prints; a fourth was making detailed measurements of the room.

"You don't leave much to chance," remarked Peters.

"This is only the beginning," replied the superintendent.

Walking to the desk, he used a pair of tweezers to pick up a receipt form which was lying beside the battered head of the corpse. Across it was printed in capitals: PAID IN FULL; and it was signed "Lucius Marplay."

"You say this is Marplay's handwriting?"

"I'm sure of it."

"Well, we'll soon know positively. The graphologist at Scotland Yard will be able to tell. When Marplay escaped from the mental home and we started looking for him we obtained samples of his writing."

"If Scotland Yard were half as efficient as it claims to be you'd have found Marplay at the start and this wouldn't have happened."

"We can't work miracles. We had nothing to go on. For all the trace of him that could be found he might have vanished into thin air when he stepped out of his taxi in Fleet Street about a week ago."

"You'd better find him now. Neither my other partners nor myself will be safe until you do."

"Paid in full," said Superintendent Wrenn, glancing at the receipt form. "He must think you owe him a tremendous debt if only death can settle it."

"We went into that with your commissioner at the time of Marplay's escape. He imagines we stole this newspaper from him. An absurd delusion; but if madmen hadn't delusions they wouldn't be mad."

They heard a high-pitched voice making querulous protests in the corridor outside and a deep, matter-of-fact voice answering them. Another plaintive outburst, then a plainclothes detective came into the room, shutting the door behind him.

"A gentleman wants to see you, Superintendent. Says his name is Craven."

"One of my partners," said Peters. "For God's sake don't let him in. He'll have hysterics all over the place."

"I don't intend to. My men need room to work. Tell Mr. Craven I'll see him in due course, officer. Make him go away. I can't be disturbed by arguments in the passage."

"Very good, sir."

The police officer who had been examining the rubber truncheon came over to Superintendent Wrenn, holding it by the leather thong.

"I've checked the fingerprints on this, sir. They're Marplay's, all right."

"You're dead sure of that?"

"Positive, sir."

"Any other prints on it?"

"None whatever, sir."

"Then Marplay is our man. Take charge of the truncheon for the present. Later on we'll have a shot at finding out where it came from. Sergeant Leet!"

A plainclothes man came forward smartly. "Yes sir?"

"From what the divisional surgeon said it seems likely that Mr. Peters discovered the body within a minutes of the murder. In that case, Marplay may still be in the building. Mr. Peters tells me he phoned the Yard as soon as he realized that Mr Ellis was dead. After that he 'phoned to the doormen on duty at each entrance to this building and the old one and instructed them to lock the doors. Unless Marplay made his getaway very quickly he'd find himself locked in. This room is on the top floor. Eight storeys, isn't it, Mr. Peters? It would take Marplay several minutes to run downstairs."

"Unless he took the lift," said Sergeant Leet brightly.

"He didn't," replied Mark Peters. "I spoke to the men running the three lifts. None of them took him down."

"What about the roof? He may have escaped that way."

"The wireless room is on the roof. It's a glass-walled cubicle, high above the rest of the building. One of the wireless staff would have seen him."

"Then, if we've got the time factor right," said Superintendent Wrenn, "Marplay is still in the building."

"Where he must have been ever since he escaped from the asylum," said Peters, with a sharp intake of his breath. "Add it up for yourself, Superintendent, your answer's bound to be the same as mine: he alighted from his taxi in Fleet Street just over a week ago; he hasn't been seen since, although his picture is plastered up all over the place and Fleet Street—and the whole of London—has been scoured for him; today he suddenly turns up in this building and commits a murder."

"Yes," agreed the superintendent, "the answer seems obvious. He must have a hiding place in the building."

"If he has," said Sergeant Leet, "it's a damned good one. We went over the place with a fine-tooth comb at the time of his escape."

"Find him this time, Sergeant Leet," snapped Wrenn, "if you have to take the building apart. There are eight constables waiting downstairs. Take them and make a detailed search of this building and the old one next door. Overlook nothing. Find Lucius Marplay. You know what he looks like?"

"Like my grand-uncle Henry, from all the photographs I've seen," said Sergeant Leet, "only pleasanter looking."

He left the room. Superintendent Wrenn walked toward a heavy old safe of clumsy design which stood in a corner.

"Bit old-fashioned for a modern office."

"I believe it dates back to the founding of the *Echo*," replied Mark Peters. "It isn't fireproof or airtight, so we don't keep anything of value in it. Ellis used it as a repository for manuscripts that might be useful one day. We occasionally buy feature articles which just miss being important copy and salt them away in the hope that a crisis in the world's affairs or a change in the political trend will make them topical. The safe's crammed full of that sort of thing. If you're interested in safes, Superintendent, you ought to see the time vault in the cashier's department. It's a beauty. You won't find better in a bank."

"About this death notice which first made you suspect that something was wrong—"

"This is it," said Peters, picking up the newspaper which had dropped from his grasp when he found the body of Sinclair Ellis.

The police official's eyebrows rose as he read the laconic announcement:

ELLIS—On the 17th of June, at his office in Fleet Street, Sinclair Ellis, aged fifty-three, of severe head injuries.

"It must have given you a shock when you read it."

"It did. A hell of a shock. That is, when I began to take it seriously. At first, I thought it was a stupid practical joke."

"How did it get into the paper? I thought a newspaper like this had a large staff of proof-readers and so on?"

"I have," said Mark Peters grimly, "but one or two of them won't be working here tomorrow."

Picking up a telephone which stood on the desk, he put through two calls in rapid succession: one to the foreman type-setter, the other to the head proof-reader. He gave orders in clipped, staccato sentences. In a few minutes the officer on duty in the corridor admitted to the room a proof-reader and a compositor. They both blinked uneasily at the body of the late editor-in-chief.

"What do you know about this?" demanded Peters, thrusting the newspaper under the proof-reader's nose.

It was a long sharp nose in the middle of a chinless face. The proof-reader was tall and skinny with bony wrists and ankles. He resembled a stork, except that storks never wear shabby blue suits and steel-rimmed spectacles. Flustered and nervous, he croaked:

"About w-what, sir? Oh, t-that, sir. Why, n-nothing, sir. N-nothing whatever, sir. I—I've never s-seen it before."

"You proofread the Births, Deaths and Marriages?"

"Y-yes, sir, b-but—"

"No buts. Either that's your job or it isn't. If it is, how came you to miss the death notice of your own editor?"

"N-no p-proof of it came to me, sir, of that I'm p-p-positive," stuttered the proof-reader, with a frightened glance at the sprawling corpse. "The d-death notices for today's *Echo* were set up yesterday afternoon. I corrected them last evening. This one wasn't among them. If it had been I'd have—I'd have—I—I don't know just what I'd have done, but I wouldn't have p-passed it. It—it must have been added after I read the proofs."

"Why didn't you recheck them before that page was stereoed this morning?"

"Well, sir, the usual p-procedure—"

"I don't want to hear about the usual procedure. Your services won't be required after today. The cashier will give you two weeks salary in lieu of notice."

For a moment the proof-reader stood staring at his employer in stunned silence, his eyes watering, his hands trembling, his mouth gulping, his Adam's apple bobbing up and down. He was trying desperately to find words with which to plead for another chance, but Mark Peters turned his back on him. With sunken shoulders the man stumbled from the room. At the door Superintendent Wrenn halted him and said:

"I shall want to speak to you before you leave the building."

The proof-reader blinked at him in a bewildered fashion and muttered:

"Oh… I see. Oh, very well. I'll wait at my—my desk."

Mark Peters was showing the death notice to the compositor, an expressionless little man in an ink-stained apron with a chunk of moustache like an untrimmed hedge overhanging his drooping mouth. The compositor was chewing a wad of tobacco and brown juice was oozing through between his lips.

"Did you set up this?"

The compositor peered at it.

"No, I didn't. Never seen it before."

"It's your job to set up the death notices."

"You, won't 'ear me denyin' it. But I never set up that un. I set the rest of these yestiddy arternoon. That un wasn't among 'em. Someun else must 'ave set it up arterwards and shoved it in the galley with the others."

"Who else sets death notices?"

"No one. Not as I know of."

"Why didn't you notice that an extra item had been added to the galley?"

"I do me work the way I bin doin' it for forty years. I got so much time to do it in an' two 'ands to do it with. When a galley's bin proofread an' corrected it's finished with, as far as I'm concerned."

"I see," said Mark Peters grimly. "Very well. You're—"

"I know. I'm fired. Well, that don't break me 'eart. I'm no ruddy mucker of a cockeyed, 'alf-starved proof-reader. I c'n walk into a job as good as this un termorrer mornin'."

The printer walked to the door. As he went out, he said something that sounded like: "Parcels to you, Mr. Peters," but wasn't.

Superintendent Wrenn glanced at Mark Peters to see how he liked that. Peters did not like it. But he forced a smile.

"Marplay must have set up the notice himself," he said. "He used to pride himself on being able to do any job on a newspaper. He could set type by hand or on a linotype as quickly as any of the men. Since we don't run a morning paper, the composing-room is deserted at night. A watchman makes a round of the building once an hour. Between rounds, Marplay would have time to set the notice and put it in the galley with those that had already been corrected."

There was a knock at the door and Sergeant Leet came in.

"I've found an office boy who admits having seen Marplay."

"Bring him in," said Wrenn. "No—on second thoughts, I'll speak to him in the corridor. No need to put the wind up him by letting him see the corpse."

Peters followed the superintendent out of the room. An undersized lad of about fifteen was standing in the corridor beside the burly plainclothes man who was on duty there. He looked scared to death. Wrenn showed him a photograph of Lucius Marplay.

"This the man you saw?"

"Y-yes sir," gulped the boy.

"You're sure of that?"

"Y-yes sir."

"Where did you see him?"

"Just about where we're standing now, sir. He was going into

Mr. Ellis' room. He smiled at me and said: 'Good afternoon.' A very nice old gentleman, he seemed."

"What time was this?"

"A few minutes after three, sir."

"It was at about ten past three that I saw the death notice," said Peters. "I must have missed Marplay by seconds."

In a tone of extreme irritation Wrenn said to the boy:

"Why didn't you ask the old gentleman what he was doing here? Or tell someone that he was prowling about?"

"Well sir, he looked as though he owned the place. I never thought but what he had a perfect right to be here."

"Don't you know that the police have been looking for this man for over a week?"

"N-no sir."

"You must have seen the posters with his photograph that are displayed all over Fleet Street. Damn it all, boy, where are your eyes?"

The boy swallowed convulsively and stared in awe at his questioner. A periodical was protruding from his pocket. Mark Peters reached forward and pulled it out. It was a twopenny blood with a lurid cover.

"This is where his eyes were. These boys are all the same. Every time they leave the building their noses are stuck in trash of this sort."

"He—he was such a nice old gentleman," stammered the boy lamely.

"You want to look out for those nice old gentlemen," said Sergeant Leet unemotionally. "Sometimes they eat little boys, if you know what I mean."

"All right, sonny, run along," grunted Wrenn, hoping that the lad would be out of sight before it occurred to Peters to discharge him. "You, too, Sergeant. Get on the job. Find Lucius Marplay!"

"We're doing our best," replied Sergeant Leet. "There's only been one bit of bother so far. Parker looked in one of the ladies' washrooms and some of the girls misunderstood his intentions."

The boy and the police sergeant hurried away. At a bend in the corridor a fat, agitated man bumped into them. It was Ambrose Craven. Shaking with terror, mopping his perspiring forehead, he waddled unsteadily to the group of men at the door of the late Sinclair Ellis' room.

"My God, Mark, this is terrible!" he wailed. "I told you he'd do it and he's done it. How can you look so calm? Don't you realize he'll kill us all!"

"I don't think there's much for you to worry about, sir," said Superintendent Wrenn soothingly. "Until Marplay is found I shall assign a policeman to escort you wherever you go."

"What good is that?" cried Ambrose Craven. "What could one policeman do against a crazy murderer?"

"He could hold him," retorted Mark Peters, "while you ran like hell."

As though the twentieth-century building were a turreted ruin, a ghost stalked through it, gibbering insanely: the ghost of a smiling, white-haired old gentleman with bats in the belfry and murder on the brain.

A thousand employees felt its chill breath on their cheeks and were shaken by the horror of its smile. A thousand whispers rustled through the building, adding theory to rumour and fiction to fantasy, making massacre out of murder; until the ghost stood in every corner, with blood-dripping knife, lurking for the unwary. A wave of hysteria swept over the clerical employees. No work was done. Every lavatory and washroom was full; the corridors and departmental offices were all but empty. Clerks and typists gathered in clusters, adding gruesome details to a rapidly growing tale of horror, about which none of them knew the simple truth. None of them, that is, but one—and in adding her own embroideries she had forgotten it. She was the telephone operator who had put through Mark Peters' telephone call to Scotland Yard.

Listening in, her mouth had opened wide, her eyes had almost popped out of her head. Turning to her neighbour, she had stammered:

"God, Batey, there's been a murder! Mr. Ellis has been clubbed to death!"

Murder!

The neighbouring operator had shrieked and swallowed her chewing gum. It almost choked her going down. While a third operator was thumping the purpling Batey's back, the first was shouting excitedly to a fourth...

Whispers tremulous with excitement; eyes peering back furtively over hunched shoulders; a tale that grew more gory, more grotesque, with every tick of the clock. The body of Sinclair Ellis became a score of hideously mutilated corpses. The dear old gentleman became a raving maniac, lusting for blood. He was running amok through the building. They were all shut in with them. The doors were locked, they couldn't get out.

Looking out of the window they saw police helmets at every entrance, Flying Squad Bentleys parked in the alley, a dense and growing crowd of curiosity seekers milling about in the street in front of the building.

And through the corridors the ghost stalked, gibbering for blood...

Joan was one of the first to hear the story. A chattering of eager young voices outside Ambrose Craven's office had brought her out, notebook in hand, and it was shouted, with all its ghastly trimmings, into her ear. For a moment her heart stood still. There was a feeling of utter emptiness in the pit of her stomach. It had come, the thing she had dreaded for days. Her father was a murderer.

The thought was horrible enough in itself but the knowledge of what must happen to him was infinitely worse. The police were bound to find him now: he would be dragged like a rat from his hiding-place, held up as a repugnant thing before the world, bullied through a trial that could only end in his incarceration in a criminal lunatic asylum. She did not think of herself, of the new stigma with which her name was smirched, of the brand that she must bear as long as she lived: daughter of a murderer. She thought only of her father, of the pass to which his poor wandering brain had brought him.

Suddenly she turned and hurried away from the other girls, who were finding a delicious thrill in the story. The thought in her mind was that she must be there when her father was found. There must be someone of his own to stand beside him through his ordeal.

When she first saw the deserted old building that had formerly housed the newspaper, she had decided that if her father's hiding place was in the vicinity that was the logical place for it. Although she knew that the police had searched it several times, she had been trying for days to find a chance to explore it on her own account, but at each attempt something had happened to prevent her. Now she hurried to the iron door on the fourth floor of the modern structure which led to the top story of the old one.

There was no one about. In desperate haste, hoping fervently that no one would come, Joan tugged at the iron door. It opened without a sound. The discovery of traces of fresh oil on the hinges made her heart beat faster. If only she could find her father before the police did! The cornices of the filthy landing on which she found herself were festooned with cobwebs, the air was dank and musty. A sound from below made her jump. Holding her breath, Joan tiptoed to the head of the stairs and listened. She heard the sound again. It echoed up the stair well; a rasping cough that started deep in a stomach, ripped through phlegm in lungs and chest and throat, and ended in a noisy spit. It came, she decided, from the caretaker in his cubbyhole on the ground floor; she had seen him once, a sunken-chested hollow-eyed little man who looked as though tuberculosis were slowly eating him alive.

For a time, Joan stood listening for the sound of footsteps on the stairs, but she heard none. Taking off her shoes, she started to creep down in her stockinged feet, but stopped at a bend where something shimmered in a shaft of dust-flecked sunlight. A spider's web almost as large as a carriage wheel, it hung across her path. To descend further she must break it. Had her father passed that way earlier in the afternoon it would not be there. The only way from the old building to the new without going out to the street was through the iron door, so if Lucius Marplay's hiding place was in the old building it must be on the top story.

Aged boards creaked under Joan's feet as she stole back to the landing she had left a moment before. There were a dozen doors to choose from. She examined the handles of each in turn. All were dusty except one. It had been rubbed clean by the recent touch of fingers.

Turning the handle, Joan opened the door and entered a large, bare room. Her first impression was: dirt. Dirt and dust. Filthy windows. Stained and faded wallpaper. Stale air.

One of her shapely white hands flew birdlike to her throat. She was staring at a trail of marks that led across the dusty floor boards from the door to the wall beside the fireplace. Not footprints; they were too small for that. They were such as might have been made by someone crossing the room on tiptoe.

Forgetting caution, forgetting the danger of being overheard, forgetting everything but the overwhelming possibility that her father might be near, Joan ran across the room and beat her hands on the wall.

"Father!" she cried. "Oh, Father. It's me—Joan—your daughter."

No answer, no sound except the pounding of her own hands, a hollow noise like the beating of a drum. Her fingers groped over the wall, exploring every inch of it. There was a sudden click and a panel slid back. With a cry which blended fear and hope, rapture and misery, Joan stepped over the threshold.

No one was there.

A dingy little room, a chair; a bookcase; a couch on which lay rumpled grey blankets; a table; a book lying open beside the remains of a frugal meal; a number of bottles, some full, some empty; tins of food and open tins that had once contained food: that was all.

Joan had found her father's hiding place. But where was Lucius Marplay?

A floor board creaked behind her. Wheeling round, she stared into the questioning eyes of a tall thin man with a small moustache. He was dressed in the sober brown which is almost a uniform with police officers who do not wear uniform. Joan's eyes dropped to his feet. They were very big.

"Yes," he said, with an edge of sarcasm to his voice. "I'm a policeman. A sergeant of the Criminal Investigation Department, to be precise. In a minute you can tell me all about you."

From his pocket he produced a Webley-Scott .33 automatic pistol. Sergeant Leet was taking no chances. Putting his free hand firmly under Joan's elbow, he pushed her further into the secret room and followed her in, holding the weapon ready for use. He whistled softly.

"So, this is where he's been hiding all this time. But where is he? And who are you? An accomplice?"

"I'm a typist. I work for the *Echo.*"

"Tell that to the marines," said Sergeant Leet. "How would a typist know about this room? Unless the job is a blind to cover your activities as Marplay's accomplice. He had to have someone to bring him food."

"I didn't know about the room. I stumbled on it by chance."

"Just stumbled by chance on something that squads of police have been tearing their guts out to find? Can't you invent a story easier to swallow?"

"I'll tell you the truth," began Joan unsteadily.

"When you start like that, I know for sure a lie is coming."

"I am a typist. Really I am. Mr. Craven employs me. But I've always wanted to be a woman reporter."

"You mean a sob sister. I've seen 'em in the talkies. And so?"

"So, I thought if I could find the murderer's hiding-place Mr.

Peters might give me a job on the editorial staff. Thinking it was sure to be in the old building, I crept away to try and find it."

"What's this?" Sergeant Leet took something from Joan's hand. It was a shorthand notebook from which she had been copying letters when she heard of the murder; she had been clutching it ever since. He flipped it over, reading a phrase here and there. "Yes, it looks as though you're a typist, all right—but that doesn't explain how you found the trick panel when half of Scotland Yard failed."

"Look," said Joan, pointing to the trail of marks across the floor of the outer room.

Sergeant Leet looked; and saw the point. He bit his lip. There would be hell to pay over this. The authorities would want to know why none of the police searchers who had been in and out of the derelict building for over a week had found the secret room. It would go easier with a certain ambitious young sergeant if he could claim the honour of finding it. He had already succumbed to Joan's youthful good looks and charm to the extent of accepting her story. It would be just too bad if a chit of a girl typist who wanted to be a sob sister were allowed to hog the credit for finding the hiding-place.

"What are you looking so down in the mouth about?" he grunted. "Just think how pleased your boss will be when you tell him what a clever little girl you've been."

"I'm beginning to see what a fool I've been," replied Joan, sensing his mood. "I'd like to crawl into a hole and hide. This may get me the sack."

"If that's the way you feel—"

"It's exactly the way I feel."

Scowling at her, Sergeant Leet rapped out: "What's your name? Who did you say you work for? Where do you live?"

He scribbled her answers in his notebook.

"All right," he snapped, "get out of here, quick, before I change my mind. And don't say a word about this to anyone or there'll be plenty trouble for both of us."

Turning his back on Joan, he picked up the book that lay on the table. It was De Quincey's essay on murder as a fine art.

Ambrose Craven did not want to go into the room in which Sinclair Ellis lay dead. He dreaded to look at the battered corpse that might so easily have been his own. He feared the smell of death that must hang like mist upon the air. But there is a morbid fascination in the things men fear, and his own terror drew him over the threshold as though it were a hand tugging at his lapels. There was no power in his trembling flesh and gaping mind strong enough to hold him back.

He did not see what the others saw. For him it was not the body of Sinclair Ellis that lay there, but the body of Ambrose Craven. He saw more blood than there was and a hundred dreadful wounds that did not exist. And when he tore his fear-thrilled eyes from the thing that was huddled over the desk they still carried to his mind pictures of imagined beastliness that made his flesh crawl.

In spite of the terror that was ripping at his vitals like bloody fingers gutting a sheep, it was Craven who noticed that something was missing.

"The curtain cord's gone!" he cried.

Superintendent Wrenn's eyes followed Craven's startled gaze to the velvet draperies that hung in heavy folds at either side of the window. Crossing the room in three strides, Peters shook them.

"Craven's right," he said, with a perplexed frown. "It's gone. A heavy cord, almost a rope. One pulled it to draw the curtains."

"Is it possible to find out how long it's been missing?" asked Wrenn.

"It was there at one o'clock today," replied Peters. "I noticed it when I dropped in to take Ellis to lunch."

"Marplay must have taken it," whimpered Craven.

"What on earth would he want with it?" objected Wrenn.

Peters said grimly:

"Perhaps for his next murder he has garrotting in mind."

Ambrose Craven looked as though he were going to be sick.

"You swine, Mark," he whispered hoarsely. "You filthy swine, saying a thing like that!"

His partner did not answer. He was staring out of the window and the veins of his neck were starting to swell. A string of profanities came hissing through his teeth. The others crowded to his side. They looked out and saw the jostling crowd that was holding up traffic in the street but nothing that accounted for the rage that was turning Mark Peters into a demon of fury before their eyes.

"What is it?" asked Wrenn sharply.

Mark Peters pointed to a team of newsboys, finding a brisk sale for their papers in the crowd. He was so angry that he could hardly hold his finger straight.

"I still don't understand," said the superintendent, frowning.

"For God's sake, man, use your eyes. Look at the posters those boys are displaying. *Evening Dispatch* posters, all of them."

"My eyes aren't as good as yours, I'm afraid. I can't read 'em from here."

"'MANIAC SLAYS EDITOR!'" shouted Peters, almost incoherent with rage. "'Exclusive to the *Evening Dispatch*!' Look down there, confound you. Can you see an *Echo* poster? No, blast your eyes, you can't. We've been scooped on our own damned murder!"

Rocket-like, he shot across the room. From the speed at which he rushed along the corridor to the lifts he might have been a star entrant in a hundred-yards sprint. He put a finger on the push button and kept it there. When the gates of one of the lifts opened, he darted in, thrust the operator aside and seized the starting lever himself. The lift dropped like a stone, stopping with a jerk a couple of feet below the second floor. Mark Peters did not wait to bring it level with the landing: he clanged open the gates and sprang out. A boy was coming out through the swing doors that led to the editorial department: he staggered back in quickly, propelled by Mark Peters' shoulder. If a giant had been coming out, he would have been barged aside as unhesitatingly. Mark Peters was in the hurry of a lifetime. For the time being he was an irresistible force—and heaven help any immovable object he encountered!

Casehardened reporters who did not care a damn for all the powers of heaven and hell felt like ducking under their desks when they saw him coming. That's Peters, that was... Before the news editor realized from the hush that had fallen that something was wrong, the managing director was standing over his desk, fists clenched, eyes glittering. A small man, Mark Peters at that moment looked immensely big.

"Let me see a copy of our special edition covering Ellis' murder," he said, each word dropping from his tight lips like a lump of lead.

The news editor's mouth fell open.

"Well?" said Peters, very quietly, very ominously.

"I—I haven't got it out yet. I was waiting for a chance to consult you."

"And what in the name of God was there to consult me about? Am I news editor of this paper, or are you? An exclusive murder story is tossed, red-hot, into your lap and you let it lie there. You're presented with the one chance in a lifetime of beating the pants off the rest of Fleet Street and what do you do with it? What do you do with it? You let the *Dispatch* filch it right under your nose! You let the *Echo* fall in the muck with a dull thud. Scooped on our own murder, by God! Look out of that window. The *Dispatch* is selling like hot cakes. Where is the *Echo?* Tell me that, you desk-bound Judas. Where is the *Echo?*"

"I couldn't go off half-cocked. The murdered man was a director of the company. I had to know what the *Echo*'s policy was to be. The position was delicate—"

"Delicate my foot!" roared Peters (or perhaps that was not the part of his anatomy he mentioned). "There's only one way to handle a story as big as this and that's to give it all you've got. If the editor of the *Dispatch* had been murdered, you'd have gone after the story hell for leather. You'd have climbed up drain pipes, bribed the police, done any damned thing to get it."

That was not all Mark Peters had to say—words tumbled out of him helter-skelter—but the news editor hardly listened to the rest of it. Wondering in a vague way what he would use for money in future to pay the food, clothing and rent bills for his wife and three children, he started to empty the drawers of his desk. When Peters ended by hissing: "You're fired!" the news editor was ready to reach for his hat and coat.

"You, Cochran, come here," said Peters, snapping his fingers to the chief subeditor, who hastened to join him. "Sit down at that desk. Get on with the job. I want an edition on the street in three minutes and extras as often as you can get them out until further orders.

"Throw out everything else on the front page and plaster it with the murder of Ellis. Lucius Marplay's fingerprints are on the rubber truncheon with which Ellis was killed and a receipt marked 'Paid in Full' found beside the body is in Marplay's handwriting. Play up these two facts. Marplay is suffering from the delusion that Mr. Ellis, Mr. Craven, Mr. Partridge and I stole this newspaper from him: emphasize that angle, it has tremendous dramatic value. You can print a contradiction—the man's crazy, of course—but give this delusion of his the prominence it deserves. We've received letters from him threatening to kill us all. Either Mr. Craven or Mr. Partridge may have kept one of the letters. If so, have it photographed and centre it at the top of the front page. See if a photographer can bribe or wheedle the police into letting him take pictures of the truncheon and the receipt. Dig out pictures of Marplay and Ellis and use them too.

"The police are searching the building for Marplay now. Detail a couple of men to keep in constant touch with them and tell the story of the search like a serial in each successive edition. If they don't find him tonight run a banner head across the front page of your last edition: WILL MANIAC KILLER STRIKE AGAIN? The suspense angle will sell as many papers as the presses can turn out. I don't care if there's nothing else in the paper when the last edition goes to press—this is our own exclusive murder and I want it played up hot and strong."

"That's the way you'll get it, Mr. Peters," retorted Cochran, reaching for a house telephone.

"And now," said Peters grimly, turning to face the men who sat at desks down the length of his newsroom, "I want to know how the *Dispatch* got the story. Since the murder the doors have been locked and no one has been allowed out or in. Who tipped off the *Dispatch*?"

A tense silence. No one spoke. And then a slack-limbed young man in a soiled raincoat and battered felt hat lounged forward.

"I did, Mr. Peters," he drawled.

"And who the devil are you? I've never seen you before."

"Oh, I don't work here. I'm a *Dispatch* reporter."

"Then what are you doing here?"

"I dropped in a while before the murder to collect a couple of quid one of the boys owed me."

"One of my reporters? Which one?"

"I wouldn't be willing to tell you that."

"I'll give you a hundred pounds for his name."

"You know what you can do with your hundred pounds," said the young man pleasantly.

"How did you get the story to your paper?"

"That was easy. I couldn't get out and none of the boys would let me use their 'phones, so I used a public call box in the hall downstairs. Tuppence in the slot. Press button A. Simple."

"You won't use a telephone again as long as you're in the building," said Peters grimly. "I'll see to that. And when I find the man you dropped in to see, I'll fire him."

"When you find him," said the young man cheerfully.

*

When Superintendent Wrenn told Mark Peters about the discovery of Marplay's hiding place by a certain bright young sergeant, Peters exclaimed:

"So that's how he used to do his little trick! What fools we've been. We ought to have remembered. But then it's almost twenty years ago."

"What are you talking about? You ought to have remembered what? What's almost twenty years ago?"

"When Marplay owned this paper, he was famous for his little eccentricities. One of them was a trick of disappearing for days at a time when he had something on his mind. No one knew where he went on those occasions, not even his wife. One moment he'd be sitting at his desk in his private room and the next he'd be gone, although no one would remember seeing him leave the building. Why none of us suspected the existence of a secret room I'm hanged if I know. It seems so obvious an explanation now."

"I'm withdrawing my men from the old building," said Superintendent Wrenn, "with the exception of the one who is guarding the street entrance and two who are waiting in the secret room to collar Marplay if he returns to it. It's quite on the cards, though, that he has other hiding holes."

"At eight o'clock tomorrow morning," said Peters quietly, "the biggest demolition gang that has ever been employed on one job will start razing the old building to the ground. If Marplay has other secret rooms, they won't be secret much longer."

*

It was evening before the *Dispatch* reporter was able to leave the *Echo* building and return to his own office. He found his news editor in conference with the managing editor and the chief reporter. They were hugging themselves with joy over the way in which the rival evening newspaper had been caught bending.

"The police have found Marplay's hiding place," said the *Dispatch* reporter, "but there's no trace of the old boy. Looks as though he's made a very slick getaway. The old coot can't be half so crackers as he's made out to be."

"We gathered that much from an edition of the *Echo* an hour ago," retorted his news editor. "What happened to you? Why the devil didn't you keep us in touch with developments by phone? We tried to smuggle in another man, but there was nothing doing. We've had to lift the rest of the story from the *Echo* as each edition came out."

"Peters had a couple of burly blokes standing guard over me with orders to knock me on the head if I reached for a phone."

The *Dispatch* reporter took a sheet of paper from the pocket of his raincoat and handed it across the desk.

"Get a load of this. A copy of it is posted up in every part of the *Echo* building."

On the paper, in block letters, the following notice was typewritten:

UNTIL FURTHER ORDERS ANY PERSON EMPLOYED IN ANY CAPACITY BY THIS NEWSPAPER WHO DIVULGES INFORMATION, NO MATTER HOW UNIMPORTANT, TO A RIVAL NEWSPAPER OR WHO CONSORTS FOR ANY REASON WITH AN EMPLOYEE OF A RIVAL NEWSPAPER WILL BE INSTANTLY DISMISSED. NO EXCUSE WHATEVER WILL BE CONSIDERED.
SIGNED
MARK PETERS

"Furthermore," said the *Dispatch* reporter, using one nicotine-stained finger to push his battered hat to the back of his head, "the Great God Peters took pleasure in personally informing me that one hell of a kick in the pants awaits any rival newspaperman, be he press lord or copyboy, who sets a foot in the *Echo* building. If Mr. Peters has got to be bumped off, he wants the story exclusive to his own rag."

"That's torn it," said the *Dispatch* news editor gloomily.

"Maybe not," replied his chief reporter. "I've just given birth to an idea. If it works, we'll go on scooping the *Echo* whether Mr. Peters likes it or not. If it doesn't—well, we've nothing to lose."

He outlined his idea in lowered tones. The others listened with attentive frowns. When the chief reporter stopped talking, the news editor rang for a copyboy and despatched an urgent fifty-word telegram.

Dusk on the evening of the murder of Sinclair Ellis. Ambrose Craven poured himself another drink. Decanter and glass clinked together and he jumped nervously. His gaze met that of his police escort. Detecting an amused glint in the man's eyes, Craven looked away quickly.

"Ring the bell again," he said irritably.

The policeman went to the desk and touched a bell-button. Craven followed close behind with the glass in his hand, taking care to keep the comforting bulk of his escort between him and the door.

"Do you want me?" asked Miss Withers, thrusting her leathery face into the room.

"God forbid."

"Well, you keep ringing."

"I'm ringing for Miss Trimm."

"Miss Trimm has been out of the office on some personal mission for quite an hour."

"Send her in as soon as she returns."

"Certainly," said Miss Withers in a I-do-my-work, I-keep-my-self-to-myself tone. "Is there anything I can do in the meantime?"

"You can get to blazes out of here."

Miss Withers sniffed. Since working for Mr. Craven she had developed an almost chronic sniff. It was the only way in which she could express her opinion of him. She was too ladylike to put it into words, even if she had known such words. The door closed behind her.

"Meddlesome old bitch," muttered Craven.

"Sir?" said the policeman enquiringly.

"Oh, nothing."

Pouring himself another drink, Craven looked up and found the eyes of the policeman on him again.

"You're not supposed to be watching me," he grumbled, in a high-pitched, exasperated tone. "You're supposed to be looking out for Marplay. If you kept your eyes on the door it would be more to the point."

"Very good, sir."

The door handle turned and Craven retreated apprehensively to the far wall. Joan came into the room.

"Where the devil have you been?" demanded her employer.

"I'm sorry I wasn't here when you rang for me. There was so much excitement going on that I—"

"You can leave the room," said Craven to his escort. He added hastily: "But don't go away. And keep your eyes open."

The policeman withdrew.

Ambrose Craven clutched Joan's cool white hands in his hot flabby ones. "I'm so glad you're here. Don't leave me. For love of God, don't leave me."

"I won't leave you," said Joan quietly.

"He'll kill me. I know he will."

"No. No. The police will find him."

"He's too cunning for the police. He's sworn to kill us: and he'll do it. I may be next."

"What did you do to him to make him hate you all so much?"

Craven stared at Joan with a half-cunning, half-stupid expression on his sagging features.

"We didn't do anything. Not anything, do you hear? The man's mad. He imagines things. All lunatics imagine things."

"You need another drink," said Joan, going to a cupboard in which Craven kept a large stock of drinkables.

Her employer followed, almost treading on her heels. He could not bear to be left by himself for a moment.

"Make it a big drink," he said shakily.

Joan made it a big drink. "I sent a boy this morning for two tickets for that show you want to see," she remarked, as she handed him the glass; "but you won't want to go so soon after Mr. Ellis' death."

Ambrose Craven's hand shook and the amber fluid splashed on the carpet.

"My God, no. It wouldn't be safe. In the crowd anything might happen. He could sneak up behind me, stick a knife in my back, and slip away before I fell. Crowds are just as dangerous as being all alone. I shan't be safe anywhere until he's found. I can't go anywhere or do anything."

"I don't think it's as bad as all that. If he stirs from wherever he's hiding the police are sure to catch him."

"Do you really think so? He's so diabolically cunning. Oh God, Joan, I'm afraid, I'm afraid. I can't think. I daren't hope. All I can do is stay here and pray to God the police will catch him before he can strike again."

"Well, you can't stay here all night. You'll have to go home sooner or later. Don't look so worried. The policeman will go with you. I'll go, too, if it will make you happier."

"Will you really?"

He hugged her gratefully. In spite of herself, Joan stiffened with repugnance. He kissed her. It was like the kiss of a slimy fat toad, but Joan concealed her disgust. This was the first time a pretty girl had volunteered to go to Craven's flat—usually he went to endless trouble to entice them there—but that aspect of the matter did not occur to him. His gratitude was such as a small boy afraid of the dark might show to someone who came to comfort him: a very repulsive small boy, one not even a mother could love.

When Joan and Craven left the office later that evening, one stalwart policeman marched in front of them and another brought up the rear. They passed Lord Noel Stretton in one of the corridors. He looked Joan in the face. No words were needed. His eyes told her what he was thinking.

The perspiring mass of human beings pushing and swaying outside the building terrified Craven. A flying wedge of policemen cleaved a passage through the gaping crowd to the door of his Rolls-Royce and he fairly sprinted to the car, his head lowered as though he were running the gauntlet. As Joan followed him a dirty hand plucked at her sleeve. She glanced sideways and saw Flinders, filthy and disreputable as ever, standing at the front of the crowd. Before Joan was swept on by the policeman who was bringing up the rear, Flinders managed to thrust a grimy scrap of paper into her hand.

When the car was weaving slowly through the tangled traffic Craven huddled himself against her so closely that she could feel his flesh trembling like so much jelly. He held her hand tightly between soft, sweating palms. He did not speak, but his mouth kept opening and shutting as though it were being worked by some automatic device.

He lived in a block of expensive service flats in Berkeley Square. Before he alighted from the car he made the two police-men who had accompanied them ascertain that the pavement and the entrance hall were deserted. Rabbit-like, he scuttled into the building, still clinging desperately to Joan's hand.

They all went up in the lift together, Craven in the middle. One of the policemen waited with Joan and Craven in the corridor outside the flat while the other went in and made sure that the place was empty.

"You've looked everywhere?" asked Craven anxiously when the searcher returned.

"I 'aven't missed a corner big enough for a mouse to 'ide in, sir."

"You've switched on all the lights?"

"Yes, sir."

"What about the windows? One of them may be open. We can't be too careful."

The policeman sighed. "I'll go and see, sir."

Craven called after him: "Be sure to draw the blinds."

In a little while the policeman returned. "It's quite safe for you to come in now, sir," he said firmly.

"You go first," replied Craven.

He was so eager to be in the middle when they went in that they all jammed together in the doorway.

In the flamboyantly decorated and furnished lounge Craven threw his hat and coat on a divan and hurried to a cocktail cabinet. He gulped down two glasses of whiskey before he thought of offering Joan something to drink. She poured herself some sherry and filled his glass again.

"I can't get drunk," said Craven despondently. "I keep on drinking and drinking but I don't get drunk. I want to get drunk. I want to forget. But I can't. I keep seeing Ellis' body. I think his throat was cut. There was blood all over the place."

He drained his glass at one swallow. Joan refilled it.

"You'll get drunk, all right, sir, if you go on like that," said one of the policemen, giving Joan a reproving look. "And you'll 'ave a terrible 'ead in the morning. I should lie down for a while, sir, if I was you."

"You two can wait in the hall," retorted Craven peevishly. "Don't fall asleep, either of you. If I shout, come in quickly."

When the door closed behind the policeman Craven switched on the radio.

"I want noise. Plenty of noise and light. Switch on that lamp over there. I told the fool to turn them all on."

Almost as soon as the valves warmed up he darted to the radio and turned it off again.

"We couldn't hear him coming with that blare going on. He

could sneak up behind us and we wouldn't hear him coming. You're not drinking."

"I'm not like you," said Joan, refilling his glass. "I'm afraid I'd become drunk quite quickly."

"Let's both get drunk. You're a sweet girl."

He dragged her to the divan. He was drunker than he imagined. If he had been a little less drunk, he would have collapsed from fear; and if he had been a little less afraid, he would have collapsed from drink. Joan pushed a cushion behind his head and another in the small of his back. He grasped her shoulders clumsily and pulled her down beside him. His flabby lips crawled over her cheek searching for her mouth. Joan did not feel at all afraid, only rather sick.

"You're a sweet girl," he muttered again. "You love me, don't you? I'm going to have you."

"I'm not so sure," said Joan, freeing herself without much difficulty—it was like wrestling with a feather bed.

Craven squinted owlishly at her. "Why aren't you sure? I can give you everything you want. I'm generous with those I like. You be nice and I'll be nice."

"I like you," replied Joan, "very much." This was even more hateful, more degrading than she had imagined it would be. "I'm very fond of you, in fact. But you don't trust me. And I'm not sure you're my kind of man."

"Don't be silly," he retorted, slurring his syllables. "Only one kind of man is any good to a girl: a man with plenty of money. I have more than I can spend."

"The kind of man I admire," said Joan, "is the man without conscience. One who doesn't beg what he wants, but takes it. One who'll lie and cheat and rob to get his own way, who regards life as war and is utterly ruthless in his dealings with others. Once I thought you were like that. That was why you fascinated me. But now—I'm not so sure. If you are, you don't trust me. You're hiding the real you from me."

She held her breath. The ruse seemed pitifully obvious. Would it work? Was he sufficiently drunk?

"I can't make head or tail of this," grumbled Craven, staring at her with muddled eyes. "You must have had more to drink than I thought. To hear you talk anyone would think you admired crooks."

"The man who rises to the top in business by bludgeoning all who stand in his way isn't a crook. He's a Napoleon."

"A Napoleon? That's what I am. If you only knew it, I'm as ruthless as the devil. More ruthless, in fact."

"Have another drink," said Joan, picking up his glass, which had fallen to the floor.

When she handed him the replenished glass she said: "The day I first saw you I felt that here was my ideal man."

"If you knew me better, you'd be certain of it. Ruthless as— as—as hell, that's me. How do you think I made all my money?"

"How?" asked Joan eagerly.

Over the rim of his glass Craven cocked a bleary eye at her. "You'd like to know," he mumbled.

"I said you didn't trust me."

"I'd trust you with my life, Darling Beautiful. But this isn't my secret only. It's Mark Peters' secret as well. And Partridge's. And Ellis'." His eyes opened wide. "Oh Christ," he groaned, "for a moment I'd forgotten about Ellis. I'd forgotten Marplay."

Trying hard to keep her voice calm, Joan said: "In the paper tonight, it says that Marplay imagines you stole the *Echo* from him."

"He'll kill us all," whimpered Craven, "one by one…like so many…flies. Oh God, I don't want to die!"

"Tell me about it," whispered Joan. "Did you really steal the paper from him?"

"It was Mark Peters' idea. It was his idea from the start. The rest of us were only—only—"

A bell rang shrilly. Ambrose Craven sat up with a jerk and the glass fell from his hand, spilling whiskey on the floor.

"Damn!" said Joan, under her breath. Aloud, she said impatiently: "It's only the telephone. I'll answer it."

"No! No!" Craven's eyes were jumping. "I've heard of murders done that way. They charge the wire with a terrific jolt of electricity. When you put the receiver to your ear you drop dead."

The bell went on ringing clamorously.

"We can't just sit here and let it ring," said Joan. "Let one of the police answer it. It's their job to take the risks. That's what they're here for."

Repressing an itch to kick him in the stomach, Joan went to the door and called in a policeman. He lifted the receiver and put it to his ear. Craven watched in morbid fascination. The man did not drop dead. In a most matter-of-fact tone, he said: "Hello?"

They heard the crackling of a voice at the other end of the wire. The policeman handed the receiver to Joan. "For you, miss."

"Who can it be?" croaked her employer hoarsely. "Who could know you're here?"

Joan did not reply. "This is Miss Trimm," she said into the mouthpiece.

"And this is Noel Stretton," replied a crisp voice. "And I'm speaking from a call box across the street. And if you don't join me in two minutes, I'm coming up to knock the stuffing out of a certain fat worm!"

When Joan came out of the lift in a towering rage, Lord Noel walked across the entrance hall to meet her, smiling cheerfully. The hall porter turned on them a beam so benignly indulgent that Joan could have screamed. He obviously thought he was witnessing a lovers' meeting.

He held the door open for them. "Good night, miss. Good night, sir."

Joan sailed out without replying, her head in the air.

Before following her, Lord Noel said: "Good night" and underlined it with a tip.

On the pavement Joan halted and looked back. The porter was still wearing the fond, smug grin of a conspirator in a romantic plot. Turning on Lord Noel, Joan said furiously: "What right have you to interfere with me?"

"None whatever."

"Then why do you?"

"It's sheer vanity on my part. I hate to admit that I was wrong. The first time I saw you I decided that you were the nicest girl I'd met for years. I'm funny that way; I believe in first impressions."

"Now that you see how wrong you were, why don't you leave me alone?"

He looked down his long nose at her. It was the most annoyingly superior trick of expression she had ever seen. She yearned to smack his face but restrained herself because she was not sure how he would react if she did.

"I don't admit I was wrong—not quite. Oh, it isn't easy to look at you in cold blood and believe in you. When we first met you were simple and unaffected and quite charming. Please don't laugh. I almost fell in love with you."

"That was kind of you," hissed Joan through her clenched teeth.

"Not at all. I couldn't help myself. But now you're a carbon copy of all the young women I can't abide. You've plucked your eyebrows, painted your cheeks, permed your hair, coloured your fingernails. All for Craven's benefit, I presume?"

"Mayn't it be because I like myself this way?"

"I'd hate to think so."

"Lord Noel," said Joan, in a choked voice, "it's kind of you to make your opinion of me so clear—"

"Not at all. I have a passion for clarity."

"—but now, will you please be good enough to leave me alone? You're a conceited, interfering prig and I hate you. Goodnight!"

Joan walked away as quickly as she could. Lord Noel sauntered at her elbow, his long legs covering ground effortlessly. After a few moments of this, Joan stopped and glared at him. In her anger she did not notice that it was starting to rain.

"Why are you following me?"

"I'm seeing you home."

"Don't trouble."

"It's no trouble."

"But I don't want you with me. I won't have it!"

"My dear girl, I'm not studying your wishes. I'm thinking of what's good for you. Having rescued you from Craven, I don't intend to give you a chance to go back to him."

"Oh!"

The exclamation, charged with fury, did not do justice to Joan's feelings; but it was all she could find breath to utter. When she looked up at Lord Noel raindrops spattered in her face, so she stopped glaring up at him and walked on at an even brisker pace. Before they had gone very far, she halted again.

"If you insist on coming with me, I shan't go home."

"Then I'll go wherever you go."

Joan's light coat and smart shoes were not made for rain and it was now pelting down heavily. Hunching her shoulders, she plodded on grimly, Lord Noel keeping easy pace with her, snug in a long raincoat.

"What's the answer to all this?" he asked in a conversational tone. "Why are you making a fool of yourself with Craven?"

Joan said nothing. There simply were not words.

"I've thought of all possible reasons I can. None of them seem adequate. It isn't that you like Craven: that's the one answer which can't possibly fit. Do you need money very badly and hope to get it from him? He'll want repayment at the rate of twenty shillings in the pound of flesh."

Rain. Rain. Rain. It came down in torrents, swept out of a sullen sky by whimpering gusts of wind. A tangle of silver wires that lashed like whips. The pavements gleamed black in the lamplight. The gutters ran with muddy water. A car went by, its tyres slapping and sucking on the greasy surface of the road. Joan sidestepped to avoid a shower of mud squirted at her by one of the wheels.

"We'd better take a taxi."

"If you think I'd go anywhere in a taxi you—"

"Nasty-minded girl. That's what comes of associating with Craven. If you won't take a taxi, let's shelter in a doorway."

"I won't even stand in a doorway with you."

Joan turned up her collar and put on her gloves which she had been clutching in a crumpled ball in one clenched fist. A scrap of paper fluttered to the pavement. Lord Noel picked it up and glanced at it. Raising his eyebrows, he uttered a low whistle. Joan snatched it from him and wadded it in her hand.

"Flinders' writing," said Lord Noel speculatively. "I'd know that demented scrawl anywhere. You have nice friends, Miss Trimm. Flinders and Craven. Two beauties."

"It's hardly your business."

"If I minded my own business life would be too dull for words. What dangerous game are you playing, Joan? I find it hard enough to understand your friendship with Craven—but Flinders! I give up. You're up to something. What is it?"

Joan did not answer. They walked on. The rain scudded down. The wind scooped up handfuls of it and tossed it playfully in their faces. Drops trickled down their cheeks, dripped off the ends of their noses.

"Your colour is running," said Lord Noel, in a tone of mild interest. "You look like a painted toy that some kid has been sucking."

"You're the most detestable man I've ever known. I hate you!"

"Well, that's better than being indifferent to me. Hatred implies a strong degree of interest."

He took off his raincoat and held it out.

"No, thank you," she said stiffly.

"Don't be a fathead. I can't let you catch your death of cold."

"Then go away and leave me to look after myself."

"I can't do that, either. You're a mystery and I shan't be happy until I solve you."

Before she realized what he was doing he slipped one of her arms into a sleeve. In spite of her struggles, he thrust the other arm into its sleeve and buttoned the coat round her. He handled her calmly, impersonally, effortlessly, as though she were a small and silly rebellious child. The coat hung on her like a tent. Her hands and feet were lost in it.

"This is unbearable!" she cried.

"If you won't use your discretion, I must use mine. If you were a child or a lunatic it would be my duty to do what was best for you without consulting your wishes—and a woman in a temper is hardly a rational being."

"Thanks!"

"Don't mention it."

"I suppose you realize," said Joan in a coldly furious tone, "that but for your persistence in accompanying me I should have been home in front of a fire twenty minutes ago?"

"Let's not go into that. It's the weak point in my whole argument. I have my reasons for sticking close to you. I like to pretend they're purely altruistic. There is great satisfaction in finding altruistic motives for doing what one wants to do."

"As long as you're satisfied."

"Thank you so much," said Lord Noel sweetly. "Here's a milk bar. Let's go in and have something warm to drink."

They paused in the doorway. Lord Noel held the door open. A warm, inviting smell came out, but Joan shook her head. They stood sheltering under a canvas awning. Lord Noel looked at Joan blandly as though they were the best of friends. Joan tried to look as though they were not even together. Remembering the scrap of paper in her hand, she held it up to the light and deciphered the sprawling writing with difficulty. It ran:

Must see you. Have news. Will get in touch early in morning.

Shredding it, she dropped the pieces on the pavement and watched the rain softening them to pulp.

"Please," said Lord Noel quietly.

"What do you mean?"

"Please tell me about it."

"I can't."

"Then there is something behind this queer attachment to Craven. Something less impossible than a liking for him."

"I didn't say so."

"Not quite. But it is so."

Joan avoided his eyes.

"If you won't come in here for a warm drink," he said, "come to my flat for one. It isn't far."

"So that's the kind of girl you think I am!"

"Hoity-toity, as Grandmother would have said. You're a funny girl. You go willingly to Craven's flat, but you're insulted when I suggest coming to mine. Why? Where does the difference come in? Is it because you know that you're really safer with Craven because nothing would persuade you to be lured into bed with a fat pig like him, whereas I—well, I'm not exactly the physically repugnant type."

"You flatter yourself," said Joan, suddenly feeling awkward.

"Oh, I know I'm an attractive young man. There's nothing quite so absurd as false modesty."

"If you dare to imagine for one moment—"

"I assure you I don't. I'm beginning to think my first impression of you was right. Beneath that rain-smeared paint you're a nice, old-fashioned girl at heart. The very mention of going to bed with a man makes you blush."

Crossing the pavement, he hailed a taxi. "Please," he said, holding the door open.

For a while Joan stood looking at him. The taxi driver stared moodily at both of them. Joan began to realize how odd she must appear with the skirt of the raincoat flapping at her feet and her hands lost inches up the sleeves. Rain dripped from the awning. It dripped down her neck. Oh, well— Shrugging her shoulders, she walked forward and climbed into the taxi. She was ready to climb out again if Lord Noel uttered a single triumphant word, but he did not speak, except to give the driver an address.

The address was that of a very large house which had been cut up into very small flats. In silence Joan and Lord Noel climbed four flights of stairs and entered a pleasant room in which a bright fire was burning. A few good prints on the wall; some photographs—one, Joan instantly noted, of an exceedingly pretty girl; deep armchairs with loose chintz covers; old brass that shone with age and polish; one wall lined with books; more books lying all over the place; a baby grand piano on which lay, open, a Chopin waltz.

"Go into the bedroom and take off your wet things," said Lord Noel casually. "That's the bedroom door over there. You'll find dressing gowns and slippers and things in my wardrobe if you need them."

Too cold, too tired, too wet, too miserable, to care whether she was being sensible or not, Joan went into the bedroom and took off her drenched coat and sodden shoes and stockings. Her dress was hardly damp, so she kept it on. Through another open door she glimpsed a bathroom. The sight of herself in a mirror almost made her weep with chagrin. The rain had made a ludicrous mess of her makeup. There were streaks of mascara on her cheeks. She washed her face, drying it vigorously on a turkish towel. In an old pair of carpet slippers, she shuffled back to the sitting-room.

Lord Noel, in a shabby tweed jacket, was making coffee in an impressively complicated apparatus at a small table in front of the fire. It smelt heavenly. Without speaking, he went to the bedroom, returned with her wet things and spread them on the high fender.

"Cigarette?" he suggested, drawing a chair up to the fire.

Joan sank into it gratefully.

"Thanks."

He held a match for her, then lit a cigarette himself and dropped into another chair. For a time they sat in silence, smoking cigarettes, drinking coffee, staring into the fire.

"This isn't how I pictured your flat," said Joan at last. "I've seen articles about it in the magazines. Where is all the chromium and glass, the cocktail bar, the window on which half the celebrities in London have scribbled their autographs with a diamond? Where are the futurist paintings, the Epstein busts?"

"You're thinking of my flat in Park Lane, the rent of which is paid by the *Echo*. It's supposed to have marvellous publicity value. I give parties in it—also paid for by the *Echo*—but I've never spent a night there. The damned place simply isn't liveable."

"I like this one better."

"That's because you're a simple soul. And so am I."

He reached out and laid a hand on one of hers.

"Now," he said, "tell me."

Joan kept her eyes on the fire. "I'd rather not."

"You must," he said commandingly. Pleadingly, he added: "Please do."

In a still small voice, she told him the whole story, beginning with her real identity and that of her father. He listened in silence to it all. He was still silent for a time after she had finished speaking. And then:

"You poor child," he said softly. "How dreadful for you."

His tone was so gentle, so compassionate, that Joan felt tears coming into her eyes. "Thanks for taking it like that. I was afraid you'd turn from me in horror."

"Good God. Why?"

"I am the daughter of a certified lunatic."

"Oh, that. There are certified lunatics in all the best families. My own uncle George suffered from the delusion that he was a barrel and spent his entire life trying to fill himself."

"It isn't funny to me," said Joan, with a break in her voice.

"Of course not. How could it be? I'm only trying to make you take it a little less seriously."

"He's not only a lunatic, he's a murderer."

"I wouldn't call it murder. That's too dignified name for the extermination of crawling things like Ellis and Craven. Besides, if he's one he can't be the other. To be responsible for his actions a man must be sane."

"I'm afraid that doesn't help much."

"You can't go on with this wild scheme of yours."

"I must."

"But don't you see, even if you were able to prove that these men wronged your father, it wouldn't help him in the least."

"I know. But it would let the world know he had some justification for killing them."

"Perhaps. But that isn't worth the risk you're running. The very thought of you and Craven makes my blood boil."

"It isn't a nice thought, even to me. But I must go on. This is something I've promised myself to see through to the end, whatever happens."

"But even if you persuade Craven to talk, there'll only be your word for what he said. That isn't evidence."

"I know. It seems hopeless. But I must go on."

"You're a dear idiot. Where do you live?"

"In Malbrouk Court. I share a tiny flat with a sort of governess-cum-guardian."

"Ever heard of a Dictaphone?"

"They use them at the office, don't they?"

"Yes. Peters dictates most of his letters into one. The words are recorded by an impression made by a needle on a revolving wax cylinder. I'm going to buy you one. Next time you lay a trap for Craven, take him to your flat instead of going to his. I'll be concealed within call in case of trouble. Beforehand we'll hide a microphone somewhere in the room, connected by wires to the Dictaphone. When you bring him to the point of talking see that he talks close to the mike and we'll have all the proof you want."

Joan's eyes were shining with excitement. "I don't know how to thank you."

"We'll talk about that later." He smiled at her. "You're very sweet."

You're very sweet: almost the words Craven had used earlier that evening. Joan shivered. "Don't say that," she begged.

Lord Noel did not ask her why not. In many ways his intuition was remarkable. He leaned forward and kissed her lightly on the mouth. She found herself wanting him to kiss her again, only not so fleetingly.

"You'd better put your things on," he said, standing up. "It's getting late and they're quite dry."

He left the room. When he returned, he went to the telephone without speaking to her and put through a call for a taxi. He took her down to it, but although he opened the door for her, he did not hand her in. The rain had slowed to a monotonous drizzle.

"I shan't see you home after all," he said, with an unsteady laugh. "You were right: I'm not to be trusted in a taxi. Not with you, at least."

He kissed her again. On an irresistible impulse, Joan took the initiative in making it a more satisfactory one. It was the first real kiss of her life.

"Darling," said Lord Noel, opening his eyes. "Darling," he said again.

Then he slammed the door of the taxi. Putting head in through the open window he kissed her on the nose. The taxi crept away, leaving him standing on the pavement looking after it.

When Joan arrived at the tiny flat in which she and Miss Trimm had managed to exist for over a week by holding their elbows in, she found Agatha waiting for her, wearing the worried frown that lately was almost habitual to her. The fireplace was littered with cigarette ends.

"Thank God you've come. Joan, this business sitting up night after night waiting for you to extricate your head from the lion's mouth and come home all in one piece is aging me rapidly. I can't stand much more of it."

"I don't think you'll have to," said Joan dreamily.

Agatha stared at her. "What's happened to you? What are you looking so damnably dewy-eyed about? You haven't—? That beast didn't—? No, nothing a hog like Craven could do to you would make you look like that."

"It wasn't Craven."

"Then who was it?"

Joan threw herself into the arms of her oldest friend. "Trimmy, hug me. Hold me tight."

Amazingly strong, surprisingly gentle, the arms of middle-aged Agatha Trimm. She stroked the girl's hair; and her large, rough hands were soft. They clung together in silence; and then Agatha said gruffly:

"Joan, darling, God knows I'm no great shakes as a mother, but I'm the best you've got. For heaven's sake tell me—"

"Oh, Trimmy, darling, shut up. Don't say a word. Just hold me."

*

Later, when they were getting ready for bed, Joan said in a faraway voice: "Trimmy, were you ever in love?"

Brushing her greying hair with harsh, violent strokes, the inevitable cigarette between her lips, Agatha said dryly:

"I'm a woman, although you might not think so."

"What was he like? Did every word he spoke thrill you?"

"Men don't waste words that thrill on a face like mine. I fell in love several times in my optimistic youth—but no one ever fell in love with me."

"Oh, Trimmy, what a blundering fool I am. I'm sorry."

"Save your sorrow, child. I got over all that long ago."

Aclock struck three, its sonorous chimes hanging heavily on the silent darkness. The uniformed policeman on guard at the entrance of the old *Echo* building stretched himself with a yawn. He took off his helmet, shook a fag-end out of it onto the palm of his hand, and put the helmet on again. He went into the dark, debris-cluttered hall to light the stump of cigarette in case one of his superior officers should come along and spot the flame of the match. He heard the caretaker coughing out his lungs in bed in the gloomy basement. 'Poor bastard' he thought, shaking his head pityingly. His own wife's uncle by marriage had coughed like that night after night for six months; and then they had carried him out in a coffin. Puffing at the fag-end, the constable turned his flashlight on the derelict lift shaft, on the dusty stairs. He put his head on one side and listened. Save for the poor devil below, the place was as silent and deserted as a graveyard.

Dead hour: the whole district was a graveyard. Dark and silent the buildings on each side of the one he was guarding and across the lane. No sound of traffic from Fleet Street a hundred yards away. The thumping of machinery from neighbouring buildings had ceased when the last editions of the morning newspapers went to press. In offices high above the street skeleton staffs of journalists still kept their vigil in case important news should unexpectedly break, but for the most part Newspaper land was sunk in slumber.

It would have been pleasant to walk down the lane to the modern *Echo* building and have a chat with the policeman on duty there, but orders were that no officer on this special duty might leave his post for an instant; and there was no telling when the sergeant might come snooping round. Soft footed, the sergeant—and harsh tongued.

A light van came slowly down the lane from the direction of Holborn, its engine ticking like a sewing-machine. The sound made a pleasant break in the hush of the night. It stopped at the curb outside the old building. The engine noise ceased but no one climbed out.

Grinding the cigarette stub under his heel, the policeman crossed the pavement and peered into the driver's cabin. No one was there. That was funny: but there was a hatch between the driving-seat and the body of the van; perhaps the driver had climbed through it. Walking round the van the policeman opened the rear doors.

A hand from inside knocked his helmet off and something hard and heavy struck him a savage blow on the head. He dropped limply to his knees, his chest sagging against the tail-board. Two hands reached out and hauled him into the van.

A few moments later a short stout man with a shock of white hair sprang out of the van and darted into the old building. He was gone for several minutes and when he returned, he was panting under the weight of a large sacking-wrapped bundle which was slung across his shoulder. Heaving it into the rear of the van, he closed the doors, climbed into the driving seat and drove off...

*

Four hours later a policeman patrolling his beat found the van parked in a turning off Kensington Gore. The constable who had been on duty at the door of the old *Echo* building was lying inside, trussed and gagged, but otherwise the van was empty.

In the course of the morning police investigators discovered that it had been stolen, late the previous night, from a lock-up garage in a Holborn mews.

On the steering wheel were the fingerprints of Lucius Marplay. The silken rope with which the policeman was bound was the curtain cord that had been missing from the room in which Sinclair Ellis was murdered.

Appointment in a Pub

Something that tickled fell on Joan's nose and she wakened with a smile. Agatha was standing beside her bed, a cigarette in her mouth, a cup in each hand.

"Tea," she said, holding out one cup. "And don't look so disgustingly rosy and rapturous or I'll pour it over you."

Brushing ash off her nose, Joan sat up and sipped the tea. She looked very lovely in a crepe-de-chine nightgown of which Agatha heartily disapproved. In Agatha's opinion there was not nearly enough of it; it emphasized rather than concealed Joan's youthful charms. Until Joan in her late teens had become stubborn about nightwear, Agatha had bought her nightgowns of sober flannel which left only her head and the tips of her toes exposed.

"What time is it?"

"Oh, about half-past nine," replied Agatha casually.

Throwing back the bedclothes, Joan slid two pink feet to the floor. "You pig, you might have called me earlier. I shall be hours late."

"If your employer keeps you out half the night, he needn't expect you to be early at the office in the morning. You've got to sleep sometime. I shouldn't have called you now, only a man keeps ringing up and demanding to speak to you. He's on the 'phone now, unless he's tired of waiting and hung up. I hope he has. I don't like his voice."

With an eager light in her eyes, Joan scrambled to the telephone, trailing a wispy silk wrap behind her. The light faded: it was not Lord Noel's voice that came to her from the other end of the wire, but the husky alcoholic whisper of Flinders.

"Miss Marplay? I've remembered it—you know what."

"Yes," said Joan quickly. "What we talked about the other day?"

"That's it. I'm scared, Miss Marplay. This is something big. I've found a paper for which Mark Peters would cut my throat. I'll be running a hell of a risk if I tell you what I know and give you the paper to prove it. You'll have to make it worth my while."

"How much do you want?"

A pause. She could hear him breathing heavily while he thought. "Can you raise a hundred pounds?"

"I might," said Joan reluctantly, "if the information is worth it."

"It's worth that and a damned sight more. Can you have it in one-pound notes by midday?"

"I think so. Where shall I meet you?"

"Do you know a pub called *The Punchbowl* in Holborn?"

"I don't know any pubs. Can't we meet in a teashop?"

"I don't know any teashops. You'll find *The Punchbowl* easily enough. Ask a policeman."

"Very well, I'll meet you there soon after one. I go to lunch at one."

"I'll be in the public bar. It's cheaper than the saloon and quieter; they don't get much trade on that side. Don't tell a soul about this or the deal's off. And don't come without the money. All in quid notes, remember."

Joan heard a click as he hung up. She replaced the receiver and slipped into the silk wrap that had been trailing behind her. Looking up, she found Agatha staring at her with a harassed frown.

"Don't worry, Trimmy," said Joan, putting an affectionate hand on the older woman's arm. "I'll be all right. I can take care of myself."

"That's what they all say," retorted Agatha broodingly, "until one day they come home in tears with a baby or wind up stiff and cold on a slab in the morgue."

The table was set for breakfast and beside Joan's plate was a little heap of parcels. Joan tore them open in impatient haste, as excited as a child on Christmas morning. They were all from Lord Noel, who had shopped for them as soon as the big stores were open and they had arrived by special messenger a few minutes before: a single American Beauty rose in a cellophane box; a pair of silk stockings, fine spun as a spider's web; a pair of walking shoes, her exact size, so dainty that they took her breath away; and a bottle of cough mixture with a note that said, "Just in case…"

"Talking about pubs on the telephone," muttered Agatha. "Receiving mounds of presents from someone you hardly know. Nice goings on."

"What makes you think I hardly know him?"

"I am familiar with everyone you've known for any length of time."

"Don't be too familiar with this man. I saw him first."

"That is not the sense in which I used the word. And let me tell you, in my young days—"

"What a memory you have, darling," said Joan, kissing Agatha's rough brown cheek.

Agatha smacked her bottom. It was not a hard smack but it stung through the crepe-de-chine. Agatha meant it to sting.

"Eat your breakfast," she snapped.

"Trimmy," said Joan, sitting down and picking up her napkin, "have we a hundred pounds in the bank?"

"Rather more than that, I hope," replied Agatha, studying the girl's face. "Why?"

Joan dropped her eyes. "I want you to give it to me."

"Whatever for?"

"I can't tell you. But I really need it. It's terribly important."

"Eat your breakfast," said Agatha again. "I'll write you a cheque before you leave for the office."

"Trimmy, you're a gem. I don't know how to thank you."

"I want no thanks," said Agatha tartly, "for making a complete fool of myself and of you."

Starting on her second egg, Joan looked for the morning paper. It was not in sight. Agatha caught her eye.

"I've burned it. You don't want to read it this morning."

Joan's lip trembled. "I suppose there's a lot in it about my father?"

"Quite a lot."

"Poor Father! I'm an unnatural beast, Trimmy. Since about ten last night I haven't spared him a thought."

"Well, that's something to be thankful for. If there were only some way to make you forget about him and this whole sorry business forever."

"It's a dreadful mess, isn't it? You've read the paper. You know he's—killed—the f-first of them?"

"I knew it last night."

"And yet, you said nothing about the murder when I came in."

"Damn the murder!" said Agatha, through tight lips. "Damn the murdered man! That's a shocking thing to say, isn't it? I'll say it again: damn everyone and everything that makes unhappiness for you! You're very young, Joan. You have your whole life to lead. I've always wanted it to be such a lovely, lovely life. Seeing all the hopes and plans I had for you kicked to pieces is more than I can bear."

*

Joan was about two hours late when she entered the anteroom she shared with the prison-matronly Miss Withers. She was wearing the Cinderella shoes and the gossamer stockings Lord Noel had sent her and his rose adorned her dress. Miss Withers, whose wrinkled fingers were racing over the keys of her typewriter, looked at the clock and sniffed.

"Has Mr. Craven rung for me yet?" Joan asked.

"He'd have rung for you fast enough—he usually does—but he has not yet put in an appearance."

"You don't like me, do you?"

"I neither like nor dislike you. Our relationship is not sufficiently intimate to give rise to either emotion."

"But you disapprove of me?"

"Most decidedly," agreed Miss Withers frigidly, giving the typewriter the hammering of its life.

Hardly knowing why she did it, except that the acid-tongued spinster was so like—and yet so unlike—her own beloved Miss Trimm, Joan unpinned her rose and laid it at Miss Withers' elbow. Then she sat down at her own typewriter, removed the cover, and pretended to be very busy. She had no work to do, for although it was Ambrose Craven's habit to ring for her at frequent intervals throughout each day, he seldom found time when they were together to dictate letters. She typed: *the quick brown fox jumped over the lazy dog.*

It was very nearly all she had ever typed on her shining new machine.

With a disconcerted expression on her lined face, Miss Withers stared at the rose. It was very beautiful. "Well, really," she thought. "The wages of sin, I suppose. One had imagined that sort of girl always received orchids." Yes, it was a very beautiful rose, but Miss Withers could not possibly keep it. Perhaps in giving it the girl had meant well—one must credit her with some decent impulses—and hurting her feelings by handing it back was out of the question; but while Joan's back was turned Miss Withers edged the flower off the desk into the wastepaper basket and dropped a spoiled sheet of paper on top of it.

The door was thrown open wide and one of Ambrose Craven's police bodyguards walked in. He stalked through to the inner room and they heard him opening more doors. The inner room was full of doors; those of a long wardrobe and a private bathroom and large medicine cupboard and an even larger cupboard which did duty as a cellar. The policeman tramped back again and said: "All clear" to his mate and Craven, who were waiting in the corridor.

Grey cheeked and hollow eyed, Craven scurried through to his private room. Over his shoulder he croaked hoarsely to Joan: "I want you."

She followed him in, shutting the door in the faces of the two policemen. She found her employer standing by the medicine cupboard, mixing himself a fizzy drink. He sent three aspirins down after it and topped them off with four fingers of neat brandy.

"I feel terrible," he moaned. "Where the devil did you get to last night? You mumbled something as you rushed off, but I didn't catch what it was. Who was the phone call from?"

"The aunt I live with was taken ill suddenly."

"How did she know where to find you?"

"She phoned the office and was told I'd left with you, so she tried your flat on the off-chance that I might be there."

"I expect she raised hell when she found that you were?"

"Oh no. Aunty's very broad-minded."

Ambrose Craven reflected that this would be a better world if the relatives of all girls were broad-minded. He aimed a kiss at Joan's mouth but she was on the alert for something of the sort and at the psychological moment she turned her head, as though by chance, and took it on the cheek. Even so, the touch of his lips was nauseating.

"We'll lunch together today," said Craven in a moist tone. He added quickly: "We won't go out. You can phone the Savoy to send it in."

"That would be lovely," said Joan, "but I've got to go home in the lunch hour and see to Aunty."

When she went back to her desk, she found Miss Withers answering the telephone. "For you," said the elder woman, handing her the receiver and avoiding her eyes. It was Lord Noel. He also wanted Joan to lunch with him. When she told him that she had another engagement she could almost feel him stiffening at the other end of the wire.

"Don't be like that again," she begged him quickly. "Trust me. I'll tell you all about it as soon as I can."

"Then you must have supper with me tonight."

"But I've already promised Mr Craven—"

"Damn and blast Mr Craven. Put him off. A bright girl like you can think of some excuse."

"All right," said Joan. "I'll sup with you. I'd love to, really."

"Darling," said Lord Noel.

Joan glanced at Miss Withers, whose hearing, she knew, was exceptionally acute. The spinster's shoulders were rising so high that her backbone was almost being drawn like a blanket over her head.

Enter Alistair Macnab

At eight o'clock that morning a hundred labourers had started ripping the woodwork out of the former *Echo* building, preparatory to demolishing it entirely. By midday they had stripped the top story to a stone shell and were gutting the third floor. The secret room on the top story had been demolished with the rest. If Marplay had another hiding-place in the old building it was certain to be discovered by nightfall. Elaborate precautions were being taken to ensure that he could not again enter the new one.

The communicating iron door between old and new had been removed and men were at work bricking up the aperture. Only employees of the newspaper and visitors who were vouched for by departmental heads were allowed to go beyond the entrance hall. Plain-clothes men stood beside the doorkeepers at each entrance; plainclothes men guarded the lifts on the ground floor; plainclothes men did duty on the roof; and a score of them patrolled Fleet Street and its environs, looking for Lucius Marplay.

Wherever Marplay was hiding, it was certainly not in the new building, for every corner of it had been searched again that morning. Every cupboard had been opened and emptied; every locker investigated. Desks had been moved out from the walls; even the safes and the time vault had been searched. There were no hidden rooms, no sliding panels, in the modern concrete structure. To make quite sure of that, the architect's plans were taken from the files and checked with detailed measurements made by a squad of surveyors. Before the police searchers finished, they were able to say definitely that there was no hiding place in the new building big enough to conceal a child, far less a grown man.

No, Lucius Marplay was not in the building. And

Superintendent Wrenn assured Mark Peters it was impossible for Marplay to enter the building. If he came within a hundred yards of it he was bound to be arrested. Peters and his surviving partners were absolutely safe. But no one could make Ambrose Craven believe it.

"A man downstairs insists on seeing you," said Mark Peters' secretary, entering her employer's room at eleven that morning.

"Who is he? Do I know him? Has he an appointment?"

"His name is Alastair MacNab, sir. You do not know him. He has no appointment. He asked me to give you this letter."

She held out a square white envelope. With an impatient exclamation, Peters took it and tore it open. His eyebrows rose as he read a letter from a private detective agency styling itself 'The New World Investigation Bureau':

DEAR SIR,

On the instructions of Dr. Hammond, proprietor and medical supervisor of the Hedley House Sanatorium, we are sending one of our most efficient operatives to give what assistance he can in the search for Lucius Marplay. While by no means admitting liability for the actions of his patient, Dr. Hammond feels that his interests should be represented by a capable investigator. We beg to assure you that you may have complete confidence in the discretion and ability of Mr. Alastair MacNab, the bearer of this letter. We shall be greatly obliged if you will afford him every possible facility to co-operate with your organization in the protection of yourself and your co-directors.

Yours faithfully,
S. BIRNBAUM
MANAGING DIRECTOR.

The secretary stood by in silence watching her employer's face anxiously. It was one of her duties to prevent waste of the great man's time and more than one of the predecessors had been instantly dismissed for neglecting that particular duty. Without a shade of expression on his hard face, Mark Peters put the letter in a drawer and said quietly:

"Show him in."

With a sigh of relief, the secretary left the room. A few minutes later she opened the door again and said: "Mr. Alastair MacNab."

The sound of heavy breathing, rather like the panting of an overloaded lorry climbing a long hill, preceded the visitor into the room.

At first sight Alastair MacNab looked less like a man than a walrus dressed up in a bowler hat and a raincoat. A spreading clump of moustache, a vapidly amiable smile, a swaying waddle: they all helped to create the illusion. He was of average height, but the bony structure of his body was not apparent; he curved outward from the neck to the hips and inward from the hips to the feet, his widest part being divided by a sort of equatorial line in the form of a keychain.

He might have been any age between forty and sixty. Impossible to imagine him as a baby, a child, a young man. Easier far to conceive that he had been born exactly as he stood. He wore a baggy suit of dark-grey cloth spotted with food stains and tobacco ash, a soiled and shapeless raincoat, a dusty bowler hat and the largest boots Mark Peters had ever seen. In one hand he carried an untidy umbrella and in the other a wicker basket about a square foot in diameter. The wicker basket struck a note of pure fantasy.

"What in the name of God have you got in there?" asked Mark Peters, pointing to it.

"Ma lunch," replied Alastair MacNab imperturbably.

"Your lunch?" Mark Peters was thrown temporarily out of gear.

"London restaurants are gey expensive," explained the Scot, breathing heavily. "I aye mak' it a rule tae carry ma ain grub when I gang oot on a case."

He looked meaningfully at Peters and then at a chair, but the newspaper proprietor was too stunned to take the hint. With unshakable self-confidence Alastair MacNab drew the chair nearer to the desk, slowly lowered himself into it, placed basket, umbrella and bowler hat on the floor beside him.

"You aren't one of Doctor Hammond's patients by any chance?" asked Peters suddenly. It appeared to be the most feasible explanation.

"I can see you and me will get on fine together," replied MacNab, his face crinkling in a smile. "I'm verra fond o' a bit joke mysel'."

"What makes you think you can find Marplay?"

"It's a matter o' temper-r-rament. In dealing wi' lunatics— and I've had conseederable exper-rience—ye hae tae pit yersel in their shoes. I've aye had the knack o' understanding whit goes on in an unbalanced br-rain."

"I can quite believe it," said Mark Peters dryly. Deep in thought, he sat looking at the Scot, who stared back at him with a bland smile that was strangely disconcerting.

"The case is in the hands of the police. I have really no authority to appoint additional investigators."

"I'm a man o' tact. I'll tak' care no' tae tread on any corns. If I succeed in finding Mar-rplay, the police are welcome tae a' the credit."

"That's very generous of you," said Peters; but the heavy sarcasm was lost on the Scot.

"I'm like that," he replied seriously. "I was never yin tae push mysel' forward."

On an unaccountable impulse, Peters pulled a scribbling-block toward him and wrote a few words on the top sheet. Tearing it off, he handed it to the Scot.

"This authorizes you to come and go as you please. I don't know why I'm giving it to you. Don't make a nuisance of yourself."

If he had been able to foresee how much of nuisance Alastair MacNab was to be, nothing is more certain than that he would have shown him the door without delay.

Almost as soon as the Scot had left the room Peters was smitten with qualms. The very appearance of Alastair MacNab ought to have rendered absurd the suspicion that he might be the accomplice of a cunning murderer, nevertheless, this was the wrong time to take chances. Ringing up The New World Investigation Bureau, Peters had a few words with Mr S. Birnbaum, the managing director.

"I can assure you positively," said Mr Birnbaum, "that Mac-Nab is the best man we've got."

"He doesn't look very intelligent."

"Perhaps not," said Mr. Birnbaum, "but looks aren't everything."

Mark Peters was unable to deny the truth of that.

A largish cigarette end lay among the sawdust on the floor of the bar. Although expecting shortly to receive a sum which, to him, amounted to wealth, the habit of years was so strong that Flinders stooped and picked it up. Straightening his back, he found the manager of The Punchbowl staring bleakly at him from the other side of the beer-slopped counter. The potman who had been in sole charge of the bar until a moment before was standing beside the manager with the detached air of one who has surrendered a ticklish responsibility into more capable hands.

The only other customer, a much-moustached little man in a bowler hat, sitting in a corner with his nose buried in a pint mug, looked up in gloomy interest. He did not take his nose out of the mug but for the moment his Adam's apple ceased bobbing up and down in the rhythm of drinking.

"What's this I hear?" said the manager, breathing heavily.

"I'll buy it," said Flinders. "What do you hear?"

"Oh," said the publican, narrowing his eyes to slits. "One of the lippy kind, eh?"

"In my youth," said Flinders, "the lippiest of the lippy. An incessant and witty conversationalist, if you'll believe me. But in miserable and embittered middle age a dour, silent, disillusioned man. In fact—"

"Never mind all that. My man says you've ordered drinks and can't pay for them."

On the counter stood a glass containing an inch of Johnny Walker; all that remained of three double Johnny's which Flinders had ordered and drunk in rapid succession. The alcoholic content of three large whiskies was the bare amount required to make him feel almost human. Before the publican could snatch the glass away Flinders picked it up and swallowed what was left in it. He put the cigarette end in his mouth.

"Got a match on you?" he asked.

An ex-prize-fighter, the publican was beginning to run to fat but still looked formidably muscular. Pushing up his sleeves, he said: "I don't want any arguments. I'll give you your choice; pay up or take a sock on the nose. Which is it?"

"I'll pay," said Flinders confidently. On one more double Johnny he would have been bold enough to spit in the publican's eye.

"Let's see your brass."

"The time," said Flinders, consulting the clock, "is two minutes past one. In three or four minutes I'll show you more brass than you ever imagined existed."

"Show me four shillings. Now."

"In three or four minutes—"

"Be damned to that for a tale," retorted the publican. To the potman he added: "This comes out of your wages. If I've told you once I've told you a dozen times, never serve these dirty tramps without first seeing the colour of their money."

"If it 'ad bin 'alf a pint of bitter I'd 'ave insisted on cash on the counter," said the potman plaintively. "But three double scotches. 'Oo'd 'ave thought the saucy 'ound would 'ave the nerve to try it on to that extent?"

"Bastards like this one," retorted the publican, "are all nerve and gullet."

Without haste he walked to the end of the bar. He raised a flap in the counter and walked through.

"In three or four minutes," said Flinders, backing away.

"In three or four minutes," hissed the publican, "you'll be sitting in the gutter wishing you'd never been born."

One hand reached out and grabbed the degenerate by the lapels. The other drew back, preparatory to launching a vicious blow.

Flinders showed teeth like a collapsed fence in a triumphant grin. "You're just in time," he said, looking over the publican's shoulder.

Joan had come into the bar. This was her first public house and she did not like what she saw of it. The Punchbowl's trade was largely with professional men and clerks, who used the saloon bar on the other side of the house. The few customers who frequented the public bar were not nice in their habits. Averting her eyes from the floor, Joan looked at the publican and his captive. The sight of Flinders made her stomach shudder. He looked as though he had not washed or changed his clothes for a month. It was, in fact, even longer than that since he had even taken off his socks; and his last wash had been an enforced bath in the casual ward of a workhouse almost a year before.

"I had a drink or two while I waited for you and I've no money to pay for them."

In silence Joan opened her handbag, took out a pound note and handed it to him. He passed it to the publican, who released him and went behind the bar to make change.

"I'll have another double Johnny," said Flinders, with an air, to the potman. "What's yours?" he added to Joan.

"I shan't have anything," she replied, hardly moving her lips.

Flinders pocketed the change and they went into a corner and sat down. The man in the bowler hat did not finish drinking his pint, nor did he take his nose out of the mug. The mug seemed to be attached to his face. He peered over the rim of it at Joan, much as a crab stares from under its shell. The potman, too, was all eyes. Never before had he seen quite so incongruous a couple as the filthy human derelict and the beautiful girl.

"Let's go somewhere else," said Joan, her flesh crawling. "I can't stand this place."

"I like it here," retorted Flinders, emptying his glass at a gulp. "You brought the money?"

"Yes. Tell me this secret that you've remembered."

"We can't do it that way," said Flinders, shaking his head solemnly. "After I told you my life wouldn't be worth that"—he snapped two dirty fingers.

"But you promised to give me the information and a paper to prove it for a hundred pounds."

"Don't get excited. I've written it all down. I have a sealed envelope here"—he touched his breast pocket — "which contains the information and the evidence."

"Does it concern the murder?"

"It concerns something that happened twenty years ago. Draw your own conclusions."

"Let me see what's in the envelope. If it's worth a hundred pounds to me, I'll pay you the money."

"That won't do. You've got to take the envelope exactly as it is and swear not to open it for twenty-four hours. There's a boat leaving for South Africa in the morning. I'm leaving with it. By this time tomorrow I'll be in mid-ocean. You can open the envelope then. I'll be safe. Peters won't be able to reach me."

"If you think I'm such a fool as to part with a hundred pounds for nothing better than that—"

Flinders wiped his nose on his sleeve. "Suit yourself. You know best how far you're willing to go to help your father."

He walked to the bar and came back with another large whiskey. Joan sat looking at him. He stared back at her with blank eyes. One of those inner voices that are forever muttering warnings to women kept telling her to rise and walk out of the place, but she paid no more attention to it than women usually do—at the time. It was absurd, she knew, to put her trust in this piece of human wreckage; but she clung desperately to the frail hope that he was telling the truth.

"Miss Marplay," he whispered, "there's dynamite in this envelope. Dynamite, I tell you."

"All right," said Joan wearily. "I'll accept your terms."

Flinders shuffled his chair round until he was facing her, his back hiding her from the inquisitive eyes of the potman and the man in the bowler hat. He spread his ragged coat to screen her even more thoroughly. His breath and the smell of his clothing were almost overpowering.

"Put the money on my lap."

Joan took a bundle of notes from her handbag and laid them on his knees. A filthy hand scooped them up eagerly and thrust them into a torn pocket. It delved into the breast pocket, brought out a greasy envelope and handed it to her.

"Put that out of sight," hissed Flinders. "Quick!"

The greasy envelope went into her handbag. Flinders stood up.

"That's the best bargain you've ever made," he said huskily. "You've bought dynamite, Miss Marplay. Dynamite! Remember I'm trusting you not to open it before I've had a chance to quit the country. I'd be killed in the explosion if you did."

Without looking at him or speaking, Joan hurried out of the pub. She wanted fresh air. Her whole being cried out for it.

With a wet, triumphant leer on his face Flinders swaggered to the bar. "Four double Johnny's," he said, producing one of the notes.

The potman put the glasses in a row on the bar. Flinders shoved aside the soda syphon and water jug that accompanied them.

"One," he said.

He swallowed the first neat whiskey in one gulp.

"Two. Three. Four."

Fascinated, the potman stared at four empty glasses.

"Give me a bottle of Johnny to take away," said Flinders.

"Yes sir," mumbled the potman, blinking.

"Make it two bottles."

The potman was speechless.

"What's yours?" said Flinders convivially, to the man in the bowler hat.

That much-moustached individual emptied his mug in a single masterly swallow.

"Pint of old-and-mild, thanking you kindly," he replied, coming over to the bar.

For the rest of the day and most of the night Flinders was on a glorious blind. He had soaked his system in alcohol so thoroughly for the greater part of his life that he could drink ten men into a state of collapse and still stand on his feet; and as long as he could stand—or even creep—he was always ready for more.

The word went round among the down-and-outs of Fleet Street gutters that Flinders was in funds and he soon found himself with almost as many friends as a Gorgonzola cheese has maggots.

In the small hours two of his friends guided the derelict's wavering footsteps into a dark alley. One of them hit him on the head with a bottle. The other caught his unconscious form as he fell and dragged it into the shadows. They went through his pockets and found eighty-nine pounds, all that was left of the hundred. It was so much more than they expected that in their excitement they divided it equally, each forgetting his previously formed intention to cheat the other.

Dinner for Two

That evening Joan dined with Lord Noel in a small restaurant on the eastern fringe of Mayfair. Soft lights, no music, good food, perfect service... Peace. Quiet. As different as could be from the elaborate meals she had eaten with Ambrose Craven in the jangling haunts of the newly rich. For the first time since she had found out about her father, Joan was able to forget everything but the moment. Almost, she was happy.

They talked a lot, but not of the murder. Lord Noel started the conversation by saying: "When you go back to your cottage you must have me down for a long week end."

Joan said: "That will be lovely."

And Lord Noel said: "What will we do?"

Joan started to tell him what they would do. Once she had begun there was so much to tell the difficulty was to fit it all in. She described the countryside, and when she found that he knew it fairly well it was necessary to describe it even more fully so that they might compare impressions. Always an eager talker when she had a sympathetic listener, Joan talked more than ever before. Her words took wings and lifted her up. For seventeen years she had lived at the cottage. They had seemed uneventful years; and it was good to realize that every day had given her something worth telling, worth remembering. In telling, remembering, she found her way back to sane and normal things. Her nerves had been taut, like a spring too tightly wound. Now they relaxed.

Three hours passed like three minutes. During the latter part of their stay, they had the restaurant entirely to themselves except for hovering waiters. The service remained perfect but the eyebrows of the head waiter became reproachful. It was long past time to go.

Ambrose Craven would have suggested a night club.

Lord Noel thought Joan ought to have an early night. In that he was perfectly correct. He was going to call a taxi, but she stopped him. They walked home with a fresh breeze in their faces and Joan went on talking. Happiness had loosened her tongue and she simply could not stop. Lord Noel was only too pleased to listen. He was beginning to be sure that he would never tire of listening to Joan.

When they arrived at Malbrouk Court, Joan took him up to be presented to Agatha. It was like an encounter between a friendly dog and a suspicious but battle-weary cat. Agatha was stiffly polite but unresponsive and ready to be downright unpleasant if the occasion arose.

"Two large packages have come for you," she told Joan.

"The Dictaphone," said Lord Noel.

Agatha looked from one to the other with eyebrows that asked a question. Joan hurriedly explained the plan to trap Craven. She was afraid that Agatha would not approve. She was quite right: Agatha heartily disapproved.

"You appear to have no more sense than my ward, young man," she remarked with pursed lips, "and that's precious little."

"I quite agree," said Lord Noel cheerfully. "If I were you, I'd put my foot down and make Joan give up this wild scheme of hers and go back to the cottage."

"I've tried that. It didn't work."

"Then, if neither of us can stop her doing what she wants to do, isn't it wisest to join in and see that no harm comes to her?"

"You're very plausible," replied Agatha stiffly. She meant it as a reprimand.

Lord Noel took off his jacket, rolled up his sleeves and set to work running a wire from the living room to the bedroom. To one end he connected the Dictaphone, to the other a concealed microphone. He patiently explained to Joan the working of the mechanism. He explained it three times. At the third telling she began to follow him. That, he said, was pretty good for a woman.

"And supposing this Craven discovers the trap that's been laid for him," said Agatha. "What then?"

"I'll be waiting in the street ready to come up at a signal."

"A fat lot of signalling Joan will be able to do if Mr. Craven turns nasty."

"It won't be anything elaborate. A simple action like walking to the window and lowering the blind."

"While she's walking to the window, he's more than likely to run after her and knock her on the head."

"Don't mind Trimmy," said Joan; "it's a habit of hers to look on the dark side."

When Lord Noel arrived home, he telephoned the *Echo* offices and enquired how the work of demolishing the old building was progressing.

He was informed that the old building was now razed to the ground.

And that no trace of Lucius Marplay had been discovered.

Ten paces to the window; ten paces to the door, like a trapped animal Nigel Partridge paced the floor. He kept hitting the palm of one hand with the clenched fist of the other. Without looking up from his desk Mark Peters said: "For heaven's sake, man, keep calm."

Partridge halted in his stride and turned to stare at his partner. "Keep calm. That's easy to say. I'm trying to keep calm. I'm doing my damnedest. It isn't easy."

"If a drink would hel—"

"I'd rather be frightened than fuddled. Oh, I know I ought to control myself—no one knows that better than I do—but put yourself in my shoes."

"In your shoes," said Peters, putting his signature to a paper, "I'd do exactly what I'm doing. I'd get on with my work."

"You're like a fish, Mark—cold blooded as hell. I'm not."

Partridge went to the door, opened it and looked out. He said something to one of the plainclothes men who were waiting in the outer room, closed the door again and walked back to the desk. "Why don't they come?" he fumed.

Peters looked at his watch. It was a few minutes after eleven on the second morning after the murder of Sinclair Ellis.

"Give them time. We only phoned the Yard eight minutes ago."

"Does Craven know?"

"I haven't told him. I don't want him having hysterics all over the place. That scared-rabbit look on his face is quite bad enough for discipline as it is."

"I suppose you think I'm another scared rabbit?"

"Not exactly. I can't blame you for having the wind up to a certain extent—but losing your head won't help you to save your life."

"You're dead right," said Partridge. With a tinge of bitterness in his tone he added: "You're always right."

Drawing a chair up to the desk, he sat down. He crossed his legs. He lit a cigarette. He took perhaps three puffs at it, then jumped up and ground it into an ash tray. He looked down at his partner. Peters was concentrating on his work.

"Oh hell," said Partridge.

He started pacing the floor again. When he reached the window, he looked down at Fleet Street. On a wall directly opposite the building a giant newspaper poster proclaimed:

ALLEGED

MANIAC KILLER

STILL AT LARGE

For a long time, Partridge stared at it. "He isn't human, Mark," he said, his voice seeming to come from a distance.

"There's nothing superhuman about him. He's a sly old fox who happens to be a little smarter than the hunters—but even the slyest fox is hunted down in the end. It's purely a question of time."

"And my time," said Partridge dryly, "would appear to be limited."

There was a knock at the door and Mark Peters' secretary ushered in Superintendent Wrenn and Sergeant Leet. With a wave of his hand Peters indicated chairs. Using tweezers to prevent leaving his fingerprints on it, he picked up a slip of paper which was lying on his desk and handed it to Wrenn, who took it gingerly, holding it by a corner with the tips of his thumb and forefinger. The paper was of the kind which the *Echo* used for proofs and in the centre of the sheet were a few printed lines which ran:

> PARTRIDGE—On the 19th of June, at his office in Fleet
> Street, Nigel Partridge, of a bullet in the head.

"My death notice," said Partridge, with a sad attempt at nonchalance.

"Found among other proofs on the head proof-reader's file about ten minutes ago," said Peters. "Heaven knows how it got there. It wasn't set up in this building, I can say that definitely. The type was set by hand and we have no hand type as small as that. All our death notices are set on a linotype. The proof hasn't been handled by anyone except the head reader. Here is a set of his fingerprints, for comparison."

Peters held out a white card on which were five black impressions. With a jerk of his head Superintendent Wrenn directed Sergeant Leet to take it. He also gave the proof of the death notice to Leet, who took from his pocket some black powder, a magnifying glass and another card on which was a set of Marplay's fingerprints. For a few minutes he studied the proof and the cards carefully.

"There are thirteen prints on the proof," he announced. "Four of them were made by the proof-reader, the others by Lucius Marplay."

A dead silence followed this pronouncement. The five men stared at each other. Wrenn was the first to speak.

"It sounds incredible," he said. His voice was husky.

"Incredible or not," retorted Partridge, "it's true. And what are you going to do about it?"

"He couldn't get into the building," said Sergeant Leet. "He simply couldn't. For the past forty-eight hours we've had the place completely surrounded."

"If he couldn't get in," snapped Partridge, "how did he manage to put that proof on the file? And if he can do that in spite of your police cordon, what's to stop him putting a bullet through my head?"

"Within twenty minutes I'll have fifty plainclothes men on duty in this building," replied Superintendent Wrenn, looking grey and worried. "By the time I've finished placing them, Marplay will have to walk through concrete walls to reach you—and that's something no living man can do."

"If he is a living man," said Partridge shakily. "I'm beginning to think—"

"Now you're talking nonsense, Nigel," said Peters.

"Perhaps I am. Perhaps it is nonsense. But if he is a living man why is it that everyone can see the things he does but no one can see the man himself?"

No one replied.

No one could think of a reasonable reply.

*

At precisely ten past one that afternoon, having waited the twenty-four hours stipulated by Flinders, Joan opened the greasy envelope for which she had paid him a hundred pounds.

It contained some blank pieces of paper.

*

That afternoon, on the top story of the building, Nigel Partridge sat alone in his private room, which was almost as impregnable as one of the vaults of the Bank of England. Bulletproof steel shutters covered the windows. Ceiling, floor and walls were made of solid concrete, with a facing of walnut plywood. There was only one way in and that was through an anteroom in which sat Partridge's secretary, Sergeant Leet and another detective. Both Leet and his colleague had unblemished records in the Metropolitan Police. The secretary was a timid but efficient young woman who had been for twelve years in her present employment. There was not the slightest likelihood that any of them were in league with Lucius Marplay.

The police had not overlooked the possibility that a mechanical device capable of firing a shot might be hidden in Partridge's room. An expert had closely examined every inch of the room and every article in it and was positive that it contained no such device.

The door between the rooms was ajar. No one could enter the inner one without passing through the anteroom. And no one who was not above suspicion would be allowed to pass.

The corridor outside was lined with detectives from the Criminal Investigation Department.

Nigel Partridge was perfectly safe. No one doubted that—with the possible exception of Partridge himself and the certain exception of Ambrose Craven, who had found out about the death notice and was sitting in his own room with his fingers in his ears, waiting for the roar of the fatal shot.

At three o'clock Alastair MacNab ambled into the anteroom. In a day and a half, he had become a familiar figure in the *Echo* building. There was hardly a part of it into which he had not pried, always with an amiable smile on his face and endless questions on his lips. He never tired of asking questions. Some of them sounded inordinately foolish.

"What do you want?" demanded Sergeant Leet unpleasantly. "Don't you know that no one is allowed in here?"

With a complacent beam the Scot placed his wicker basket on the secretary's desk and started fumbling in a pocket.

"I hae a wee pass that Mister-r Peter-rs gied me. It allows me tae gang wherever-r I please."

"It doesn't allow you to come in here. No one's allowed in here. Hop it."

"There's a wee question I'd like tae ask Mister-r Par-rtridge—"

"Outside," said Leet firmly.

"Oh, verra weel."

Still beaming, the Scot picked up his basket and waddled out of the room. When he had gone the secretary looked at Sergeant Leet with a puzzled frown. "His lunch is alive."

"What are you talking about?"

"He's supposed to carry his lunch in that basket. I put my hand on it and felt something moving inside. His lunch is alive, I tell you."

Sergeant Leet stared hard at her for a moment.

"It is," she insisted. "I felt it moving."

"All right," he responded. "His lunch is alive. Well, that's his business. He's a queer fish. If he likes live bait, it's got nothing to do with me. I'm only here to see that he keeps his nose out of Mr. Partridge's room." He jumped up. "'Afternoon, Mr. Peters," he said.

Mark Peters was standing in the doorway smoking a long cigar. "Everything all right?"

"Yes sir."

"That's good. Don't leave him alone for a minute."

From the inner room Partridge called: "Mark, come here."

Peters walked through, leaving the communicating door slightly ajar. Craning his neck, Sergeant Leet heard scraps of conversation:

"Mark, I'm frightened."

"Buck up, old man. There's nothing to worry about. You're too well guarded."

"I know. I keep telling myself there's no danger, But—I— Oh, I know it's silly, but I can't help it."

"Then why not have a couple of the Yard men here with you?"

"No. I don't want them sitting staring at me. It would drive me mad. Besides, if they can stop Marplay they'll stop him before he gets in here. But will they be able to stop him? —that's the question that's beginning to turn my brain. Will they be able to stop him? Or shall I go the same way as poor Ellis?"

Sergeant Leet heard the loud slap of a hand striking the desk; and the voice of Mark Peters saying: "Nigel, you've got to brace up. If you keep on like this you'll go to pieces."

And then, after an interval, the weary voice of Nigel Partridge: "Sorry, Mark. I'll try to control myself."

"Would you like me to stay with you?" That was Peters speaking.

A long pause and then Partridge's voice, strained and hoarse: "No. I don't want anyone. I'll see this through alone."

In a few moments Peters came out, leaving the door ajar. Sergeant Leet did his best to look as though he had not been listening.

"Don't let anyone in," said Peters. "He doesn't want to be disturbed. Keep your ears cocked, though, and run in if you think anything's wrong. Take no chances. This Marplay is as cunning as the devil."

"He won't pass us, sir," replied Sergeant Leet positively.

A few minutes dragged by uneventfully. The outer door opened again and Superintendent Wrenn put his head into the anteroom. "Everything all right, Sergeant?"

"All correct, sir."

"Good. Keep your eyes peeled."

"We will, sir."

The strain of sitting still and doing nothing but wait, wait,

wait, became too much for the secretary. She put a sheet of paper in her typewriter and began to type a letter which her employer had dictated earlier that day. To the overwrought detectives it sounded like the clatter of a machine gun.

"Stop that!" said Wrenn sharply. "We don't want any noise."

The words were hardly out of his mouth when there was a great deal of noise in the inner room. A loud report, a thud, the sound of many articles falling on the floor...

For a moment they stared in consternation at the partly open door: and then Sergeant Leet dashed into the inner room, the others close behind him. A few paces from the desk Leet halted and stood staring at what lay there. The secretary screamed and fainted.

Across the desk sprawled the lifeless body of Nigel Partridge, blood trickling from a hole above the right eye.

On the floor, in a jumble, lay a telephone, a cigarette box, an ash tray, pens, pencils: all, apparently swept from the desk by his arms as he fell.

Near the head of the corpse lay a receipt form on which was pencilled in block capitals: PAID IN FULL. It was signed 'Lucius Marplay.'

As soon as he realized that Partridge was dead, Superintendent Wrenn looked round swiftly for the murderer.

But although they had run in within seconds of hearing the shot, although there was only one way in or out, there was no one in the room except the police officials, the secretary and the corpse.

The murderer had not slipped out when they ran in, that much was certain. Sergeant Leet's colleague was still standing in the doorway and no one had passed him.

It was incredible, unbelievable, fantastic, impossible...

Nevertheless, on the face of it, Partridge had been shot by someone who was not there!

Black Magic?

Never before had Superintendent Wrenn felt so utterly defeated as he did at that moment. It was his first encounter with an invisible murderer. He remembered a book he had once read, *The Invisible Man*, by H. G. Wells. At the time he had found it entertaining but far from credible. Now he actually caught himself wondering whether Lucius Marplay had discovered some secret means of making himself invisible; some fabulous drug, like the one in the book. "Before I know where I am," he told himself grimly, "I'll go potty and start climbing the walls."

He turned limply to speak to one of his subordinates and found a score of faces staring into the room in morbid fascination. Among the gaping intruders were some *Echo* reporters, a few filing clerks and typists, and half a dozen of the detectives who had been on duty in the corridor. In the foreground stood Mark Peters, looking white and shaken for the first time that Wrenn remembered. Beside him, Alastair MacNab, no longer beaming amiably, but with a tight, hard look on his round face. Behind the staring faces the anteroom was packed to suffocation. Wrenn could hear some of his men shouting, ordering out those who had no business to be there, but none of the intruders were paying any attention. They all wanted to look. Those at the rear were standing on tiptoe, stretching their necks to see over the heads and shoulders of those in front.

Wrenn turned savagely on Sergeant Leet. "What is this? A peepshow? Clear them all out."

The secretary who had fainted was still unconscious. When there was room to work, Wrenn detailed two of his assistants to take her to the first-aid room on one of the lower floors. One of the detectives who helped carry her down returned for her personal belongings. When he picked up her handbag he was surprised to find that it was quite heavy. Fingering it—the bag was made of cloth ornamented with steel beads—he felt something hard and bulky inside. He opened the bag, looked in, and uttered a startled exclamation.

"Look at this, Superintendent."

Wrenn looked. He put a hand into the bag and brought out a small pearl-handled revolver. Flipping open the cylinder, he saw that it contained five live cartridges and one which had recently been discharged…

*

"Looks like a .25 bullet," said the divisional surgeon, turning from the body and holding up a bloodstained probe in which was a small round gory object.

"The revolver found in the girl's handbag is a .25," said Superintendent Wrenn.

"Good God, sir," protested Leet. "You can't possibly imagine—"

Ignoring his subordinate, Wrenn said to the doctor: "Can you give me some idea of the range at which the shot was fired?"

"From a distance of six or eight feet at least. At close range there would be marks of burned powder round the wound—and you can see for yourself that there are none whatever. From the angle at which the bullet entered his head I should say that the shot was fired from the door."

"The door was ajar," muttered Wrenn, almost to himself. "The secretary was sitting within two feet of it."

"And we were sitting facing her, Parker and I," retorted Sergeant Leet hoarsely. "If she'd made a move, we'd have seen it. Hang it all, Chief, you were in the anteroom yourself when the shot was fired. The sound came from in here."

"Oh, shut up," snapped Wrenn. "Do you think I don't know all that?"

Turning to another subordinate, he handed him the revolver and the bullet. "Rush these to the Yard as fast as you can. Tell the ballistics expert I want his report as quickly as he can give it to me. Wait there while he's making his tests and bring the report back with you."

"Maybe I'm crazy," mumbled Leet, "but if the bullet matches the gun—"

"If it does," Wrenn almost shouted, "it won't make sense. And can you tell me two facts in this whole damned case that match and that do make sense?"

Sergeant Leet was silenced.

*

After the first excitement all but a privileged few were excluded from the room in which Nigel Partridge lay dead. Mark Peters was one of those allowed to enter. He said nothing, but stood for a while taking everything in. When he knew all the police knew about the murder—which was precious little—he hurried to the newsroom and marshalled his staff to prepare an elaborate account of the crime, to occupy the entire front page of the *Echo*. It was a big story, involving many factors. He intended it to be the biggest story the *Echo* had ever printed. Sure that it was exclusive, he took time to do the job properly. A subeditor was assigned to elaborate the facts of the crime from details which Peters supplied; another brought up to date the obituary of Nigel Partridge; a third rehashed the murder of Sinclair Ellis and the events that had led up to it. There were more than twenty men hard at work on different angles of the story when a reporter ran into the room excitedly waving a copy of the *Evening Dispatch*.

Peters snatched it and flattened it on a desk. He read the headlines that were spread across the top of the front page. With a strangled cry of inarticulate rage, he crushed the newspaper into a ball.

The *Dispatch* had once more scooped the *Echo*, this time with a full report of the killing of Nigel Partridge illustrated by a photograph of the scene of the crime, showing the police bending over the body—a photograph which must have been taken immediately after the murder.

In a white-hot fury Peters snatched up a telephone and put through a call to the editor of the *Evening Dispatch*. But although he raged and stormed, the voice that answered him remained cool and detached.

"I have my sources of information," was all the editor of the *Dispatch* would say.

"If you won't tell me the name of the Judas who gave you that story, you'll have to tell the police."

"I doubt it. The identity of my informant has no bearing on the murder. The police will have to bring heavy pressure to bear before I divulge it, very heavy pressure indeed. I doubt if they'll care to do that. Freedom of the Press, you know—you wrote an able editorial on the subject not long ago. Awkward questions in Commons, and all that sort of thing. No, no, Mr Peters, I really don't think either the police commissioner or the home secretary will care to make a major issue of what amounts to guerrilla warfare between two newspapers. Sorry, and all that."

Mark Peters slammed down the receiver. He said something short, sharp, profane.

He honestly felt that the person who had enabled the *Dispatch* to scoop the *Echo* was a greater criminal than the murderer.

But although he stormed and raved through the building, he did not find out who that person was. The doorkeepers and the plain-clothes men on duty at the entrances were prepared to eat their hats if a newspaperman had set foot in the place.

*

Almost two hours after the murder Sergeant Leet remembered the secretary's peculiar statement that there was a living thing in Alastair MacNab's wicker basket. Thinking it over, he became curious and went to look for the Scot. There was so little else to investigate, he felt he might as well investigate the basket. He found Alastair MacNab sitting at an open window in an otherwise deserted corridor, feeding with breadcrumbs the pigeons that strutted on the sill. The basket lay on the floor at his feet. Without saying anything, Leet knelt and opened it. There was nothing in it except some crumbs.

"If it's a bite tae eat ye're looking for," said the Scot affably, "I'm sorry tae tell ye I've jist scoffed the lot. I'm a wee bit late wi' ma lunch the day. If I'd stoppit tae eat earlier I micht hae missed something."

About to rise, Leet noticed something round and black lying on the floor. He picked it up. At first sight it looked like a waistcoat button. At second sight it still looked like a waistcoat button, but there appeared to be no way to fasten it to a waistcoat. There were indentations like thread holes on it, but they did not go through. The reverse side was smooth and solid.

Alastair MacNab reached out calmly and took the 'button' from the puzzled police sergeant. With one finger he pressed it into the middle of his waistcoat. When he took the finger away the 'button' remained where he had put it. It matched exactly the other buttons on his waistcoat.

"An invention o' my ain," said the Scot blandly. "Nae needle or thread requir-red. A boon tae the bachelor."

"How does it fasten?"

"I canna tell ye that," replied MacNab archly. "It's a dar-rk secret until the patent is gr-ranted."

*

Toward nightfall the detective who had been sent back to Scotland Yard with the revolver and the bullet returned with a report from the Criminal Investigation Department's expert on ballistics. The report was final, definite and conclusive: the bullet in Partridge's head had been fired from the revolver found in the handbag.

Wrenn went to interview the secretary, who was being detained in a waiting room, showed her the report and asked her how she explained it. She did not attempt to explain it. She sat staring at the revolver and shaking her head like one of those dolls with wire spring necks.

"I've never seen it before," she declared tearfully. "In fact, I've never seen a revolver before. It's the first revolver I've seen. I don't know where it came from. I wouldn't know how to fire it. I don't know anything about revolvers. I've never seen one before."

"All right, all right, all right," growled Wrenn irritably. "There's no need to tell me the same thing over and over again. I believe you. You've never seen a revolver before."

"That's what I said," wept the girl. "I've never seen a revolver before."

Night had fallen. With jerky strides Ambrose Craven paced the floor of his private room. He sat down, he jumped up. He paced the floor again. Turning on the light he went to the window, intending to draw the blinds. With his hand raised he suddenly realized what a perfect target he was offering, and scuttled across the room into a corner, as far from the window as he could go. His scalp prickled. His knees were weak as water. His hands were clammy. His heart kept jumping like a Mexican bean. Queasy stomach; throat dry as the Sahara; jangling nerves; eyes darting like a water bug: he had all the symptoms of panic-stricken cowardice. He wanted to cry, to laugh, to shout, to yell. He wanted to scream and scream and scream, to empty his fright on the startled air.

Opening his mouth, he let out one terrified yelp. The two policemen who formed his bodyguard came running in from the anteroom with drawn automatics. The weapons frightened him so much that first he could not speak. When they saw that Craven was alone in the room, the policemen looked at each other significantly. One of them put a finger to his head.

"Not you," stammered Craven. "I don't want you. Go away, both of you. I want Miss Trimm."

Leaning back into the anteroom, one of the policemen said to Joan: "You'd better come. I think he's going off his head."

When Joan came in Craven ran to her, clutching her and whimpering like a fear-demented child.

"Send them away," he wailed. "I'm afraid of them. I don't trust them."

Joan signalled with her eyes to the policemen and they withdrew, leaving the door open.

"I can't trust anyone," whimpered Craven. "Not anyone at all. They're all in league with Marplay, every one of them."

"You can trust me," replied Joan. Saying it, she felt like Judas.

"You'll stay with me, won't you? You won't let anyone get at me?"

"I'll stay with you."

"I'm afraid to be here. I'm afraid to go home. I'm not safe anywhere. Partridge was murdered, even with the police guarding him. They're all traitors. I'll be the next to die. I know it. If I could only hide from them all... But, wherever I go, they'll follow. And they've all sold themselves to Marplay."

"Come home with me," whispered Joan. "No one will find you there."

"They'll follow."

"No, they won't. I'll find a way to throw them off."

Craven's flickering eyes searched her face. "If you really think it would work—"

"Trust me," said Joan. Again, she felt like the lowest of traitors. "I must leave you for a moment, but I'll be back."

"Hurry," pleaded Craven. His forehead and the backs of his hands were wet with perspiration.

Joan went downstairs to Lord Noel's glass-walled cubicle.

"He's almost out of his mind with fright," she said. "I think he'll talk. I'm taking him to my flat."

Lord Noel stood up and reached for his hat. "I'll be there as soon as you are."

"Telephone Miss Trimm," said Joan, "and remind her that she must go out."

"Right."

Returning to the anteroom of Craven's office, Joan said to one of the policemen: "Mr Craven's going home. Will you have his car brought round to the front door?"

The policeman nodded and left the room. Joan gave him time to be well out of the way then she went to the inner room and fetched Craven. They hurried to the goods lift, with the other policeman at heels.

The goods lift deposited them at the side door.

"You told my mate the front door," said the policeman, looking at Joan.

Without replying she hurried Craven to her two-seater, parked a short distance up the lane.

"What's the idea?" demanded the policeman suspiciously. "First you send my mate to fetch Mr. Craven's car and then you—"

"Mr Craven's going home in my car," said Joan quietly. "He wants you to follow in the Rolls."

"It can't be done. Orders are to keep close to Mr Craven."

Joan settled in the driving seat Craven huddled beside her. She turned the ignition key.

"You're welcome to come with us," she said, pressing the self-starter. "Climb into the rumble seat."

"What about my mate?"

"We'll stop at the front of the building and pick him up with the Rolls."

Frowning uncertainly, the policeman walked to the back of the car and tugged at the lid of the rumble seat. Before he realized that it was locked Joan put the engine in gear, depressed the accelerator and let in the clutch. The car jumped forward and went down the lane rapidly. It happened so suddenly that the policeman was dragged off his feet and almost fell on his face when he lost his grip on the handle of the rumble seat lid.

The little car took the turning into Fleet Street without slackening speed, shot under the radiator of a bus, missed a safety island by a fraction of an inch, and swerved into the stream of traffic on the other side of the road, causing the drivers of three other vehicles to scratch paint and dent mudguards in their frantic efforts to get out of the way. With the nonchalance of a little girl cutting out paper dolls, Joan carved fantastic patterns in the traffic. She heard a police whistle blowing behind her but did not look back. She was keeping her mind on her driving—although all who saw her thought she had lost it.

During the next few minutes, she made the two-seater do incredible things. Her driving was a model of how not to drive: seeing a film of it would have cured most reckless motorists for life, if it did not put them off driving completely. She took hair-raising risks and got away with them, sailing past red lights as though they were not there, blithely ignoring all the other vehicles on the road. Rounding a corner into a deserted street, she drove half its length and turned into an alley which she followed to the next street. There, having shaken off the pursuit, she slowed down and, from that point to Malbrouk Court, drove with decorum.

At Malbrouk Court she took the two-seater straight into the basement garage and parked it in its usual position.

"This is where I live," she said, turning to Craven. "And you see we haven't been followed."

Ambrose Craven did not reply. He had fainted.

It took Joan a few minutes to bring him round and even when he regained consciousness, he remained in a semi-stupor. Her driving had shocked all feeling out of him. He was numb, like a large and misshapen lump of putty. He followed her into a lift, walking like a somnambulist, and they went up to her flat. Joan led him to a chair close to the table on which the microphone was hidden in a bowl of flowers. He dropped into it heavily. His breath was coming in grunts.

"My God!" he said limply.

Joan brought him a tumbler half full of whiskey and he drank it like water. Going to the window, she raised the blind, the prearranged signal to let Lord Noel, waiting in the street below, know that they were in the flat. If the blind was lowered later, he was to come up in a hurry. But, looking at Craven, Joan felt quite sure that she would not have any trouble with him. Her employer was punch-drunk from the craziest motor drive of his life. She had taken him for a ride with a vengeance.

"You're safe here," she said. "No one at the office knows where I live and I'm quite certain I threw off the pursuit. My aunt's gone out. We're alone."

Craven only looked at her. In silence he handed her the empty glass. She refilled it. Touching the switch that made the Dictaphone start recording, she said:

"I know how you must feel. The murder of Ellis…the murder of Partridge…the dread that perhaps you will be next. Poor man! Your nerves are bound to be on edge."

Tears rolled down Ambrose Craven's podgy cheeks.

Joan thought: how can I make him talk? What's the best opening gambit? While she was wondering, Craven began to talk of his own accord.

"It's all Mark Peters' fault," he whimpered. "It was his idea from the start."

"Tell me about it," said Joan, holding her breath.

She was afraid that whatever Craven told her would be too incoherent to be of value. She expected him to stammer, to evade vital points, perhaps to dry up altogether. But Craven was ready to talk. He spoke in a low voice, but clearly and intelligently. He seemed to want to get it all off his chest.

"It happened so long ago…twenty years ago. You must have been a baby then. It was Peters' idea. He's mad, you know. The kind of madman who's crazy for power. The rest of us must have been a little mad, too, to listen to him. We all had good jobs on the paper under old Marplay. Peters was business manager, Ellis news editor, Partridge circulation manager. I was in charge of advertising. Marplay paid us well. We were satisfied, all of us but Peters—or thought we were until Peters persuaded us differently. He wanted power. To be the business manager of a big newspaper was nothing to him. He had to be proprietor. But he had no money. He could raise some; we could all raise some; but not enough. It takes a lot of money to buy a London newspaper. You've no idea how much money it takes. Especially so flourishing a newspaper as the *Echo* was even in those days. And Peters wanted the *Echo*. He's utterly ruthless when he wants something. There's no doubt about it: he's mad. It's a dangerous kind of madness.

"For about a year Marplay went away and left the four of us to run the paper. His wife had had a baby after they'd both given up hoping, and he would hardly leave her for an instant. Marplay's absence was what gave Peters the idea. He couldn't work it without us, so he asked Ellis and Partridge and me to come in with him. At first, we didn't like the idea, but Peters talked us into it. You can't stop him when his mind's made up. He talked and talked and talked. That man could make you believe that the moon shines by day and the sun by night. He made us believe that his scheme was so safe and simple that even if it failed no one could ever prove that we had been guilty of treachery. We all had comfortable incomes, but none of us were rich. He showed us how we could become rich. We couldn't refuse a fortune that was there for the taking.

"Peters set the ball rolling by deliberately causing expensive blunders in the business management of the paper that lost it thousands of pounds. Ellis let the other papers scoop us on one big news story after another and printed some libellous articles, involving the *Echo* in half-a-dozen lawsuits, costing enormous sums in damages. In one way and another I estranged some of our biggest advertisers and revenue dropped like a stone. Partridge contrived a sort of creeping paralysis in his department which caused the circulation to shrink to a third of what it had been. The *Echo* always arrived late at the newsstands, after our competitors had sold out. There was breakdown after breakdown in the printing department—Peters arranged that.

"In the middle of all this Marplay came back. He couldn't understand what had happened to his paper. It never occurred to him that we were sabotaging the *Echo*; and that was the only answer that explained everything. He trusted us. In some ways he was very simple. The *Echo* was in a muddle and nothing he could do made it any better. He was pulling one way; we were pulling the other. Peters was cunning. He schemed so cleverly that Marplay even began to blame himself for some of the blunders.

"Marplay had a nervous breakdown. While he was in a nursing home, we made hay of the *Echo*. When he came back, we handed him a tangle that even a wizard could not have unravelled—and he was still a sick man. He went completely off his head. We hadn't planned that, but it helped a lot. What was left of the *Echo* went into liquidation. By that time, it was worth so little that the money we could raise was sufficient to buy it. After all, what was more natural than that Marplay's most trusted employees should gamble their savings on the slim chance of saving the business on which their bread and butter depended?"

Joan's hands had been wrestling with each other on her lap. Now she rose and walked across the room. She felt sick. Craven went on talking but she no longer heard what he was saying. It came to her as dull rumbling without form, without meaning. For a time, she stood by the fire, holding on to the mantelpiece.

The doorbell rang shrilly and she came to herself with a start.

In a trembling voice Craven said: "For God's sake, don't answer it."

Without looking at him Joan went to the tiny vestibule and opened the door of the flat. On the threshold stood Mark Peters. He came in, shutting the door behind him.

"You'll pardon the intrusion," he said quietly, looking her straight in the face. "I've come for Mr. Craven."

He was no bigger than one of his office boys, but his eyes and mouth made Joan feel utterly helpless. There was an indescribable something about him which made her feel that no one, nothing, could stop him doing whatever he wanted to do. It would be worse than useless to deny Craven's presence in the flat. Joan stood aside and let Peters go into the sitting room.

Craven was cringing back in his chair in terror. When he recognized his partner, he relaxed with a sob. "Mark! I thought—"

"You thought it was Marplay? Serve you right if it had been. You poor fool, what are you doing here? There's a police alarm out for you and this girl. She's suspected of kidnapping you. By doing this idiotic disappearing trick you've got yourself into the headlines of every paper in London. You've crowded the murder of Partridge almost off the front page."

"How did you find us?"

"The police searched the files at the office for this young woman's address. There was no record of it. I took the liberty of searching your desk—and found it in your engagement book."

"Why didn't you bring the police with you?" asked Joan. Her mouth was dry.

"It didn't happen to suit my book. I wanted to find out first what you were up to. Suppose you explain."

Fumbling for words, Joan began: "It was only that—that—"

"Don't tell me. I'll work it out for myself. What's this?"

Mark Peters knelt and hooked a finger under the flex that ran along the skirting board and through the door of the bedroom. He tugged at it and the bowl of flowers went over. The microphone fell out and clattered on the floor. Joan made for the window. With his free hand Mark Peters grabbed her ankle and dragged her back.

"Don't go away," he said softly, rising to his feet.

His voice was very quiet, but Joan's blood ran cold. He gripped her arm tightly. "Let's see where this leads," he said, following the line of the flex with his eyes.

He took her with him into the bedroom. On one of the beds stood the Dictaphone, its cylinder still revolving. Mark Peters pushed Joan into a chair. He did not bother to hold her; he seemed quite sure that she would stay where he had put her; and he was right. Raising the Dictaphone needle, he slid it to the beginning of the record and set in operation the mechanism that made it utter what it had recorded.

He listened in silence to the voice of his partner explaining how they had stolen the newspaper from Lucius Marplay. His facial expression was calm, impassive, almost detached.

"Very interesting," he commented. Stopping the mechanism, he removed the record from the Dictaphone.

They went back to the sitting room.

"You talk too much, Ambrose," said Peters chillingly, "but it would appear that your conversation hasn't bored your young friend in the least. In fact, she was so interested that she took the trouble to make a permanent record of it."

Ambrose Craven stared stupidly at Joan; his mouth wide open. The asinine expression on the face of his partner seemed to annoy Mark Peters more than anything else. Leaning forward, he hit Craven across the mouth with the back of his hand.

"You bloody fool!" he exclaimed.

When he turned to Joan, Mark Peters' mouth was set in a tight smile. "I don't grasp your motive for getting this poor fool into a corner and making him talk. How did you know he'd have anything worth recording to say? What's behind this? Blackmail?"

"I—I—"

"Trying to think of a plausible lie?"

Joan stared at him hopelessly. Her eyes dropped to the record in his hand. After all her trouble, it was lost to her. Peters would see that she never had a chance to get another—even if Craven could ever again be persuaded to talk.

A light flickered in the dark eyes that were watching her shrewdly. "How old are you?" Peters demanded suddenly.

She did not answer. Peters studied her face.

"There is a look of him about your mouth. You have his eyes. You're just about the age his daughter would be. In fact, you are his daughter, aren't you— Miss Marplay?"

"Miss Marplay!" screamed Ambrose Craven.

"Yes, my dear Ambrose," retorted Peters, mimicking his partner's voice to perfection, "your young friend is the daughter of an old friend who has promised to end your life rather suddenly."

For the second time that evening Craven fainted.

"Poor, weak, cowardly wretch!" said Mark Peters. "Don't bother with him, Miss Marplay. He's happier unconscious. Lately, you know, he's been almost out of his mind with fear. That's why he came out with the farrago of nonsense you took the trouble to record."

"It wasn't nonsense."

Putting the record under his left armpit, Peters used his right hand to take a cigar case from his breast pocket.

"You don't mind if I smoke?"

Joan shrugged her shoulders. Pinching the end of his cigar, Peters struck a match and lit it. He exhaled cloud of blue smoke. "Where is your father?" he asked, in the same conversational tone.

"You don't think I know that," said Joan, staring at him.

"I'm not a fool, Miss Marplay. A child like you isn't in this alone. I doubt if you have the brains to think of trapping Craven with a Dictaphone. And it's quite impossible for your father to have accomplished all he has without assistance. You've had the free run of the *Echo* offices, where so many inexplicable things have happened. Oh, you're Lucius Marplay's accomplice, all right. I have no doubt of that."

"You can think what you like," retorted Joan.

Her heart was thumping. Over Mark Peters' shoulder she had seen the door of a cupboard behind him opening very slowly. She averted her eyes lest their expression should warn Peters that something was happening. She had no idea who was coming out of the cupboard. It might be anyone—even her father. She dared not look again.

"Don't move," said a deep voice behind Mark Peters.

Something cold, round, metallic was jabbed firmly against the back of his neck. It felt like the muzzle of a revolver.

Mark Peters stood very still. A hand took the Dictaphone record from under his arm.

Out of the corner of his eye Peters saw a mirror hanging above the mantelpiece. In the mirror he saw his own reflection and that of the person who was standing at his back: a middle-aged woman in a tweed jacket and skirt holding the point of a dumpy umbrella against his neck. The ferrule of the umbrella was the round, metallic object that felt so cold.

Swinging round on his heel, he made a grab at her. Miss Trimm struck him on the head with the umbrella. The blow was a hard one—it bent a number of the ribs—but it did not stop him. Dropping the umbrella, Miss Trimm turned and ran into the bedroom with the record in her hand, slammed the door and turned the key in the lock. Mark Peters took a few swift backward strides and launched himself at the door, using his shoulder as a battering-ram. The force of the impact tore a ragged hole in a flimsy panel. He put his hand through, groped for the key and unlocked the door.

Now was Joan's opportunity to signal to Lord Noel to come to their assistance; but she decided to leave him out of this. She did not want Peters to imagine that Lord Noel was another of her father's accomplices. The umbrella had proved useless as a weapon. Picking up a large and comfortingly heavy vase Joan went into the bedroom.

Agatha was standing by the open window, keeping Peters at bay by lashing out at him with her feet and her right hand. In her left hand she grimly held the precious record. Her face was dour and determined; it looked like a sharp piece of flint.

Going close to Peters, Joan picked out with her eyes the precise place on the back of his head where she intended to hit him.

And then a hand came through the window and snatched the record.

They heard feet clattering down the fire escape that ran up the side of the building. Agatha and Peters put their heads out of the window simultaneously. They saw a dim shape going down the iron stairs at breakneck speed. It was too dark for them to see whether the thief was short or tall, thin or fat, man or woman. They brought their heads back into the room and stared at each other.

"You can put that down now, darling," said Agatha dryly, addressing Joan, who was standing like a statue with the vase poised in her uplifted hand. "You ought to have socked him with it sooner. It's too late now—unless it will relieve your feelings."

Joan lowered the vase. "Who was it?"

"Too dark to tell," replied Agatha.

"It might have been anyone," said Peters dully.

Agatha shut the window. She looked at Peters with an unpleasant light in her eyes. "That's that," she said. "We haven't formally met, Mr. Peters, but I've overheard sufficient to gather who you are. You'd better go as quickly as you can."

Mark Peters brushed some dust off his coat. Ruefully, he eyed a tear in the sleeve. "Good night," he said, with a smile that was no more than a muscular contraction.

"And take your fat friend with you," said Agatha.

Peters left the room. In a few minutes they heard the outer door shut. They came out to the sitting room. It was empty.

"I heard only one pair of feet crossing the floor," said Agatha. "Your friend Craven must still have been unconscious. How in the world did a little man like Peters manage to drag that great lump out of here all by himself?"

"He must be stronger than he looks," replied Joan.

Feeling weak and a little dizzy, she put a shaking hand to her forehead. "What were you doing in the cupboard?"

"Looking for wild flowers," snapped Agatha. "What did you think? Good God, girl, you don't imagine I'd any intention of leaving you on your own? I felt in my bones that something would go wrong." She added irritably: "What on earth are you mumbling about?

"I'm counting up to a hundred to give Peters a chance of leaving the building before I call Lord Noel. I don't want them to run into each other. Ninety-eight...ninety-nine..."

Crossing to the window, Joan lowered the blind.

"I've been dead wrong all my life," said Agatha, picking up the dumpy umbrella. "I always thought one of these made a dependable weapon in any emergency. Mother used to say there was nothing like a good long hatpin, but I was of the umbrella school."

Laying it on the table, she took a packet of cigarettes from her pocket and offered one to Joan.

"Thanks."

They smoked in gloomy silence until a knock door heralded the arrival of Lord Noel.

"What's happened?" he asked, looking from one long face to the other.

"You may well ask," said Agatha. "A fine sentry you turned out to be."

Joan told him the whole story. He bit his lip.

"I was concentrating on watching the window. From the position I'd taken up I couldn't see the entrance to the flats."

"If we'd both been murdered," said Agatha cuttingly, lighting a fresh cigarette on the stump of the first, "I expect you'd have gone on watching the window for days. That would have been trying for you."

"Go as far as you like," mumbled Lord Noel. "I deserve it. Joan, I'm terribly sorry."

"That's all right. Don't mind Trimmy. She's only upset about having lost her last illusion: that a woman with an umbrella is a match for any man. You carried out your part of the plan. You've nothing to feel humble about."

"To be quite truthful, I was in two minds whether to come up without waiting for the signal. You see, I thought I saw Flinders ducking into the alley that runs down the side of the building—"

"Then it must have been Flinders who stole the record!" exclaimed Joan.

"—I was about to follow him when I saw that comic Scot who's suddenly started hanging about the office—MacNab, I believe his name is."

"Then the comic Scot may be the thief," remarked Agatha.

"Or my father," said Joan in a subdued voice.

"Let's hope it was your father," responded Agatha.

"It may have been anyone," said Lord Noel hopelessly.

"Anyone but us—and Peters," agreed Agatha.

"At least that's something to be thankful for," said Joan. "Peters hasn't got it."

With a moody frown Lord Noel took a gold case from his pocket and extracted a cigarette.

"Sorry," he said. "I'm forgetting my manners."

He offered the case to Joan, who shook her head. He offered it to Agatha. She had not finished the cigarette she was smoking, but she took one for later.

"Well," said Lord Noel, snapping the case. "What do we do now?"

"That's easy," said Agatha. "You go home and Joan and I have a hot drink and go to bed."

"Mayn't I stay for just five minutes?"

"Not for one minute."

"Please, Trimmy," said Joan.

"You're pests, both of you. I'm tired and I want to go to bed. You can stop and have a cup of cocoa, young man. That is, if you like cocoa."

"I'm crazy about cocoa," said Lord Noel.

"It's a perverted taste for a man. I'd be careful of him, Joan. He can't be normal."

Agatha went to make the cocoa, leaving them alone.

"Darling," said Lord Noel, as soon as her back was turned.

Agatha put her head round the door and said: "You might at least wait until I'm properly out of the room."

But neither of them heard her.

They were drinking cocoa in front of the fire when the bell rang again. Agatha said something which the others hoped they hadn't heard correctly and went to answer it.

Alastair MacNab was standing in the corridor. "Guidevening," he said pleasantly.

"What's good about it? And who are you?"

"The name, dear-r-r ledy"—raising his hat with a gallant flourish— "is MacNab. Alastair-r-r MacNab, at your ser-r-rvice. I'm a pr-r-rivate detective to trade. And you are Miss Tr-rimm, I pr-resume?"

"If I'm not, a shocking mistake must have made in the dim and distant past. What do you want?"

"That's an awfu' guid smell," he murmured, sniffing the air.

"It's a pity you didn't bring your bloodhounds. They might have enjoyed it."

"I've nae bluidhounds," said the Scot seriously. "I've a wee Aberdeen terr-rier, but he aye bides at hame."

"Well, that's something to be thankful for. I've always said dogs are more intelligent than men."

"Dae ye mind if I come in?" asked Alastair MacNab, walking in.

"Oh, dear me, no," replied Agatha, shutting the door and following him into the sitting room. "We're used to people popping in and out just as they please. I wonder you trouble to ask. Most of them don't."

"Guid evening, m'lord. Guid evening, Miss Marplay," said Alastair MacNab with a cheerful beam. Dead silence. They all stared at him.

Apparently oblivious to the impression created by his use of Joan's name, the Scot placed his dusty bowler hat and shapeless umbrella on the table and unbuttoned his soiled raincoat. The gold chain across his ample middle looked as though it should have an anchor attached to one end of it. He produced a well-coloured meerschaum and blew into it.

"I see ye're smoking, so maybe ye'll no' mind if I light my pipe. There's naethin' like a pipe tae create a comfortable atmospher-re."

"Did you say Miss Marplay?" asked Agatha, in a hushed voice.

"That's the young leddy's name, is it no'?"

"How did you know?" demanded Lord Noel.

"It's my business tae ken such things. That cocoa smells awful guid."

"Perhaps you'd like a cup," said Agatha, in a poisonous tone.

"Ye're sure it widna pit ye tae ower much trouble?"

"Dear me, no. Didn't you know—we're running a restaurant. Anything you don't see, ask for. You're sure you'd really like cocoa? There's nothing else you would prefer?"

"Now that's verra kind of ye. To tell ye the truth, I'm no' just that fond of cocoa. I'll hae a wee drap of what I see in this bottle, since ye ask me."

Walking across the room he picked up the bottle of whiskey Joan had brought in for the benefit of Ambrose Craven. Lifting the glass that lay beside it, he sniffed it and put it back again.

"I'd better hae a clean tumbler. That'll be the yin Mr. Cr-ra-ven was drinking oot of."

"You seem to know everything," said Joan grimly.

Alastair MacNab looked at her with a kindly twinkle in his eyes. "I wish I did, my bonny wee lassie, I wish I did."

It was all too much for Joan. She fetched a clean glass and handed it to him.

"Soda? Or do you prefer water?"

"I'll no' tr-rouble ye for either, my dear," he replied, pouring himself a generous measure. "There's twa things I like naked and whiskey's yin o' them." When no one laughed, he added apologetically; "That's a wee bit joke, ye ken."

With the glass in one hand, his pipe in the other, he walked across the room and drew a vacant chair nearer to the fire.

"This is whit I like. A warm fire, a drop o' something worth drinking, pleasant company like yersels. Ye'll no' mind if I light ma pipe?"

"We never mind anything," said Agatha in a strangled voice. "Not anything."

"Look here," put in Lord Noel. "How did you know that this young lady's name is Miss Marplay?"

"When I became inter-rested in Lucius Mar-rplay," replied the Scot cheerfully, "I found oot he had a daughter-r aged aboot twenty. I went tae some tr-rouble tae tr-race her wher-r-reabouts during the past twenty years and discover-red that she had been living in a countr-ry village, and that on the day of her father's escape fr-rom the mental hame she came tae London with her companion, a Miss Tr-r-rim. At the *Echo* office this mor-rning I found oot that a young and pr-retty Miss Tr-rimm had started working there aboot the same time. I pit twa and twa together. They aye mak' fower, if ye've a guid heid for figures."

He turned gravely to Joan. "There's jist yin question I'd like ye tae answer, my bonny lassie."

Lord Noel stood up. "Miss Marplay isn't answering questions. You've had your little joke and scrounged a drink and now you'd better go before I lose my temper."

Alastair MacNab paid no attention to the indignant young man. He was staring at Joan with the solemn eyes of a Scots collie. His gaze was kindly, almost fatherly.

"I'll answer your question," said Joan. "What is it?"

"Do you know where your father is?"

None of them noticed that he had dropped his atrocious accent.

"I haven't seen him since I was a baby. I've no idea where he is. If I had, I'd go to him."

"I believe you," he said quietly.

He drank the rest of his whiskey. Setting down the glass, he stood up and retrieved his hat and umbrella.

"I'd like a wor-rd or two with you, dear-r lady," he said to Agatha, his burr as strong as before. "But not tonight. We auld folk will hae a quiet chat by oorsels at a later date. Wid tomorrow evening suit ye? We could meet at a corner hoose. It wid gie me a chance tae return your warrum hospitality. We'll no need a chaperon, I'm thinking. We're baith auld enough and ugly enough to be trustit."

"Mr. MacNab," Agatha hissed through her clenched teeth, "I've stood for a lot, but if you think—"

"If it's ma wife ye're worrying aboot, dinna fash yersel. I'm a puir lone bachelor. The Strand Cor-rner Hoose, then. Tomorrow evening at eight."

The door closed behind him.

'Well!" said Joan.

"What a blighter," said Lord Noel.

For once Agatha could find no words.

A Hand Beckoned...

In the still of the night Joan awoke with a start. Some odd, unfamiliar sound had roused her but she could not think what it was. At her ear, magnified by the silence, she heard the tick… tick…tick…of the bedside clock. Rolling over, she squinted drowsily at the illuminated dial. Almost three. From the core of the building came the droning whine of the lift taking a late home-comer to an upper flat; from a flat nearby, the gurgle of bath water running away. Overhead, someone dropped a shoe on the floor, following it, after a lengthy interval, with another. Familiar noises, all these, for Malbrouk Court went late to bed. Night sounds floated up from the street, accustomed sounds that could not have penetrated her slumbers. That which had wakened her was none of these: in her mind lingered a vague impression of a summons. Thinking that Agatha might have called out, Joan turned her head and looked at the bed on the other side of the room. Agatha was fast asleep. Snoring. The bedclothes rose and fell in time to the rhythm of her snores. It came again: an insistent tapping. Not loud, but clearly defined, like fingernails on glass. A few sharp taps. A silence. More tapping. Another silence.

Lifting her head from the pillow, Joan looked at the window. She saw a pale blur—a face—pressed close to the outer side of the pane. A hand beckoned to her. Slipping out of bed, she stole to the window. Agatha had shut and securely fastened it before they went to bed. "I may be a jittery old woman," Agatha had said, "but I'm taking no chances." Joan put out a hand with the intention of rousing Agatha, but on the point of touching the older woman's arm, she hesitated and drew back.

She was unable to see the face at the window clearly, but it appeared to be round and elderly and the hair that topped it was white. Her heart missed a beat. After all these years was her father separated from her by only a thin sheet of glass? In doubt, Joan looked at Agatha again and the face made frantic negative motions. Joan did not know what to do. If her father was outside, it would not be Agatha he would want to see but his own daughter. He would be unwilling to trust another woman, a stranger to him. But—was it her father? She switched on the bedside lamp. The face vanished. Going to the window, Joan peered through the glass, but there was nothing to see. Although feeling that the action was foolish, she pushed back the catch and opened the window. Leaning out, she saw a short, plump figure standing on the fire escape a dozen feet below.

A low, urgent whisper floated up to her, so plaintively gentle that her heart melted.

"Joan, my dear…come to me…I need you…I want you…"

A lost soul pleading with her for salvation. An Ishmael yearning after the love of his own kind.

"Joan…I need you…"

A small voice in her brain warned her to be wary but she would not have heeded a hundred such voices. All she knew, all that mattered, was that her father had come to her, that he wanted her, needed her. Putting on slippers and a wrap, she climbed out on to the fire escape and started to go down.

As she approached the figure receded. For a moment she wondered whether it was merely a figment of her own imagination, but when she faltered and stood uncertainly motionless in the darkness she saw it halting and beckoning to her again. Another whisper came to her, too pitiful to be ignored.

Down three flights she crept, the beckoning figure always a few yards in front of her. They reached the ground and stood looking at each other in the lane that ran along the side of the building. Two hands were held out to her in a supplicatory gesture. Joan ran toward them.

They fastened on her neck.

It happened so suddenly that she had no time to cry out.

Fingers like steel gripped her throat relentlessly, squeezing, squeezing, squeezing; a giant top spun dizzily in her brain; she dropped, numb and senseless, to her knees.

*

Afterwards it was very cold and she was lying on the ground, gasping for air. Every breath tore savagely at her lungs. Tears were streaming down her face. Her heart and brain were empty. Someone was patting her shoulder and saying:

"It's all right, Joan. It's all right."

Agatha…

Agatha was bending over her, in a long flannel nightdress. There were tears in her eyes too. Above her the sky, spangled with stars.

"Then I didn't dream it," Joan croaked painfully. It hurt to talk.

"Ssh, darling. Don't even think of it. Try to rise. Lean on me, I'll hold you up."

"Where is…he?"

"He's gone. When I awoke and found the window open, the light on, and you missing I ran down the fire escape without stopping even to put on my slippers. When I realized what was happening to you, I went berserk. It was more than he could face. He ran.

"You fool," she added, with a sob. "You damned little fool. You almost scared me out of my wits."

The lowest section of the fire escape had swung clear of the ground and the bottom rung was out of reach. Agatha held Joan up—the girl was almost a deadweight—and they staggered together to the employees' entrance, which was on that side of the building. There was a night watchman on duty at the door, but he was fast asleep. Shivering with cold, they crept past him and slowly climbed the long flights of stairs.

When they were inside their own flat Joan said in a stricken tone: "It was my father. It was my father. He wanted to kill me. Oh, Agatha, he wanted to kill me."

Agatha held her tightly.

"Hush, darling. He's mad. He didn't know what he was doing."

At Scotland Yard

At eleven o'clock that morning Miss Trimm had a foul cold and a worse temper. A few hours after their nocturnal adventure she and Joan had been roused out of bed again by two C.I.D. detectives who brought word that their presence at Scotland Yard was urgently required and who refused to take 'No' for an answer. The reason for this summons was that Mark Peters had taken the trouble to inform the police of Joan's identity and the deputy commissioner had a number of questions to put to Lucius Marplay's daughter. He did not seem at all disposed to accept the answers. From half-past nine—when Joan and Miss Trimm reached Scotland Yard—until eleven, the talk had been going round and round and, as far as Agatha could see, it was coming out nowhere. In exasperation she boiled over:

"I keep telling you, Miss Marplay hasn't seen her father since she was a baby. Not since she was a baby, do you understand? Perhaps plain English isn't good enough for you. Perhaps you'd like me to repeat it in French or Hindustani."

To emphasize her words, she pounded with her clenched fist on a desk. It was the deputy commissioner's desk and that important official was glowering at the indignant spinster across it, hunched up in his chair, his elbows on the armrests, his hands pressed together under his chin. Bushy brows drawn down over sunken grey eyes; his pale, clean-shaven face had a formidable expression. Agatha Trimm was not impressed.

"It's no good looking at me like a dyspeptic bloodhound," she snapped. "You don't frighten me in the least."

In the background, Superintendent Wrenn watched his chief with bated breath, waiting for an explosion. Joan was more at ease. She knew Agatha of old. In any argument, against any adversary, she was prepared to back Agatha to come out on top. The explosion did not come. Instead, with a long-drawn sigh, the deputy commissioner said patiently:

"My dear Miss Trimm, I quite appreciate your point of view, but I must remind you that we are investigating two murders and that Miss Marplay's father is suspected of having committed them. I would point out that it is quite impossible for Lucius Marplay to have done all the things he is known to have done without the aid of an accomplice with free access to the *Echo* building."

"About a thousand people are employed by the *Echo*. Why pick on Joan?"

"Surely that's obvious. She is Lucius Marplay's daughter. Immediately after his escape from the mental home she took great pains to obtain a job in the *Echo* building. On her own admission she hadn't been brought up to earn her living. Why should she want a humble job as a typist, except as a means of assisting her father?"

"She's already explained all that. What she told you is the truth—only you're determined not to see it."

"You must admit that her story doesn't sound rational."

Agatha leaned forward and transfixed him with a needle-sharp eye. "Sir George, have you a daughter?"

Taken aback, the deputy commissioner stammered: "I have."

"How old is she?"

"Nineteen next birthday."

"And do her actions always seem rational to you?"

"Well..." The deputy commissioner smiled ruefully. "Perhaps not always."

"Very well, then."

"I see your point," he admitted.

Agatha picked up her gloves, handbag and umbrella.

"Miss Marplay and I are rather tired," she said flatly. "Unless you have other questions of importance to put"—she placed great emphasis on the word "importance"—"we won't intrude on you further."

"We'll let you know if we wish to see Miss Marplay again," said the deputy commissioner. "And perhaps you'll be good enough to let her come alone."

"If you wish to interview Miss Marplay alone," retorted Agatha, "it will be necessary for you first to obtain a warrant for her arrest. I don't think you're likely to do that. Good day, gentlemen!"

On their way downstairs Joan said to Agatha: "I'm glad you didn't tell them about what happened early this morning." She faltered and added: "About Father. I don't want anyone to know about that ever."

Agatha did not speak. She pressed Joan's hand. That was sufficient.

Coming out of the building they were met by Lord Noel. They were surprised to see him, for at this hour he was usually busy at the office.

"I've got the sack," he explained. "Peters must have seen me last night, although I didn't see him. An hour ago, he sent for me and told me that my services were no longer required."

"Oh, Noel," gasped Joan, "I'm sorry."

"Don't be," he smiled. "I'm not. Scribbling society gossip is no job for a manly young fellow like me. In any case, we're both in the same boat. Peters asked me to tell you that you needn't come to the office again. He's sending you a week's salary in lieu of notice."

Meanwhile, in the deputy commissioner's office a third person was on the point of joining the ranks of the unemployed. Superintendent Wrenn was offering his resignation to his superior, but Sir George refused to accept it.

"I know how you feel, Wrenn. Your failure to find Marplay; that poor devil being murdered yesterday almost under your nose; the editorials condemning police inefficiency that are in all the papers this morning... What with one thing and another you must be feeling pretty low; but I'm convinced that no other officer could have done any better than you did. So, carry on, Wrenn."

"Thank you, sir."

"Not at all. But for God's sake, Wrenn, find Lucius Marplay. The home secretary has been on to me. He, in turn, has had an awkward time with the P.M. Cables from Washington informed him that the American papers are playing up this business hot and strong—and you know how fidgety criticism in the American rags always makes the Prime Minister."

A telephone bell rang. Superintendent Wrenn answered it. He talked into the mouthpiece for moments then hung up and turned a grim face to his superior.

"Another death notice, Sir George. This time it's Ambrose Craven's."

Rendezvous with Death

Three cars in close formation swung past the main entrance gates of the aerodrome: a Rolls-Royce limousine and two Flying Squad Bentleys. Front and rear cars were packed with plainclothes detectives armed with Webley-Scott .33 automatic pistols. The blinds of the Rolls-Royce were drawn and Ambrose Craven was hunched up in the rear seat between Mark Peters and Superintendent Wrenn. Craven's grey lips were moving but he did not say anything. In his mind's eye he was seeing a few lines of type on a sheet of proof paper:

Craven—On the 20th of June, at his office in Fleet Street, Ambrose Craven, aged fifty-one, of poisoning.

This was the twentieth of June—but Craven was going to fool Lucius Marplay. He was not going to be at the *Echo* office for the rendezvous with death. An airplane had been chartered to fly him to Budapest; it was waiting at the aerodrome, ready to start. In a few minutes it would carry Ambrose Craven up to the skies, nearer to his Maker, but reassuringly far from the man who had designs on his life. A very safe plane—Craven had insisted on that—with two powerful engines and two trustworthy pilots. No other passengers. In the air and later, in Budapest, Ambrose Craven would be safe.

And yet...

A hundred 'and yets,' a hundred horrible possibilities, passed in procession through his fear-jangled brain. Even now he did not feel safe. He knew that even in the air, even in Budapest, he would not feel safe. Not until Marplay was caught, not until Marplay was hung by the neck until he was dead, not until

Marplay was buried six feet deep with a slab of marble on top would Ambrose Craven breathe freely again.

And even then, there would be times…in the dead of night… in his room alone…whenever there was a silence…wherever there was darkness…times when icy fingers would wrap themselves round the heart of Ambrose Craven and he could cower with fear and know in every tingling nerve that Marplay had come for him, even though Marplay was decaying bone in a damp grave.

As long as he lived, he told himself, he must never be in the dark. Never, never, never be alone. And yet, whom could he trust? He could trust no one, no one at all. Tears sprang in his eyes, the self-pitying of a coward who has died a hundred deaths and knows he has a hundred more to die.

Passing the square white booking hall and administration building, the cars took a road curving in a wide semicircle to the rear of the aerodrome. On one side tall poplars stood in line like a guard of honour; the other was bounded by a high wall surrounding the landing field. At the back gates a man in uniform was standing in the roadway. He signalled and the cars went through without slowing down.

In the centre of the field the airplane waited, the blades of its propellers spinning in the sunshine, a transparent, shining wheel. No one within fifty yards of it, except the pilots who were to take it up. The cars drove onto the field and halted. From the Bentleys sprang ten detectives who clustered in a body round the rear door of the Rolls-Royce. Superintendent Wrenn alighted, glanced swiftly to right and left, then helped out Ambrose Craven, who stood uncertainly on the running board before diving into the middle of his police escort like the first bather of the season taking a reluctant plunge from a springboard. Peters followed, and they moved in a huddle to the airplane.

One thorough search of it had already been conducted, but

Craven insisted on another, so two of the detectives and one of the pilots climbed in and went through the motions to satisfy him. The other pilot, finding some difficulty in keeping his face straight, helped Craven into the straps of a parachute and assured him that the plane was the safest that human ingenuity could devise.

At the last moment Craven demanded his cigarette case. It was in a waistcoat pocket and before it could be reached the parachute harness had to be unfastened and his overcoat and jacket unbuttoned. The pilot did these things and more: he put a cigarette between Craven's lips and struck a match. Nothing for Craven to do except inhale. But he did not inhale. His mouth fell open and the cigarette dropped to the ground. His mouth remained open, like that of a dead fish. His eyes were starting out of his head. He was staring at a slip of paper in the pilot's hand.

"W-where did you g-get th-that?"

"It was in your cigarette case, sir."

"It—it wasn't th-there before."

Superintendent Wrenn snatched the paper and read aloud what was written on it:

DEAR CRAVEN,

We have an appointment at one p.m. in mid-air. I shan't be late.

LUCIUS MARPLAY.

"Damn!" said the pilot. The match had burnt his fingers.

With a moan, Ambrose Craven fainted.

A few minutes later, after careful examination of the paper, Sergeant Leet announced: "The writing is that of Lucius Marplay and Marplay's fingerprints are all over it."

"You're positive of that?"

"Absolutely, sir."

"What do we do now?" said Wrenn hopelessly.

"Load him into the plane and send him off to Budapest," replied Mark Peters, rolling his cigar to a corner of his mouth with a twist of his lips. "This is sheer bluff. Marplay can't possibly reach him in an airplane."

"Perhaps not, but if he came to in mid-air he'd die of fright." Wrenn turned to one of the pilots. "I suppose it isn't likely that someone has tampered with the engines?"

"Not only unlikely but impossible, Superintendent."

"Nevertheless," said Wrenn, "I'm afraid the trip to Budapest is off. But I'm damned if I know what else to do with him."

"Lock him in a cell at the nearest police station," suggested Peters. "If Marplay reaches him there we'll know there are supernatural influences at work."

"No, a cell would scare the life out of him too. Mr. Craven is a delicate plant. We'll be lucky if he doesn't die on our hands through sheer fright, if nothing else. Well, put him back in the car for a start. We'll make up our minds as we go along."

In the car, Craven came to. At first, he could only sit and gape in terror from Wrenn to Peters and from Peters to Wrenn. Afterwards he demanded to be taken home, but almost in the same breath he changed his mind. If Marplay could reach him in mid-air, Marplay could reach him at home.

"You might try a submarine," said Mark Peters caustically.

Craven sobbed noisily. The cars turned into Hyde Park and went round and round while the question of where to take the doomed man was thrashed out. Wrenn suggested Scotland Yard, but Craven very quickly said: "No," although he could give no definite reason for being afraid to go there.

"We really ought to take you to a barber," remarked Peters. "You've a two-day growth of stubble and I'll swear you haven't washed lately. If you've got to die, at least die clean."

"You swine, Mark," wept Craven.

"Well, make up your mind. It'll soon be lunch and I'm hungry."

"I can't eat," whimpered Craven. "The death notice said: 'by poisoning.' I mustn't risk eating anything."

"Look here," said Superintendent Wrenn suddenly, "the best thing is to go to your office. Even if you hide somewhere today there'll still be tomorrow all the other days until Marplay is caught. You can't go on living in fear indefinitely. Come to your office. I'll surround you with men. There'll be twenty pairs of eyes watching you every moment. If Marplay should come he won't be able to reach you. How could he, in a room packed with guards? If he comes, he'll be caught—and that will be the end of him."

"You must be mad!" cried Ambrose Craven. "Ellis was murdered at the office. So was Partridge."

"The superintendent's right, Ambrose," said Peters. "After all, no one was there to see what happened to Partridge. He wouldn't have anyone in the room with him. In your case it'll be different. To reach you Marplay will not only have to walk through walls, he'll have to penetrate a barrier of flesh-and-blood as well."

"I believe he can do even that," Craven mumbled brokenly.

"If he can, there's no hope for you—or for me, either. We're both doomed wherever we go. Oh, for God's sake, man, take a grip of yourself. If there's a way to stop Marplay, it's the way the superintendent has suggested. Surround yourself with armed men, shoulder to shoulder. Stand in the middle of them. What can happen to you then? Do you think he's going to drop from the ceiling?"

Ambrose Craven did not know what to think. All he was capable of knowing was a gnawing dread beyond the realms of reason. The discussion might have gone on indefinitely had it not occurred to him that a car was not a very safe place in which to be when danger threatened. In a car, anything might happen. If he had to get out of it suddenly, he would find himself in the naked daylight. That was a particularly unpleasant thought.

They went to the *Echo* building. Before Craven was willing to go upstairs it was necessary to clear everyone out of the top story and post guards at the landings of the front and back stairs and at each lift gate.

There was an element of absurdity in the elaborate precautions taken to keep Craven from harm, but few of his protectors were aware of it. They were too determined not to be caught napping this time to see the slightest degree of humour in the situation. Policemen lined the corridors, policemen filled the anteroom to Craven's private office, policemen stood shoulder to shoulder round the walls of the office itself.

In the middle of the room, with fifty eyes on them, sat Craven, Superintendent Wrenn, Mark Peters and the divisional surgeon, who had his little black bag ready to hand. Time ticked away. One o'clock…two…three… There was still no sign of Marplay. Waiting, waiting, waiting… They were all on edge, none more so than Ambrose Craven. It would not have been so bad if there had been anything that he could do to distract his mind; but there was nothing he could do. Nothing was safe. His flesh quivered at the horrors his brain conjured up.

Even Mark Peters was feeling the strain. He rose, went into Craven's private washroom, and laved his hands and face in cold water. Returning, he sat down again and lit a cigar. It was fascinating to watch his long, clean fingers nipping the end, manipulating the match.

Always a dandy, Craven began to feel like a leper. All those eyes on him; and he with filthy hands, dishevelled clothing.

If he looked in the mirror, he would see a haggard, grubby, unshaven face: the face, in fact, that his guards were seeing. His vanity rebelled at the thought. Looking round at his guards, he was almost reassured that there could be no danger. After all, how could Marplay possibly reach him? Before he started imagining fantastic ways whereby Marplay could reach him, he rose quickly and said:

"I think I'll freshen up."

The washroom, his wardrobe, his toilet cupboard, had all been examined already. To make quite sure, they were carefully overhauled again, and nothing was found that was in the least degree suspicious. Under the watchful eyes of his protectors, Craven shaved and washed and powdered, brushed his hair, took in a notch in his abdominal belt, donned fresh linen and a pressed suit. It took a long time. He kept stopping to make sure that he was still alive.

When his toilet was almost complete, he suddenly uttered an agonized gasp and fell flat on his face. Something dropped from his hand and rolled across the floor. Mark Peters picked it up and placed it on the desk.

At first the others thought Craven had fainted again. They all stood staring at his prostrate form, with the exception of the divisional surgeon, who went down on his knees beside it. A brief examination told him that Ambrose Craven was dead. There was a stupefied look on his face when he announced the fact.

"Heart failure?" suggested Wrenn.

But even as he spoke, he was sure that it was not heart failure.

"Poison. Hydrocyanic acid, I think. He has the symptoms— and there's a definite smell of almonds." The divisional surgeon spoke like a man in a dream.

"But how?" Wrenn almost screamed. "How? How? How?"

That was the question. Craven had neither eaten nor

drunk. He had not even smoked. How had the poison been administered?

"He was using a scent spray when he fell," said Mark Peters. "It dropped from his hand. I picked it up and put it on the desk."

"That's the answer," replied the divisional surgeon. "No other is possible. Hydrocyanic acid gas in the scent spray."

The scent spray and every other toilet article which Craven had used were rushed to the laboratories at Scotland Yard to be analysed. The scent spray contained an expensive brand of perfume; that was all. The other articles were equally harmless.

When a minute examination of the corpse was made a receipt form was found in one of the pockets—"PAID IN FULL—Lucius Marplay."

Lull Between Storms

This time the *Dispatch* did not scoop the *Echo*. Both papers reached the street simultaneously with identical accounts of the murder. Someone had copied the *Echo* story as it was written—or stolen a proof—and managed somehow to smuggle it out of the building, although main door and side door were watched and no one was allowed to leave the building without a pass; although trusted employees at the switchboard were listening to every outgoing telephone call. Mark Peters made no efforts to find out who had achieved the seemingly impossible. The problem was too much for him. He gave it up. He turned it over to Superintendent Wrenn. Surely, he said, the person responsible for this minor mystery must know a great deal about the major mysteries.

Wrenn telephoned his superiors at Scotland Yard. The deputy commissioner telephoned the home secretary. The home secretary tried to get the editor of the *Evening Dispatch* on the wire. But the editor of the *Dispatch* was away on leave of absence for an indefinite period; and so was the news editor; and so was the managing editor. And their deputies were very sorry, but they did not know where to reach them. And they were sorrier still, but no one else in the *Dispatch* office knew who was supplying the newspaper with the accounts of the *Echo* murders.

*

That evening Miss Trimm went out at a quarter to eight without telling Joan where she was going. She was clad in her best and carried a handbag which she used only for state occasions. When she was leaving the flat Joan said softly: "Give my regards to Mr. MacNab."

Agatha did not reply. The force with which she slammed the door was more expressive than words. On her return—shortly after eleven—she was wearing what Joan called her 'graven-image face.' Severe, blank, it told nothing. Removing her outdoor things, putting on her fleece-lined house slippers, lighting a cigarette, she kept her lips tight, her eyes expressionless.

"You aren't fooling anyone," said Joan gleefully. "I know where you've been."

"How many times must I tell you," said Agatha, pursing her lips, "that slang expressions do not become a young lady."

"Oh yeah?" mocked Joan. "Come off it, Trimmy. Don't try to change the subject, you fast cat. That stony countenance doesn't fool me—you've been out on the tiles."

"Oh Lord, give me patience," said Agatha, rolling her eyes. "My good girl, supposing I have been out with Mr. MacNab—"

"Let's not suppose," retorted Joan. "Let's admit it, quite, quite frankly."

"Very well. I have been out with Mr. MacNab. We conversed for a while over a cup of tea. Surely such conduct offers no grounds for coarse innuendo. I simply felt it expedient to meet the man and find out what he had to say to me."

"Your appointment at the Strand Corner House was for eight. It's now ten past eleven. You didn't spin out one cup of tea for three hours."

"We went to the pictures. Mr. MacNab holds the view that one can talk more freely in the dark anonymity of the pictures."

"Did he hold your hand in the sentimental bits?"

"It was a news theatre. Mickey Mouses and travelogues."

"There's romance in travel," said Joan.

Agatha gave her a look.

At twilight on the following afternoon Joan and Miss Trimm were at tea in their flat when the telephone bell rang. Joan answered it and heard the apologetic voice of the hall porter.

"A man down here, miss, wants to speak to you. Not being by any means sure that you'd want to see him, I've taken the liberty of refusing to let him come up. He's dirty and ragged and impertinent and he won't give his name."

"Tall and thin?" asked Joan, thinking of Flinders.

"No, miss. Short and on the stout side."

"Ask him what he wants with me."

"He says he's got an important letter for you, miss. If you ask me, it's a try-on."

"I'll be down directly," said Joan, hanging up.

When she came out of the lift she found the porter, lofty in uniform and medals, standing guard over a grubby little man.

"I am Miss Marplay. You have a letter for me?"

The grubby little man took off a bowler hat green with age and showed her a soiled envelope in the lining. Joan held out her hand for it but he shook his head.

"A certain little matter comes first. The bloke wot gimme the letter said you'd cough up 'alf a quid on delivery."

"Who gave you the letter?"

"'E might be a little fat cove wiv white whiskers," answered the grubby little man, "and then again, 'e might not. 'E might be a young bloke wiv a red nose an' white spats, but I don't think so."

"In other words, you've no intention of telling me?"

"You've guessed it, lady."

"And if I refuse to pay the ten shillings?"

The grubby little man put his hat on his head with the letter in it. "No 'alf quid no letter."

"Shall I take it from him, miss?" suggested the porter, flexing his muscles.

"Try it, cock," said the grubby little man cheerfully, "and I'll give you a kick that'll cripple you for life."

"I'll give you the ten shillings," said Joan hastily. "You'll have to wait while I go upstairs for it."

"Witing don't bother me. As long as this big bleeder keeps 'is 'ands off me, I'll wite wiv pleasure."

The hall porter fumbled in his hip pocket and produced a worn leather wallet.

"I'll gladly lend you the ten shillings, miss, but if you'll excuse the liberty, I should think twice before parting with it. If you ask me—"

"Nobody's asking you, cock," said the grubby little man.

A ten-shilling note passed from the porter to Joan and from Joan to the grubby little man, who pocketed it quickly, handed over the letter, and lost no time in taking his departure.

"I hope you haven't made a mistake," said the porter, more hurt than angry.

Joan tore open the envelope and glanced at the sheet of paper which it contained.

"No," she said quietly, "I haven't made a mistake."

Although Agatha looked enquiringly at her when she returned to the flat, Joan said nothing. Shortly afterwards Agatha left to keep an appointment. She did not say whom she was meeting; but Joan could guess. Half an hour later Lord Noel dropped in for a cup of tea and Joan silently handed him the sheet of paper. On it was pencilled in crude block letters the following notice:

FOR SALE BY AUCTION
ONE USED DICTAPHONE RECORD
ONLY CASH BIDS CONSIDERED
THE BEARER OF THIS MESSAGE WILL RETURN
AT TEN O'CLOCK TONIGHT AND GIVE THE
ADDRESS WHERE THE AUCTION IS TO BE HELD.

"Flinders," said Lord Noel, when he had read it. "One can't help admiring his consummate nerve."

"For sale by auction," repeated Joan. "That means, I suppose, that he's inviting others."

"It wouldn't be an auction if there were only to be one bidder. I wonder who the others are. Peters, for one."

"My father, perhaps, for another," said Joan, in the hushed voice she always used in mentioning Lucius Marplay.

"It isn't likely that Flinders knows where to find your father—although your father may know where to find Flinders. For cool cheek, this beats everything. Flinders must be crazy. He's simply asking for trouble. Have you shown the notice to Miss Trimm?"

"No. I didn't want her to start fretting. You know how worried she always is when she imagines that I'm running risks."

"Almost as worried as I am myself. But this time there won't be anything to worry about. You won't attend this auction."

"I must. I want the record."

"Let me see to it."

"I've got to go myself, Noel."

"Idiot," said Lord Noel. "Very well, I'll go with you."

"There's only one thing: I haven't much money."

"I could raise some, but it wouldn't be enough. Peters could outbid us even if we sold or pawned everything we own."

"Then Peters will get the record," said Joan hopelessly.

"Not necessarily. I won't bid in terms of cash."

"What do you mean?"

"I intend to offer Flinders a valuable skin for the record; his own. If he doesn't want the hiding of his life, he'll hand it over."

At ten o'clock that night they were waiting impatiently for the messenger to return. Joan had instructed the night porter to send him up as soon as he appeared. At a quarter past ten, at twenty past, at twenty-five past, they were still waiting. It was almost half-past ten when the grubby little man arrived. He was so drunk that he could hardly stand; but not so drunk that he forgot to demand another ten shillings before handing over a second grimy envelope. Lord Noel kept a firm grip of the messenger's sleeve while Joan tore open the envelope. On a grimy scrap of paper was written:

14 HAGGARD STREET
KNOCK TWICE

"Why didn't you bring this half an hour ago?" asked Joan.

"I was busy," replied the grubby little man with a loud hiccup. He buckled at the knees and would have fallen if Lord Noel had not held him up.

"Busy getting drunk," said Lord Noel angrily.

"I 'aven't any other business, wot I knows of."

"Do you know the contents of this note?"

"I don't know 'em and I won't want to know 'em. I think it's funny business, meself."

"When did Flinders give it to you?"

The grubby little man looked owlish. "I don't remember menshuning that name."

"When did he give it to you?" repeated Lord Noel, shaking him roughly.

"This smorning. There were three of us. We each 'ad to

deliver two envelopes apiece. One in the arternoon, the other at ten sharp tonight."

"Is this what you call ten sharp?"

"I was never one to be fussy about time…used to say, w'en I 'ad a wife—"

"Never mind that. I only hope the others were as unpunctual as you."

"Bill wouldn't be. Bill would be early, if a 'E'd spent 'is 'alf quid by eight o'clock and us others wouldn't lend 'im a bean. You're ruddy lucky I'm as early as I am. If I'd 'ad the price of anover pint I'd 'ave been anover ten minutes."

"To whom was this Bill supposed to deliver his two envelopes?"

"Your guess is as good as mine, guv'nor."

"We'd better go," said Joan quietly.

They all went down in the lift, the grubby little man chatting amiably. Lord Noel held his captive until they were outside the block of flats, then he relaxed his grip and the grubby little man collapsed on the pavement. By the time he staggered up, waving his clenched fists and offering to fight, Joan and Lord Noel were in a taxi which was disappearing round a corner.

They alighted from the taxi at one end of Haggard Street. A dismal blind alley in the neighbourhood of Victoria, it consisted of two rows of flat-fronted, three-storied houses of crumbling brick, dilapidated and gloomy. A for-sale board hung at one of the dark, un-curtained windows of number fourteen, which had an air of having been untenanted for years. From the pavement a flight of dirty stone steps mounted with rusty iron railings to a chipped and blistered door. Knocker and doorbell were green with neglect.

Making a wry face at Joan, Lord Noel went up the steps and knocked twice. The sounds echoed through the decaying house, but there was no answer. Pushing up the flap of the letter box, he peered through. The hall was dark. Nothing stirred. He listened carefully but did not hear a sound. He tried the handle and the door swung back, creaking on rusty hinges.

Taking a small electric torch from his pocket, he ran the beam over the narrow hall and the flight of stairs that ascended from it. Bare, dusty floor boards. Stained walls. Smell of decay. Training the light on the floor, he saw the tracks of many muddy footprints leading from the door to the stairs. Turning, he found Joan standing at his elbow.

"I don't like the look of this," he said quietly. "You'd better wait outside."

"I want to stay with you," she replied.

Gripping his arm, she added shakily: "What was that?"

Listening with tensed muscles, they heard faint sounds overhead. They might have been made by a mouse scratching in the wainscot; or a man tiptoeing across an upper floor.

"Anyone there?" called Lord Noel, turning the ray of the torch upward.

His voice echoed through the place, coming back to him with a hollow, mocking intonation.

"I'm going up to reconnoitre. You'd better wait outside. I don't like this."

"Neither do I, but I'm coming with you."

"If that's the way you feel, we'll both wait outside until someone else comes along."

For a moment they stared in silence at each other and then Joan darted to the stairs and started to grope her way up with one hand on the shaky banisters and the other on the clammy wall. Muttering something uncomplimentary under his breath, Lord Noel followed her, the light of his torch cutting the darkness. As soon as he joined her, Joan stood aside to let him go first. She clutched his hand tightly. He could feel her trembling. "Stubborn little idiot," he hissed.

They went up a step at a time. At the first of the two upper landings Lord Noel shone his light round the walls and into the corners, revealing a bare passage, another flight of stairs and four doors, one of them standing open.

Walking to the open door, he shone the light inside. It fell on something that looked like a bundle of rags. He ran the light over it: there was a battered hat at one end, a pair of worn and broken boots at the other, a shapeless heap in the middle.

"Only a bundle of rags," he said, in a hoarse whisper that seemed to fill the house.

He was lying. Joan knew that he was lying. Rags do not bleed. From the crumpled heap was creeping a dark, glossy stream that looked chillingly like blood. A stream that fed a dark, glossy pool, gradually widening on the dusty floor boards.

"Stay where you are," said Lord Noel. He did not know whether he whispered it or shouted it.

Crossing the room, he shone the light on a livid face with twisted lips that were turned back, revealing decayed stumps of teeth. It was the face of Flinders; and a single glance told him that Flinders was very dead. Someone had come earlier to the auction and opened the bidding with a knife thrust. The knife was still sticking in the breast of the corpse. In its hand was an automatic pistol.

Lord Noel knelt and examined the pistol as closely as possible without touching it. There was no smell of burnt powder. It had not been fired recently. A dirty forefinger was pressing tightly on the trigger, suggesting that Flinders had died in the act of trying to shoot the person who knifed him. But the pistol had not fired—Flinders had forgotten to release the safety catch. It was like Flinders to make so clumsy and final a blunder.

Not far from the body lay a heap of black fragments, almost ground to powder; the remains of a Dictaphone record smashed beyond repair.

Neither Joan nor Lord Noel had heard footsteps behind them and they were unaware that someone was approaching until a calm voice behind them said: "Anither murder-r. When will this shocking business end?"

Whirling round, they saw Alastair MacNab standing behind them, leaning his weight on his ancient umbrella. They had no way of telling whether he had come from upstairs or downstairs.

Rising to his feet, holding the light focussed on the Scot, Lord Noel said suspiciously: "How do you know it's murder? From where you were standing you could scarcely see the body."

"I hae an insteenct for such things," replied MacNab without the slightest change of expression.

"Or did you find the body before we did? Was it you, perhaps, who killed him? We heard someone moving overhead. It may have been you."

"Ye've a verra suspeecious mind, laddie," said Alastair MacNab calmly.

"We'd better call the police," said Joan.

Lord Noel motioned to Alastair MacNab to go first and the three of them went downstairs. The Scot opened the front door.

"It's a gey sma' world," he said. "Look who's here." Mark Peters was standing on the steps, one hand raised to the knocker, the other holding a cigar stump.

"The auction's over," said Lord Noel grimly. "Someone has finished off the auctioneer with a knife."

"Flinders is dead, is he?" said Peters. He did not sound in the least surprised. "Well, it was a dangerous game he was playing."

"How do you know the corpse is Flinders?" demanded Lord Noel quickly.

"I presume you received an invitation to come here similar to the one that reached me," replied the newspaper proprietor blandly. "Didn't you suspect at the time that it came from Flinders?"

There was no answer to that.

Joan and Lord Noel in the lead, Peters and McNab close behind, they walked to the corner to look for a policeman or a telephone-box. A short distance along the next street they saw a blue-uniformed, helmeted figure. They hurried to meet him and Lord Noel hastily told what they had found in the empty house. It was a little too much for the policeman to take in all at once. His startled mind fastened on one point.

"You say that while two of you were examining the body a third came on the scene," he said slowly, his eyes travelling from face to face; "and when you opened the front door, a fourth person was standing on the threshold?"

"That's what I said," agreed Lord Noel impatiently.

"Four of you," said the policeman, counting noses. "But I can only see three. Where is the other?"

In some bewilderment, Lord Noel looked at Joan and then at Peters and then he looked where Alastair MacNab should have been—but at some point on the short walk the Scot had disappeared. None of them, not even Peters, had seen him go.

The policeman herded in a body the three who remained to the nearest telephone, which he used to report to Scotland Yard. He marshalled them back to Haggard Street, keeping a wary eye on each of them. Almost outside the house they were joined again by Alastair MacNab, who came out of the darkness twirling his umbrella, with a guileless look on his round face.

"Where have you been?" the others demanded in chorus.

"I'd rather no' answer that," said the Scot, with a meaningful nod at Joan, "in the presence o' a ledy."

When the first contingent of detectives arrived from Scotland Yard, they went up to the room in which the body lay, taking Joan, Lord Noel, Peters and MacNab with them. Not long after they entered the room the Scot stooped and picked up something.

"What's that?" asked one of the detectives instantly.

"A wee clue," replied Alastair MacNab, handing the detective a cigar band. Mark Peters uttered a short caustic laugh. He held up a fresh cigar which he had lit a moment before on the stump of the other.

"I dropped that band when we entered the room," he said.

Alastair MacNab regarded the newspaper proprietor with a crestfallen look on his solemn face.

"Maybe I'm no' sae muckle o' a detective as I thocht," he admitted ruefully.

Omar Khayyam Expressed It

An all night-session at Scotland Yard. Endless questions asked and answered, none of the answers making the mystery less deep. Wrenn interviewed Joan, Lord Noel, Mark Peters and Alastair MacNab individually; and then he interviewed them all together. Neither method elicited much. Their stories varied in detail but were identical in substance: a ragged man had brought a letter announcing the auction and later he had returned with an envelope containing the address at which it was to be held. In Joan's case the messenger was short and stout; in Peters' case, of medium height and thin; and the man who had come to MacNab was "a big, gaunt feller, wi' a red nose."

The knife in the dead man's chest was examined and on it were found the blurred but distinct fingerprints of Lucius Marplay. That did not surprise Superintendent Wrenn. He had begun to feel haunted by the ubiquitous but disembodied spirit of that plump and white-haired certified lunatic. Squads of police were despatched to make a round of the cheap lodging houses of central and outer London with the purpose of finding the ragged messengers who had delivered notes from Flinders. Lord Noel, Peters and MacNab went with them to identify the men. While they were gone, Wrenn had another talk with Joan. When it began, he felt that he was wasting his time. Long before it was over, he was sure of that. No matter how often he asked the same questions, framing them in a variety of ways, he got the same unilluminating answers.

A lioness rampant, Agatha arrived, imperatively demanding to see her cub. She was shown into a waiting room, left to cool her heels. After a time, she departed; but she soon returned with a solicitor who talked heavily about the rights of the individual until they were both admitted to the room in which Joan was being questioned. The solicitor cautioned Joan to say nothing except on his advice. Agatha went further and told her to say nothing whatever.

"There's no need to tell her," groaned Wrenn. "She's been saying nothing in a great many words for the past hour."

Meanwhile the police searchers invaded one unsavoury doss house after another. In a 'fourpenny flop' too foul to describe they found Joan's grubby little man. He had been on a glorious drunk and when wakened wanted to fight, but soon sobered up when he found himself in the clutches of the hard-eyed heavy-handed men from Scotland Yard. Meekly, he told them where to find the down-and-outs who had delivered Flinders' messages to Peters and MacNab.

Bundled into cars, the unhappy trio of vagrants were taken to Scotland Yard. In the entrance hall Lord Noel met a reporter he knew, who was waiting about in hopeful anticipation of good copy. He had a paper under his arm: an early edition of the Morning World, which was run in double harness with the *Evening Dispatch*. Before Lord Noel was ushered in by one of the detectives, the reporter handed him the paper. Lord Noel looked at it while he was being marched upstairs. Although the murder of Flinders had happened less than two hours before, and although the police had taken precautions to prevent the news leaking out, an amazingly complete account of it was spread across the front page of the morning newspaper published by the *Dispatch*.

Threats, abuse, arguments, even a measure of coaxing, failed to extract much from the three human derelicts who had been brought in. The truth was that they did not know very much. Flinders had told them he had a stunt on; knowing Flinders they had been pretty sure that it was a fishy stunt; knowing Flinders, they knew better than to pry into the nature of it; he had given each of them two envelopes to deliver and assured them that ten shillings would be handed over by the recipients on delivery of each envelope; they had delivered the envelopes and speedily drunk up the money: that was all they could tell.

Since none of them had solicitors to harp on their rights they were taken downstairs and lodged in cells for further questioning. Being none of them given to brooding on the morrow, and being one and all accustomed to infinitely less homely lodgings, they curled up on the hard beds and were soon fast asleep.

The others, Joan, Lord Noel, Peters and MacNab, were permitted to go home. When they left Scotland Yard, however, they were shadowed by detectives—two apiece—who had instructions to keep track of their movements until further orders.

In the small hours of the morning Wrenn had a tense interview with two of his superiors. They went over the case, starting with the escape from the mental home, finishing with the murder of Flinders, until they were all heartily sick of it.

With a heartfelt sigh the deputy commissioner said at last:

> "About it and about and evermore,
> Came out at the same door where in I went…"

"I beg your pardon?" said Wrenn.

"Poetry," said the deputy commissioner wearily.

"Oh," said Wrenn. He thought, but did not say, that this was a nice time for poetry.

"About this MacNab," remarked the deputy commissioner. "I think he merits considerable attention."

"I intend to investigate his antecedents fully in the morning, Sir George."

"You ought to have attended to that when he first appeared on the scene."

"Well, Sir George, he was vouched for by Mr. Peters."

"Who admits he was only going on a letter from Sam Birnbaum of The New World Investigation Bureau. A shady customer, this Birnbaum, from all accounts. It didn't occur to you, I suppose, to find out from the proprietor of the mental home whether he instructed Birnbaum's agency to act in the matter?"

"There have been so many other things—"

"You'd better attend to this particular matter without delay. You may use my phone."

In a few minutes Superintendent Wrenn turned from the telephone with a long face. He had roused Dr. Hammond, the proprietor of the mental home, out of a deep sleep and had been ticked off with humbling completeness.

"Doctor Hammond says he never even heard of The New World Investigation Bureau," he reported. "And he has not instructed any agency to act for him. He sounded annoyed that we should think so."

"Get hold of MacNab immediately," said the deputy commissioner.

"Yes, Sir George. That ought to be simple. I have two men trailing him, with instructions to report by phone every hour."

But finding MacNab was not so simple as it sounded. When the detectives who were shadowing him telephoned to Scotland Yard, it was to report that they had lost him. The Scot had taken a taxi and they had followed in another but when the first taxi drew up at its destination MacNab was not in it. At some point en route at which his vehicle had turned a corner he must have jumped out quickly before the pursuing taxi came in sight. The shadowers had gone on to the Scot's lodgings, but Alastair MacNab was not there...

Summoning a Flying Squad car, Superintendent Wrenn made a hurried journey to Sam Birnbaum's house at Brixton. After prolonged pounding on the door, Birnbaum came down in his nightshirt. His eyes bulged when he saw the irate police official, but he hastily opened the door wider and welcomed him in.

"Well, Superintendent," he said effusively, "this is an unexpected pleasure."

But he did not look pleased. He led the way into the dining room and bent to poke the ashes of a crumbling fire. "Sit down," he urged. "Have a drink. Have a cigar."

"You can skip all that," snarled Wrenn. "Where's MacNab?"

"MacNab?" repeated Birnbaum, frowning as though he were hearing the name for the first time.

"Yes, MacNab," bellowed Wrenn; "the man you sent to the *Echo* with a letter to say that Doctor Hammond wanted him to help in the search for Lucius Marplay."

"Oh, MacNab," said Birnbaum brightly, as though that wasn't the name he had heard the first time. "What about MacNab?"

"He's missing. Where is he?"

"How should I know, Superintendent? You don't think I keep him in my pocket? At this hour if he's got any sense he's in bed, where I was until you dropped in. If he isn't there I wouldn't know where to find him."

"Do you mind if a couple of my men search your house?"

"Have you got a search warrant?"

"I can get one."

"I wouldn't put you to all that trouble," said Birnbaum affably. "Go on—search the place. See if I care. If you find MacNab, I'll tell you what I'll do: I'll eat him for you, bones and all."

While two plainclothes men were going through the house from basement to attic, looking under beds and into cupboards, Wrenn had a heart-to-heart talk with Sam Birnbaum. He began it by saying: "I've been talking to the proprietor of the mental home. He tells me he never heard of your agency. What do you say to that?"

"I don't say anything to it. Not until I talk to my lawyer."

"How long has MacNab been working for you?"

"Maybe two years, maybe three. I'm not sure."

"What other cases has he worked on?"

"Now, Superintendent, you don't expect me to answer that offhand at a moment's notice."

"Your files at the office will supply the answer."

"Maybe they will, maybe they won't. You know how it is in my business: sometimes you keep records, sometimes you don't. It all depends on the case."

"You'd better get your clothes on," said Wrenn, his mouth tightening. "You're coming with me to Scotland Yard."

"If you haven't a warrant—" began Sam Birnbaum, shaking his head slowly.

"I'll get one while you're dressing."

"On what charge?"

"Fraudulent misrepresentation," snapped Wrenn. "Obstructing the police in the execution of their duty. Suspicion of complicity in four murders. I'll think of a couple of other charges in due course, but these will be good enough to hold you for a while."

All the smiling evasiveness oozed out of Sam Birnbaum, leaving him an abject, sadly troubled and apprehensive little man.

"Look, Superintendent, don't be so hasty," he pleaded. "I'll tell you the honest-to-God truth."

"It had better be the honest-to-God truth," declared Wrenn, "or I'll put you through the hoops and over the jumps until you wish you'd never been born."

"This MacNab came into my office the morning after the

murder of Ellis. I'd never seen him before. I wish to hell I'd never seen him at all. He laid two hundred pounds in notes on my desk. He told me what he wanted in return. It was a very little thing he wanted me to do, Superintendent, only a very little thing. A letter to Mr. Peters, that was all he wanted. He told me what to write. He had it all written out already, all I had to do was copy it and sign it. He assured me positively— definitely—that he wasn't up to anything illegal. He swore it. Things have been pretty bad with me lately, Superintendent. That two hundred pounds might have been sent straight from heaven to save my life. Could I hand it back to him? I appeal to you, Superintendent, as a police officer and a gentleman: could I? Considering that I didn't have to do anything illegal for it—or, anyway, only a little bit illegal."

"And that's all you know about MacNab?"

"If I should drop down dead at your feet this very minute, Superintendent, that is positively, absolutely all I know about the gonof."

Sam Birnbaum did not drop down dead.

Perhaps for once he was telling the truth (although a lie or two one way or the other had never been known to weigh heavily on his conscience).

Mr. MacNab "Explains"

At a quarter to eight that morning Mark Peters arrived at the *Echo* offices. Walking along the top floor corridor to his room he fumbled in a pocket for his key ring. The outer door of his private quarters was usually unlocked when he arrived but this morning, he had come over an hour earlier than was his custom and his secretary was not due until nine. He turned a key in the Yale lock of the outer door and adjusted a knob which put the catch out of action. He walked through the anteroom, unlocked his private room with another key—one of old-fashioned design —and pushed open the door. On the threshold he halted, drawing in his breath with an angry hiss. His brows came down in a straight line over his smouldering eyes.

Someone had contrived to enter his private room before him. It was Alastair MacNab; and the Scot was going through the drawers of a desk with commendable—if misplaced—efficiency. He badly needed a shave. Looking up with a complacent beam, he said:

"Guid mornin', Mr Peter-rs."

"What the devil are you doing here?"

"Dear, dear, I hope ye're not angry. It was yersel that gied me permission tae gang where I pleased. I jist took ye at yer word."

Forgetting his key ring, which was dangling from the key in the lock, Peters came into the room.

"I didn't give you permission to go through my personal papers."

"Hoots, there's naethin' verra personal about them that I can see. They're a' strictly business."

"How did you get in? Both doors were locked. I attended to that personally before I left last night."

"That's a verra simple lock on yon door," replied the Scot placidly, pointing over Mark Peters' shoulder. "I could open it wi' a hairpin."

"There's a Yale lock on the outer door. You didn't open it with a hairpin."

"No, I had tae use twa sheets of celluloid and a table knife."

"What are you talking about? Two sheet celluloid and a table knife? You can't manipulate a Yale lock as easily as that."

"That's where you're wr-rong. That's where a lot of people are wrong. It's verra simple. Ye push the sheets of celluloid into the crack between door and lintel—"

Mark Peters walked to his desk and sat down. He let the Scot go on talking. For one thing, he was interested in the lock trick; for another, he wanted to detain MacNab for a while without resorting to force. At eight o'clock Superintendent Wrenn was coming—they had arranged the appointment the previous night—and he could supply whatever force was necessary. Until he came, it was easiest to let the Scot have his head. Alastair MacNab needed no encouragement to talk. Resting his elbows on the desk, he gave Mark Peters a rambling but illuminating lecture on the fine art of unlocking doors without a key and with the simplest of tools.

He was still talking when Wrenn and Sergeant Leet arrived a few minutes later. At sight of him their eyes opened wide. The Scot was not in the least put out. He interrupted his discourse to say:

"Guid mornin', Super-rintendent. Mornin', Sergeant"; and went on as volubly as before.

"Where have you been?" demanded Wrenn. "I've had men scouring London for you all night."

"Dear, dear, I'm sorry ye were pit tae all that trouble. I spent the night in var-rious par-rts of this verra building."

"How did you get in without being seen? The detectives on duty at the doors were watching for you."

"When I was appr-roaching the building, a fight started in the lane. There were half-a-dozen toughs cur-rsin' and blindin' and throwin' bottles. Hoots, it sounded as though mur-rder were being done. The detectives at the side door went tae stop it and while they were gone I jist walked in and cam' upstair-rs."

"I heard this morning about that fight. It was all noise and nothing else. When my men came up the toughs melted away. I believe you arranged it to draw them off."

"Ye've a suspeecious mind, Super-rintendent," said MacNab calmly.

"I had men patrolling the corridors all night. How was it that none of them saw you?"

"I took care o' that," replied the Scot simply.

"H'm. Well, there's still a great deal for you to explain. I've seen Birnbaum. He admits you're not employed by him and that his letter to Mr. Peters was a pack of lies. You paid him two hundred pounds to obtain the entree to this building."

"It was worth it," said MacNab.

All this was news to Peters, but he said nothing. There was, however, an angry glint in his eyes. He did not like to be fooled, especially by so apparently stupid an individual as Alastair MacNab.

"What's your game, MacNab?" demanded Wrenn.

"I'll tell ye the gospel truth," began the Scot.

"There's a lie coming, Chief," said Leet. "Look at his eyes. He's cooking something up."

"It's my natur' tae lee," said Alastair MacNab bluntly. "I've been a leear frae birth. But this time I mean tae pit my car-rds on the table. I've a surprise for ye, Super-rintendent. I ken hoo Par-rtridge was killed."

"How?" asked Wrenn quickly.

The others held their breath.

Alastair MacNab shook his head.

"I canna tell ye in so many wor-rds. I'll hae tae show ye." He glanced about him. "This room is verra similar tae the yin in which Par-rtridge was shot, is it no'?"

Mark Peters said quietly: "The two rooms are almost identical."

"Guid. I believe Mr Par-rtridge's desk was bit nearer the window. Dae ye mind if we shift this yin?"

"Go as far as you like," said Peters. He rose and moved out of the way.

"Thank ye kindly. Gie me a hand, Sergeant."

Sergeant Leet glanced enquiringly at his superior. Wrenn nodded. Shrugging his shoulders, Leet took a grip of one end of the desk and helped MacNab to move it. Arranging it to the Scot's requirements took time. He was finickingly particular about the task. Before he was satisfied it was necessary for Leet to go down on his hands and knees and take a number of exact measurements. The Scot placed a chair in the approximate position that Partridge's chair had been when he was shot. He rearranged some of the articles which were lying on the desk, took some away, added others.

"That's mair like it. Dae ye mind sittin' doon for a meenit, Mister-r Peter-rs? You can be Mister-r Par- rtridge. Dinna get the wind up, I'll no' shoot ye."

Without a word Peters sat down at the desk.

"The door was slightly ajar-r," said the Scot.

Taking the hint, Leet went to the door and opened it.

"This room is soundpr-roof, is it no'?"

"Yes," said Peters. "And so was Partridge's room."

"That's fine."

The Scot picked up the telephone. He balanced it on one hand, at a level with his chest.

"This is precisely like the phone that was on Par-rtridge's desk?"

"All our phones are identical," said Peters.

"Thank ye."

Wrenn was standing near the window, Lee at the door. Without anyone noticing it—their eyes were on the telephone—MacNab edged closer to Leet. In an incredibly swift movement, he ripped the telephone cord from its connection and threw the instrument to Leet, who had three alternatives: to let it hit him, to step aside, or to catch it. Leet followed a natural instinct: he caught it. At the exact moment that the sergeant's hands reached out for it MacNab hooked a foot behind his knees and pulled his legs from under him. Wrenn dashed forward—and tripped over his subordinate, who had fallen in his path.

Dodging a hand Leet thrust out to grab his ankle, MacNab ran out of the room, slammed the door behind him and turned the key in the lock. He sat down at the desk in the anteroom and uncovered the typewriter. The men he had tricked were pounding on the door behind him but with unflustered calm he inserted a sheet of paper in the machine and typed a few lines, poking at the keys with one finger of each hand. He signed the paper with a name that was not his own. Folding it, he went to the door and adjusted the lock so that it would fasten behind him. He went out of the anteroom, shut the door, shook it to make sure that it was locked, and walked briskly down the corridor.

A few minutes later, one of the switchboard operators having reported that the light on her board connected with Mark Peters' telephone was glowing incessantly and that she could not get an answer when she plugged in, a detective came up to investigate. Realizing that something was wrong, he summoned assistance and smashed down the outer door. Almost simultaneously Wrenn and Leet succeeded in their frenzied efforts to break through the inner door.

By that time Alastair MacNab had walked nonchalantly out of the building by the main entrance, handing a pass signed by Superintendent Wrenn to a detective who was about to stop him. At least the pass appeared to be signed by Superintendent Wrenn. It bore his name and even Wrenn was forced to admit that the writing was amazingly like his own.

Once more London was scoured for Alastair MacNab. And again, the police failed to find him.

*

That night, when the presses had stopped and most of the *Echo* employees had gone home, a two-seater car drove up to the side door of the building and a very clean, very brisk young man stepped out. He explained to the doorman that he was a salesman for a new type of vacuum cleaner and that Mark Peters had given him permission to demonstrate it on the premises. The two detectives who were stationed at the door came forward and he gave one of his cards to each of them. He handed another engraved card to the doorman.

"Any time you'd like a demonstration of our smaller model in your own homes," he said chattily, "you need only give me a ring. No obligation to purchase."

He displayed his credentials: a letter of authorization on the notepaper of a well-known firm; a letter apparently signed by Mark Peters, asking him to hold the demonstration that evening; a metal badge which said that this was Anti-Dirt Week; a wallet containing his driving license, some personal correspondence, and even a photograph of his wife. One of the detectives went to the car and poked about inside it. He found nothing he would not have expected to find in such a car with the exception of a large and brand-new vacuum cleaner, dismantled and packed in cases, which did not differ much from most other such contrivances as far as he could see. Even the young man looked exactly what he claimed to be: and the selling of vacuum cleaners attracts—or produces—a very definite type. The detective had opened his door to one of the species in his day—and shut it again in their faces—and he claimed to be able to spot them a mile off.

"Well, I don't know nothing about it," said the doorman, picking his teeth with a sharpened matchstick. "Nobody ain't said nothing to me about no demonstration. Mr. Peters is gone and so is nearly everybody else. There ain't nobody left in the building who'd know anything about it."

"Then supposing I leave the cleaner and come back tomorrow?"

The doorman looked at the detectives who shrugged their shoulders.

"That's up to you," said the doorman, chewing reflectively. "Only, I don't take no responsibility for nothing."

"I suppose there isn't a carpet I could test it on, to make sure that it's in working order?"

"You can't go upstairs without a pass. Nobody can't. It's a rule. And all the rooms with carpets in 'em is upstairs."

"Wait a minute," said one of the detectives. "Isn't there a carpet lying rolled up in the passage back there?"

"That come out of Mr. Partridge's room," said the doorkeeper. "It was taken up when you blokes pulled the room to pieces, looking for cloos."

"If I could just run the cleaner over it—" said the clean brisk young man.

"I don't see why not," said the detective who had already spoken. "Our men are finished with it. For one thing, it would prove that the blooming thing is really a vacuum cleaner. We've got to know positively what it is before we let him leave it. It might be a ruddy bomb."

"Do what you like," said the doorman, excavating his molars again. "I don't take no responsibility for nothing."

Under the watchful eyes of the detectives, the clean, brisk young man assembled his machine, inserted the plug in a power point, and gave the carpet a thorough cleaning. While he worked, he kept up an incessant flow of chatter, pointing out the advantages of having a similar cleaner—one of the smaller models—in every well-conducted home. The detectives were not impressed: the broom and dustpan method was good enough for them, as long as their wives were the ones who had to wield dustpan and broom. In due course the young man rolled up the carpet again, spread some sheets of paper on the floor, disconnected the dust-bag of his cleaner, and emptied on to the paper a truly impressive mound of dirt. He began to explain the infinite variety of germs that lurk in dirt, but the detectives had had enough. They escorted him back to the side door—he took the parcel of dirt with him—and said 'Good night' very firmly. Before he drove away, the young man handed out some brightly printed circulars advertising the exceedingly efficient cleaner which he had used.

Twenty minutes later the young man climbed the stairs of a dingy office building in the city. Although it was late, there was still a light in one of the offices. He rapped three times on the door, paused, and rapped again, twice this time. The door opened and he walked in.

"It was as easy as kiss my foot," he said, placing the parcel of dirt on a table.

"You're sure it was the right carpet?" asked Alastair MacNab, with hardly a trace of accent.

"Positive."

"Good work, my lad."

Alastair MacNab telephoned for a taxi. When it came, he put on his hat and coat and went down with the parcel under his arm. Giving the driver an address, he climbed in. When the taxi drew up at its destination, he told the driver to wait. Mounting the steps of a modest dwelling house, he rang the bell. The trim maid who admitted him ushered him without delay into a laboratory at the rear of the place, in which the occupier of the house, a practising analyst, was busily at work.

"This is what I want you to analyse," said the Scot, handing over the parcel. "How soon can you let me have a report?"

"What is it?"

"Dirt."

The analyst did not look at all surprised.

"There are a lot of ingredients in dirt. It may take me the best part of the night."

"I'll make it worth your while."

"Very well. Return in the morning about seven."

The taxi conveyed the Scot back to the grubby office in the city. Another visitor was waiting to see him: a middle-aged man in a wing collar and a shabby frock coat.

"About that agreement you wanted me to look into," he said, putting on steel-rimmed spectacles. "I have all the particulars here—"

Last Man In

Another morning. Another death notice. This time that of Mark Peters. It appeared suddenly, apparently from nowhere, like a rabbit conjured out of a hat. The head proof-reader was quite certain that it was not on his file when he looked through it at the commencement of his day. Before the paper went to press, he looked through the file again and then sent a boy to Mark Peters' office with it—an arrangement that been in force since the murder of Nigel Partridge. The boy was accompanied by two detectives, one on either side. No one else came within a yard of him on his way upstairs. But when Wrenn and Peters examined the file, there the death notice was. It uncanny.

"'At his office in Fleet Street'," Mark Peters quoted grimly. "Well, that at least is incorrect. I may die, it won't be here."

"I don't know what to say," groaned Wrenn hopelessly. "I don't know what to do. I did my best for Mr. Partridge. He died. I did my best for Mr. Craven. He died."

"If I die, you can write down Lucius Marplay as a supernatural force. I'm going to make it as difficult as possible for him. I have a yacht moored down the Thames above Canvey Island. No one knows I own it—I'm certain of that. I acquired it under another name some months ago; and I never talk about my private affairs. With the co-operation of the river police, I think we can set Mr. Marplay a ticklish problem."

"He's already achieved the impossible."

"I know. But I've come to believe that the secret of his power lies in this building. I don't know in what way that may be. I can't imagine how. But I honestly think that outside this building his black magic won't work."

"May I say, Mr. Peters, how much I admire your courage?"

"If I am to die," said Peters, "squealing won't help."

An hour later three launches put out from Westminster. Two of them were filled to capacity with Scotland Yard men and river police. Mark Peters sat in the third, with Superintendent Wrenn, and the inevitable divisional surgeon. The newspaper proprietor was wrapped in a heavy greatcoat, smoking a long cigar. The third launch also contained a considerable quantity of electrical equipment. They chugged down the Thames as quickly as their heavy loads would allow, their prows smoothly parting the murky yellow water, leaving wide fan-shaped impressions on it that melted on the embankments at either side of the river. The sky above was clear and blue; if this was to be Mark Peters' last day on earth, it was a day worth looking at...

Peters took a slip of paper from his pocket and passed it to Wrenn.

"What do you think of this?"

The police superintendent read the following laconic message:

I shall meet you on the yacht. LUCIUS MARPLAY.

"It's uncanny," he muttered. "Utterly uncanny."

"I could have sworn no one knew about the yacht," replied Peters. He said no more until the launches were nearing the yacht and then he remarked quietly:

"I don't want to make a fuss, but your men had better search her before I go aboard."

"Of course," Wrenn answered quickly.

But he knew that his men would find nothing. What had they ever found, since the beginning of the case?

This search was no different from the others. Every part of the yacht was inspected under Wrenn's supervision and the searchers found no trace of Lucius Marplay. They were already convinced that Marplay could strike without making an appearance, so that meant precisely nothing. Mark Peters came aboard and went to his cabin accompanied by Wrenn. He opened a locker and took out a bottle of Napoleon brandy. Sergeant Leet had already opened that locker and smacked his lips at the rows and rows of bottles which it contained. He had counted a dozen rows at least; and the locker was about six feet long. Making a rough calculation, he had estimated that it must contain about two hundred bottles. Enough booze, he had reflected enviously, to keep an average man delightfully blotto for many months. Peters poured some of the brandy into two glasses and offered one to Wrenn, who shook his head.

"Drink it," said Peters, thrusting the glass into his hand. "It's the real thing. You may never get another chance."

Wrenn did as he was told. Peters was right. It was the real thing. But when Peters started to refill his glass, he shook his head again, this time more positively.

"No, thanks. I want to keep a clear brain for the work at hand."

"If I survive this day," said Peters, putting the brandy back in the locker, "I'll give you a bottle."

Outside, on the deck, men were installing a battery of searchlights. Wrenn was taking no risk of being surprised when darkness came. But he felt in his bones that everything he did was in vain, that nothing would stop Lucius Marplay until his vengeance was complete.

The yacht had been moved to the middle of the river and anchored there. To left and right were stretches of water, patrolled unceasingly by the river police launches. On either side the river lapped clay banks which rose to footpaths and dipped again to low-lying fields with no cover that would enable a man to approach unseen. Two detectives scanned the fields through telescopes. Not even a sparrow in a furrow escaped their vigilance.

Uneventfully the day dragged by. Peters sat in his cabin, smoking and reading. Wrenn paced the deck with a troubled frown, so nervy and irritable that an uninformed spectator would have thought it was his life that was threatened. Every now and then he hurried into the cabin to make sure that all was well with Peters. On one of those occasions Peters lost his icy calm for the first time since they had read the death notice.

"This may be the last book I shall ever read," he snapped. "For the love of God let me read it in peace."

In a sky ablaze the sun sank down, a ball of brass melting over a fire, and the grey of twilight settled on the countryside. Twilight faded into dusk, dusk into darkness. The moon rode out, the stars blinked down. Like broad blades, the searchlights cut the darkness, carving great slabs out of it, making synthetic slices of daylight that shifted with every moment. The river police launches circled incessantly, their lights on yacht and river banks in turn.

Occasionally other boats came up or down the river and if they were disposed to linger—the display of illuminations was enough to rouse the curiosity of the least inquisitive river traveller—the police speedily moved them on.

Not long after nightfall a rowboat appeared out of the gloom, came into a patch of brilliant light thrown by one of the searchlights and headed straight for the yacht. At once a launch shot towards it and for a few moments the two vessels rocked on the water side by side. Wrenn snatched a telescope from one of his subordinates and trained it on the rowboat. It had a solitary occupant clad in a raincoat and a bowler hat. He was talking to one of the river police, apparently explaining something.

Leaning over the rail, Wrenn sent a shout across the water:

"Bring that man on board."

The police launch headed for the yacht with the rowboat in tow. In a dazzling bath of light Alastair MacNab climbed a rope ladder to the deck.

"Guid evening, Super-rintendent," he said cheerfully, tipping his hat.

It was all Wrenn could do to keep from smashing his fist into the Scot's broad, beaming face.

"Put handcuffs on this man," he snapped to two of his subordinates. "Not like that—put his hands behind him first. Take him to the stern—and see that he stays there. I shall hold you accountable for him."

Meekly enough the Scot put his wrists out behind him and allowed them to be manacled together. He did not seem to mind in the least. The detectives marched him to the stern and he leaned comfortably against the rail. The mooring rope of the rowboat was tied to the anchor chain of the yacht.

Wrenn went on patrolling the deck. He simply could not keep still. One end of his beat was the rail against which MacNab was leaning, the other the cabin in which sat Mark Peters. Thus far Peters was alright. At frequent intervals the superintendent glanced through an open porthole and saw him serenely reading and smoking. The cigar smoke, curling through the porthole, smelt good.

Nine o'clock…ten…eleven…

Midnight. Still nothing had happened. Nothing, that is, but the arrival of Alastair MacNab. By this time Wrenn was quite sure that the Scot was Lucius Marplay's tool. It must, he reasoned, have been through him that Marplay had achieved his seemingly impossible feats. When Partridge was murdered, when Craven was murdered, MacNab had enjoyed the run of the *Echo* building. Since his escape from the mental home, Marplay had only been seen in the building once, to the best of

Wrenn's knowledge: by an office boy, outside the door of Sinclair Ellis' room, on the afternoon of the first murder. It was utterly impossible for him to have come and gone in the building since that day; at least one of the detectives who were posted about the place would have been bound to have seen him. They had eyes in their heads; they were all watching for him, or for any person who even remotely resembled him. No, for Marplay to have done in person the things which had been done was quite impossible. Easier, far, to believe that MacNab had done them at Marplay's orders. And this time the Scot was powerless. His hands were linked behind him with steel cuffs and chain. A burly armed guard stood on either side of him.

Even while he assured himself that MacNab was powerless, Wrenn began to doubt it. He had reached the stage when he doubted everything; he would have to stop and think before acknowledging the truth of even so obvious a fact as that black was black and not white. He strode to the stern, twisted MacNab round and stared down at the handcuffs. He tested them his fingers. They were all right. They were securely fastened.

There was nothing to tell him that the Scot had already slipped his hands out of them and put them back again. Getting out of handcuffs without unlocking them was a trick MacNab had learned from a sideshow performer at a country fair in the days of his youth...

Muttering to himself, Wrenn turned on his heel and started to walk back to Peters' cabin. He had taken no more than two paces when he suddenly shouted and broke into a run. The door of the cabin had opened and Peters had stumbled out, struggling with someone.

A light focussed on the swaying figures, and then another; the man with whom Peters was fighting was short, plump, white haired—it was Lucius Marplay—

A knife gleamed in Marplay's hand; his hand was upraised, the blade pointing at Mark Peters' chest. Peters was holding the wrist grimly, winding a leg round the knees of his adversary… The knife dropped and skittered across the deck...

It all happened swiftly, in the time it took Superintendent Wrenn to run less than fifty feet. Peters tore himself free. His fist shot out with all his strength behind it, landing on Marplay's jaw. Marplay went back; back against the rail, hitting it with a thud that sent a shiver down its entire length. He went over, over the rail, turning a somersault in mid-air. A mighty splash sent a spray of water up on to the deck.

Wrenn grasped Mark Peters' arm.

"Are you alright?" he gasped.

"I'm…alright… A…little…winded…"

From the launches, from the yacht, the blades of light were slashing downward, a dozen of them cleaving the darkness at the spot where Marplay sank. Bubbles were coming up, bursting on the surface of the yellow water. A score of eyes were peering downward, watching for the rise of a short, plump body. But no body floated up. Only bubbles; bubble of air, of the breath of life. . . .

"He must be entangled in the weeds," said Wrenn hoarsely.

MacNab's custodians at the stern had their eyes more on the activities at the bow than on their prisoner. The Scot thrust a shoulder against one and then the other. The handcuffs dropped to the deck with a clatter and he sprinted forward, throwing off his raincoat. About fifteen feet from where Wrenn stood he vaulted the rails and dropped feet first to the water. He went down, down…

His bowler hat came up. The surface of the water was churned by the kicking of his feet as he swam to the bed of the river. For a moment the surface was still, and then it was broken by his bobbing head. He shouted something and disappeared.

A launch sped to the spot. River police were leaning over the side, looking down, reaching out. MacNab's head bobbed up again. One of the river police grabbed his hair and tugged. The launch almost tipped over. MacNab was dragging something with him. Another river policeman grasped his arm and he was pulled into the launch. A second head appeared on the surface, followed by a pair of shoulders. They belonged to Lucius Marplay; his eyes were shut, he looked like a corpse. The Scot was clutching Marplay's collar grimly; to break the hold, they had to prise MacNab's fingers apart. When they opened the fingers Marplay almost sank again, although two men had a grip on his arms. They hauled him in. He seemed to weigh a ton.

Alastair MacNab stood up, water dripping from him, his trousers sticking to his legs. "Will he live?"

"Sit down," grunted a voice. "You're rocking the boat. He'll probably live. He's breathing already."

"Lend me a pencil and a piece of paper." MacNab's teeth were chattering, but there was little trace of his former accent.

"What in hell do you want with pencil and paper at a time like this?"

"Never mind that. Let me have them."

"I've met some crazy people in my time," said one of the river police. He held out his hand, with a notebook and pencil in it.

"Thanks."

The launch slid to the side of the yacht and the divisional surgeon scrambled down the ladder, carrying his black bag. Shouts were coming from the yacht. The Scot was scribbling busily in the notebook. Someone touched his arm and said:

"They want you to go on board. I'll hold the ladder."

"Eh?"

"I said they want you to go on board the yacht."

"Half a mo'," said MacNab, still scribbling.

"The superintendent wants you. He won't wait."

"He'll have to wait," retorted MacNab.

Standing up, he took a step toward the ladder. He took another step sideways and jumped out over the water. He landed with a crash in the rowboat, which rocked perilously and almost capsized. From under the seat, he dragged out his wicker basket, opened it, and fumbled about inside. There was a whir and something shot up into the sky...

MacNab turned, to find the launch gliding alongside the rowboat. The river police had their truncheons out and were ready to use them.

"Alright," he said. "Where's this blooming ladder?"

It All Sounds Very Simple

Wrapped in two blankets, looking perfectly cheerful after his impromptu cold bath, Alastair MacNab shuffled into the cabin where Wrenn, Mark Peters and Sergeant Leet awaited him, the latter armed with a shorthand notebook. In a neighbouring cabin the divisional surgeon was working on Lucius Marplay, trying to restore him to consciousness. Wrenn gave the Scot a long, hard look and said:

"Perhaps you're ready to talk."

"I'm always ready to talk. A loose tongue has never been one of my failings."

"You've lost your accent."

"I can get it back if you prefer it."

"Are you ready to talk sense?"

"I'll tell you the truth as far as I know it. It may not sound like sense."

"It is my duty to caution you that anything you say will be written down—"

"I know the rest. In any case, you're wasting time. You'd better speak your little piece to Peters."

"What do you mean by that?"

"It's a long story."

Mark Peters said nothing. His dark eyes regarded the Scot with an unfathomable expression. He selected a fresh cigar from a box at his elbow. He did not light it; once he had chosen it, he seemed to forget it; he sat pinching it gently between his long fingers.

"To begin with," said Wrenn, after an odd glance at Peters, "supposing you tell where you got the sample of my signature you copied this morning on a pass enabling you to walk out of the *Echo* building."

"When deep in thought you have a habit of scribbling designs and sometimes your name on odd pieces of paper. You were doing it at the Yard the other night when questioning me. You dropped the paper into a wastebasket. When no one was looking I retrieved it, thinking it might come in handy."

"And just who are you?"

"The name is Alastair MacNab. There's no cod about that. I'm a reporter, employed for twenty-four years by a Glasgow daily newspaper. The *Dispatch* brought me south by plane on the night Ellis was murdered. Mark Peters was barring all rival newspapermen from the *Echo* building; the *Dispatch* reporters in especial were marked men. No need to tell you how I got myself in. You know that. I deliberately made a guy of myself. I don't normally look the bloody fool I've appeared to be lately. In the wicker basket I had a carrier pigeon. It took a comedy character to get away with a gag like that. Concealed beneath my waistcoat I had a tiny camera—it looks like a toy but it cost eighty quid. The lens projected through a buttonhole and was capped with a fake button.

"From the first I was suspicious of Mark Peters. It wasn't natural for so clever a man to allow a mug like me the free run of his office. A man with nothing on his conscience would probably have shown me the door. Why should Peters be so willing for me to remain, unless to prove himself ready to clutch at any straw that might help to find Lucius Marplay?"

Turning, Wrenn stared at Mark Peters, who returned his gaze calmly.

"The man's mad," said Peters.

"A small boy caught in a cupboard with jam on his face and hands," said Alastair MacNab, "swears he's not been near the jam pot, hoping desperately that if he protests his innocence long enough he will be believed, although his guilt is obvious.

That's all very well for a small boy; but an intelligent man, Mr. Peters, should know when he's at the end of his tether."

"Show me the jam on my face and hands," said Peters softly, quietly.

"Last night," replied the Scot, "a young friend of mine took a vacuum cleaner to your office and used it on the carpet that was in Partridge's room at the time of the murder. I had the dirt analysed; it contained traces of burnt powder of the kind to be found in fireworks of the loudly banging variety. Another of my colleagues took the trouble to look up the terms of your partnership agreement with Ellis, Craven and Partridge. Furthermore, if you recall a cigar band I picked up in the room in which Flinders was murdered, a band that had come off one of your own special brand—"

"I recall it," said Peters huskily, toying with the cigar in his hand. "I dropped it a moment or two before you picked it up."

"Oh no, you didn't. I found the body before Noel and Miss Marplay did, although it didn't suit my book to say so at the time. When I found Flinders dead the cigar band was lying beside the body. I pretended to 'find' it later to see what you would say. You killed Flinders. You killed Ellis. You killed Partridge. You killed Craven. Tonight, you tried to kill Marplay."

"You fool," laughed Peters. "I wasn't there when Partridge was shot. Superintendent Wrenn will tell you that. He and his subordinates heard the shot and ran in—"

"They ran in," said MacNab, "and no one was there except the corpse. There was only one way in: the door by which they had entered. The room was practically a concrete box with but one opening in it: the door. To make sure of that, the police stripped the panelling from walls, floor and ceiling and tested the solid concrete beneath with pneumatic drills. Therefore no one but Partridge was in the room when the shot was heard. Partridge could not have shot himself, for there was no gun in the room. It was established beyond doubt that there was no mechanical device in the room capable of firing a shot. Therefore, Partridge was not killed at the time the shot was heard. The sound heard was simply an explosion. The police took it for a shot because they were half expecting one and because there was a bullet hole in Partridge's head. Partridge must have been killed when someone was in the room with him. You were the last person in the room before he was found dead. Therefore, you killed him!"

"There's no need to be melodramatic," responded Peters suavely. "I'll admit you've worked up quite a plausible case. But can you explain how I could have planted a bullet in Partridge's head without a shot being heard then and there? Even a silenced revolver makes a noise, you know. And the door was ajar. There were three people in the anteroom. They must have heard him talking to me until the moment I left the room."

"With regard to that last point, you're pretty clever at impersonating the voices of your partners."

Before Mark Peters could reply the divisional surgeon came in. He told them that Lucius Marplay would live; he had regained consciousness, but was still very weak; it would be some time before he could talk.

"One would almost think Marplay was determined to drown," remarked the doctor, with a puzzled frown. "When we undressed him, we found under his jacket a curious garment somewhat like a life belt. Only it wasn't a life belt. It was made up of pouches, each containing a lump of rock salt. That explains why he sank so quickly and did not come up again; had, in fact, to be dragged up. There's something else that strikes me as odd: his legs and arms are quite stiff with cramp, as though for a considerable time before he went into the water he had been confined in a narrow space."

"If his legs and arms were stiff with cramp when he fell overboard," said MacNab at once, "how could he have used them to struggle with Peters?"

"He couldn't," replied the divisional surgeon blankly. "He couldn't possibly have used them."

"Then the struggle was faked. Peters must have used Marplay as a dummy, to put on a show for those who were watching. And Marplay must have been confined somewhere in this very cabin until the time came to put on the show."

"But where?" demanded Wrenn, who by now taken an automatic from his pocket and was watching Peters closely. "We searched the cabin."

Alastair MacNab let his eyes rove round the walls. "What about that locker? It's big enough to hold a couple of men."

"It's full of bottles," said Sergeant Leet in a thick voice. His mouth felt full of tongue.

"I wonder," said MacNab. He opened the locker: and it certainly appeared that every inch of it was occupied by rows and rows of bottles. He took some of them out, and found that there were actually six rows, backed with a mirror which made them look twice as many. Behind the mirror was an empty space large enough to hold a man. Turning his head, the Scot looked meaningfully at Mark Peters.

"Yes," said Peters dryly, "the jam is thick on my face and hands. I'm not a fool. I know when I am beaten."

"Before you go any further," said Superintendent Wrenn, "it is my duty to warn you that anything you say will be written down and may be used in evidence at your trial."

"Very, well," said Peters, with a faint smile. "I might, perhaps, decline to say anything, but with what you already know, with what Marplay can tell, it would only be a matter of time before you discovered the rest; or enough, at least, to hang me. I've lost, so I might as well lay down my hand. You may start writing, Sergeant.

"On the afternoon when the first death notice appeared I went to Ellis' room to show it to him. Ellis was lying across his desk unconscious. A rubber truncheon lay on the floor. Marplay was standing beside the desk looking down in horror at Ellis. The previous night he had set up the death notice when the composing room was deserted. He had come that afternoon to Ellis' office to kill him, but had only knocked him out. In a dazed voice he told me that at the very moment he hit him he suddenly realized, fully and for the first time, exactly what he was doing. For years in the mental home, he had worked out ingenious schemes of murder, pretty much as another man might have exercised his wits with crossword puzzles. A sort of mental game, exhilarating to play at, but when translated into action it became different altogether. It became murder—and in a sudden return of complete sanity Marplay realized that he could not do murder.

"Then and there I saw my chance to rid myself of Ellis and my other partners. MacNab has said something about our partnership agreement: the clause to which he presumably referred was one providing that on the death of a partner his share in the newspaper must pass to the surviving partners, who are obliged to pay into the dead man's estate one fourth of the sum for which we originally bought the *Echo*: a mere fraction of its present value. I realized that if I could wipe out my three partners the *Echo* would be mine for a song. The *Echo* is my life. It means more to me than anything else in the world. Its growth has been stunted by the conservative policies of my partners. It was worth any risk to me to have it under my sole control.

"Picking up the truncheon, holding it with a handkerchief

to prevent leaving my fingerprints on it, I struck Marplay with it, knocking him out. Then I used it to bash in the brains of Sinclair Ellis. Dropping the truncheon on the floor, I ripped down a curtain cord and securely trussed Marplay. Gagging him with the handkerchief, I locked him in the large safe which was standing in a corner of the room. It wasn't airtight; there was little danger that he would suffocate. I wanted him alive. He was going to be useful to me.

"At three o'clock in the morning, when everything was quiet, I returned in a stolen van. I was roughly disguised as Marplay. You know how I disposed of the policeman on guard at the side door of the old building. Going in, I crept through the old building to the new one, taking care not to be seen, and returned the van carrying the bound form of Lucius Marplay. I have a house in the country twenty miles out of London which I bought some time ago under an assumed name. No one knows I own it. It stands in its own grounds a mile from the nearest village. I had not troubled to install a caretaker. I took Marplay to that house and from that night until late yesterday evening, when I moved him to this yacht, held him prisoner there. Every night I went there and fed him and made sure that he could not escape. When I wanted his fingerprints on a knife or a paper it was easy to secure them. And if I required him to write something, he was easily persuaded by a little refined torture. Most of the time since the first murder two detectives have followed me about, but it wasn't hard to throw them off when I really wanted to do so.

"The death notices and all that sort of mumbo-jumbo only mystify as long as one believes that Marplay contrived them. You can imagine how easy that sort of thing was for me.

"By the way, I used my Marplay disguise later, in an attempt to get rid of his daughter. The attempt was almost successful, but her companion intervened at the crucial moment. I don't suppose you know anything about that. The girl, thinking her assailant was her father, would keep quiet for his sake."

Superintendent Wrenn drew a deep breath. "How did you shoot Partridge without the shot being heard at the time?"

"I didn't shoot him. I struck him on the head with a weapon rather like a hammer, only with a long sharp spike. It made a round wound, like a bullet hole. In the point of the spike was a cup into which I had fitted a bullet. A wire from the cup ran up a groove to the head of the hammer. After hitting him all I had to do was pull on the wire and withdraw the spike, leaving the bullet embedded in his brain. To cover the sound of the impact, I made a slapping noise on the desk with my other hand."

"I heard the slapping noise," said Leet huskily. "I thought you were striking the desk to emphasize what you were saying."

"But the bullet had rifling marks on it," protested Wrenn. "Our ballistics expert is positive that it been fired from a revolver."

"Your expert is right. Only it was fired the night before the murder, into a bale of cotton wool, from which I retrieved it. I did that because if there been no marks of rifling on the bullet, your expert would have known immediately that it did not come from a gun. I had the revolver in my pocket when I came into the anteroom after the alarm was given and, in the confusion, putting it in the secretary's handbag was simple."

"The shot we heard? The crash of things falling from the desk? How did you manage those?"

"Before I left the room I balanced the telephone, an ash tray, and some other articles on the edge of the desk. I placed on the ash tray a capsule filled with gunpowder. A capsule made of lead which could be relied upon to melt to almost nothing on combustion, with a slow fuse attached, which I lit. When the fuse burnt down there was an explosion—the 'shot' you heard—and the balanced articles toppled over.

"As for the murder of Craven, I prepared two methods of disposal for him. The first, a scent spray filled with hydrocyanic acid gas, one good breath of which would be sufficient to kill him on the spot. The second, a poisoned cigar. The cigar was not a very good idea; using it would have been extremely risky. Fortunately, it was not necessary to use it."

"But I had the scent spray analysed. The report stated that its contents were harmless."

"Your expert analysed the scent spray I placed on the desk. That was not the one I picked up from the floor. A little sleight of hand, Superintendent, rendered childishly simple by the fact that you were all staring at the body."

Mark Peters sighed. With brooding eyes, he looked at MacNab.

"My scheme was supremely audacious," he said, with a touch of vanity. "But for you, I believe I should have carried it through successfully. But for you, Marplay would now be at the bottom of the Thames, held down by the weight of the rock salt in the curious garment he was wearing. After a while the rock salt would have melted and his body would have floated up for burial as the corpse of a homicidal maniac. These literal-minded policemen would never have dreamed of suspecting that the murderer was not Marplay, but me. They might have wondered at the odd garment the sodden corpse was wearing beneath his jacket, but they would never have guessed for what purpose it had been devised. But for you—"

He sighed again.

"You're a good newspaperman, MacNab. I wish you had been with me on the *Echo*." From Mark Peters, that was high praise.

Wrenn said suddenly: "You mentioned a poisoned cigar you prepared for Craven but did not use. What happened to it?"

Mark Peters smiled. "This is it," he replied—and bit deeply into the end of the cigar with which he had been toying.

*

Afterwards, when there was no doubt that Peters was dead, Superintendent Wrenn said dejectedly:

"There were still a lot of points I wanted him to clear up."

"You'll have to work them out for yourself," replied Alastair MacNab.

Sir John Retires in a Huff

Above the treetops the spire of the village church tapered to a cloudless sky. On a lawn three centuries old, smooth as a carpet, figures in white were playing tennis, darting and leaping as though their bodies were made of fine springs. On the terrace of the rose-brick manor house two old gentlemen sat in canvas chairs watching the play with wistful eyes. One of them sighed and reached for a decanter which stood on the table between them.

"Not so much soda in mine, Sir Charles," murmured his companion sleepily. He listened for the swish of the syphon and raised a warning hand when he heard it. "That's enough. Don't drown it."

Sir Charles poured a second whiskey-and-soda and settled back in his chair to enjoy it.

"That's Joan Marplay playing on the second court —young Stretton's her partner."

"Nice girl, Joan Marplay. And Stretton's a fine young feller, even if he does earn his livin' writin' piffle for the papers."

"They make a charmin' couple," said Sir Charles. "Shouldn't wonder if they made a match of it."

"Funny about Marplay," mumbled his companion, taking a sip from his glass.

"Dashed funny," agreed Sir Charles.

"Oddest thing I ever heard of, the way he turned out to be innocent after all. I still don't understand why he was never tried for knockin' out the first chap with his rubber truncheon. After all, he did do that."

"I expect the police thought he'd been punished enough. He was put through the mill pretty thoroughly by that bounder Peters, you know."

"Funny about the will Peters left."

"Bequeathin' his money and the newspaper to Marplay? Yes, that was rummy. It only goes to show…" The drowsy voice of Sir Charles trailed into silence.

"It goes to show what?" asked his companion irritably, after a long pause.

"Eh? What did you say?"

"Oh, never mind. Let it drop. Tell me, what is Marplay's present status? Is he barmy, or is he sane?"

"No one knows—yet. I believe a couple of brain specialists are at the cottage now, making up their minds about that."

Sir Charles began to nod. His eyes closed; his mouth opened. The other old gentleman went on talking for a time and then he, too, dozed off.

After a while Joan and Lord Noel sauntered up from the tennis court. They went round the side of the house and through a gap in the garden hedge into the fields, to a short cut which ran to the cottage.

"Sorry I broke up the game, Noel," said Joan, "but I'm impatient to hear what Sir John Digby and the other specialist have to say about Father. I wish they'd let me stay while they talked to him."

"My dear, I quite understand. But let's not walk quite so confoundedly fast. There's a question I want to ask you."

"I think I know what it is," said Joan, looking up at him with a grave face. "Please don't ask it now."

"Why not?"

"Because what I reply must depend on the verdict of the specialists. If they say my father is sane my answer will be yes. If they say he's…mad"—her voice broke when she uttered that word—"my answer will be no."

"Darling, what earthly difference—"

"I'm sorry, Noel," said Joan firmly, "but that's the way it must be."

Passing a spinney of young larches, they saw Miss Trimm and Alastair MacNab sitting on a fallen tree, deep in earnest talk. Joan called out to them and they scrambled to their feet and came out of the spinney looking guilty and embarrassed. Joan linked arms with Agatha and they walked on together, the men following a short distance behind.

With a shrewd glance at the older woman, Joan said: "Do I hear wedding bells?"

Agatha arched her back. "I don't know what you mean."

"Oh yes, you do. There's a look in Alastair's eye—"

"My dear girl," retorted Agatha stiffly, "I'm not responsible for the eyes of Mr. MacNab. I believe he has a slight cast in one of them, if that is what you mean."

"You're dodging the issue, Trimmy. Be a man, my girl. Tell the truth and shame the devil. He's asked you to marry him, hasn't he?"

Miss Trimm didn't say yes and she didn't say no. She said: "Why should I want to marry?"

"Spare my blushes," said Joan.

"Oh, that," replied Agatha scornfully. "I wasn't thinking of that. You don't, when you're my age. At my age a woman marries for comfort or for the company of a man. I have ample means for comfortable existence and in this enlightened age I can surely enjoy all the male society I desire without the inconvenience of having a man under my feet at all hours of the day and night."

For the moment Joan carried the argument no further. They were in sight of the cottage and her eyes were hurrying on ahead of her feet. She saw Sir John Digby coming out of the cottage, slamming the door behind him. His face red with anger, his whole body bristling with indignation, he entered his car, which was waiting at the garden gate. Joan ran toward the cottage as fast as she could but by the time she reached the gate Sir John's elderly Daimler had driven away. The other brain specialist was coming down the garden path. Joan rushed to meet him.

"What's the matter?" she demanded. "You haven't— My father isn't—"

"My dear young lady, I'm delighted to be able to tell you that your father is as sane as I am—and probably saner."

"Then why did Sir John rush away like that? What made him so angry?"

The specialist smiled.

"Your father offered to show him some card tricks," he replied.

THE END

THE MAN WHO CAME BACK

It was midnight, and along the Great West Road a powerful touring car speeded, its glaring headlights cleaving a path through the darkness. Crouched over the wheel was a man of about thirty, whose stern grey eyes were focussed on the road ahead.

Suddenly the wall of darkness which flanked the road was broken by a splash of white which appeared about thirty yards in front of the speeding car and resolved itself into a girl in a white coat. The driver's face whitened and his teeth bit into his lower lip as he stood on clutch and brake.

With difficulty, the driver regained control of the car and drew it to a standstill. Climbing out, he walked back to where the girl lay at the side of the road. As he bent over her, she stirred, and her eyes opened.

"What happened?" she asked huskily.

"I was going rather fast," the man replied. "You appeared suddenly on the road…It was all I could do to pull up in time. As it was, the car skidded and the rear mudguard gave you a nasty jolt."

"I remember now. I was running away from 'The Hog.'"

She glanced over her shoulder anxiously, then rose to her feet. The man breathed a sigh of relief.

"How do you feel? You aren't hurt, are you?"

"A trifle shaken, that's all. I'll be alright in a moment."

"Will you think me a heartless brute if I leave you, then?" He looked down the road with a peculiar expression in his eyes. "I assure you I must. It's a matter of—well almost, life and death."

"Oh, but I want you to help me. You must help me," she cried.

"I help you?" he laughed mirthlessly. "You don't know what you're saying. I can't help anyone."

"Oh, yes, you can!" she insisted. "You've got a car. I live three miles down the road—back the way you've come. I must get home at once. I simply must! Please take me."

"Please don't question me," he replied in strained voice. "But it's quite impossible. If I'd killed you, I should never have forgiven myself. But I can't do what you ask. Think what you will of me; I'm callous—a heartless brute—but I can't."

"You can't leave me like this!" she cried. "You've got to take me home. You've got to, do you hear? You've got to!"

With a quick movement her hand dived into one of the deep pockets of her overcoat and reappeared in a moment, clutching something sinister and formidable-looking, which gleamed darkly in the moonlight. She said: "I'm sorry, but you've forced me to do this."

"You're going to force me to drive you back at the point of the gun?"

"Just that. I'm sorry, but you've asked for it."

"Alright," he said. "You've played your trump card. Now I'll play mine."

With unsteady fingers he unbuttoned his dark overcoat and threw it back. Beneath he was wearing a shoddy suit of drab grey material, of unmistakeable cut. A number was stitched in red upon the breast pocket. "Take a good look."

"You're—you're a—"

"I'm an escaped convict," he said hollowly. "From Greyhurst, the prison just off the road, eleven miles back. I stole this car and overcoat to make my getaway."

Watching the girl's face, the convict saw surprise and uncertainty, but no trace of fear.

"Your duty, I suppose you know, is to detain me here—shoot me, if necessary, if I attempt to escape. You owe it to society to see that I'm put back where I belong. I shan't stand much chance of escaping if you choose to stop me."

The hand holding the automatic dropped to the girl's side and the weapon slipped from her fingers and clattered on the road. The convict climbed out of the car and picked it up; offered it to her.

"Aren't you afraid?" he asked. "Now that you know—what I am?"

"No." Her eyes searched his face. "You won't hurt me. You're not a bad man. If you were, you wouldn't have stopped when you knocked me over. You'd have gone on—escaped—without a thought for me."

"In that case" —he swung the automatic above his head— "we'll dispose of this." It flew in a glittering arc from his fingers into the shadows of the moor.

"You'd better go," she urged. "If you don't, they'll catch you."

"Thanks, but I've changed my mind. I've got you to consider now."

"They may not know yet that you've escaped," she said. "But they'll find out soon. If you delay the cordon will be drawn across the road and it will be too late."

"You said you were running away," he responded. "What did you mean by that?"

"I was running away from 'The Hog'. That's the name we've given to the General Manager of the firm I work for. Anything more hog-like is difficult to conceive. Little piggy eyes, a fat stupid face, a huge fleshy neck, and a large, loose mouth. Ugh!"

"I see. That doesn't quite explain why you happen to be running away from him after midnight on the Great West Road?"

"Oh, what does it matter? Don't you realise you've got to get away at once?"

"For a moment, let's forget that I'm an escaping convict and remember only that I am a man. Tell me the rest of the story, please. Where is 'The Hog' now, for instance?"

"If he's where I left him, he's sitting in a car on a side road a quarter of a mile from here, nursing a broken head," she replied, with an effort at calmness. "I inflicted the injury with the butt of his own automatic—the one you've just thrown away. That's why I'm not anxious for him to find me. We were out in his car. He parked in the sideroad and began to make love to me. There was a struggle, during which I somehow got possession of the automatic he always kept in one of the side-pockets of the car. I hit him with it as hard as I could and he flopped back on his seat as though he were dead. I bolted. I wanted to get home as fast as I could."

Ignoring her anxiety on his behalf, the man said:

"What I can't understand is why, if you hate him, you went out in the car with him."

"You can't understand because you're a man," she replied bitterly. "I didn't go because I wanted to. I had no choice. I support my grandfather—we're alone in the world—and I can't afford to lose my job. Especially without a reference, and The Hog wouldn't give me one. Now do you see?"

"Your grandfather knows—" he hesitated —"about this man?"

"Grandfather doesn't know about anything except his wonderful invention. If I'd told him, he would have made me throw up the job long ago, and then how would we have lived? He knows 'The Hog' though and hates him. Grandfather worked for our firm for years. He retired eighteen months ago—the oldest and finest mechanic the National Transport Company ever had."

The convict stared at that.

"The National Transport Company?" he repeated.

"Yes," she said in a puzzled tone. "We run buses all over the country."

"Your grandfather—" he swallowed—"is his name Sam Jarvis?"

"Yes, that's right. You know him?"

"I knew him," he answered. "One of the best old chaps that ever breathed."

"Then you're one of grandfather's friends—?"

"A convict," he said, "has no friends. The manager of the National Transport Company," he continued, "used to be an elderly man named Simmons."

"He retired a year ago, just after I joined the firm."

"He had two assistants, Stephen Grey and Aubrey Marcus."

"I never knew Grey," the girl replied. "He was put in prison for embezzlement some years ago. Mr. Marcus is the present manager."

"Get in," he said. "I'm going to take you home."

"Why should you put yourself in danger of being caught and sent back to that awful place for my sake?"

"For two reasons," he replied. "Because I'm making myself responsible for your safety, for tonight, at least. And because—"

"Yes?" she prompted.

"In prison," he said harshly, "the chief impulse of my life was hate. And the man on whom my hated was centred—the man I loathe more than anything in the world—is Aubrey Marcus!"

They were silent until the car approached the sideroad on which she lived. He turned the car down the road, which was little more than a lane, lined on either side by hedges of wild rose. In a few moments they came to a cottage in the centre of a garden. None of your prim, landscaped gardens, this, but a patch crowded with flowers—hollyhocks, lilacs, roses, tall sunflowers.

"You can't go back now," she said. "Even if the alarm isn't

out for you yet, the owner of this car will certainly have missed it. You haven't a chance of escaping if you venture back upon the Great West Road."

"I can't sit still and surrender tamely," he pointed out.

"That car," she went on, "is our greatest problem. We've got to dispose of it, somehow, at once. I know! About half a mile down the road you'll find a cart track leading across the moor. Follow it for about five hundred yards, then drive over the moor to the left. A short distance across the moor you'll find a clump of gorse. Drive the car behind it, and it won't be visible from the cart-track or the road. When you've done that, come back."

"I won't come back. It's splendid of you to suggest it, but I'm not cad enough to take advantage of your kindness."

She faced him squarely. "You've helped me at the risk of your own freedom."

"I'm a convict—a criminal."

"I'm not your judge. I don't ask what you've done. It's enough for me that you helped me when I needed help, and that you need help yourself. If you were caught, I'd blame myself for making you bring me back, and spoiling your chance of escape."

"I'm a coward, a miserable coward. I ought to get as far away from here as possible, as quickly as possible. I ought to be man enough to keep you out of my trouble. But—I'll come back."

She watched the bobbing taillight of the car out of sight before going on tiptoe to the cottage. When he returned, she met him at the door with a finger to her lips. She led him into a low-ceilinged, raftered room, which was faintly lit by an oil lamp which stood on a table in the centre. One end of the table was covered by a checked tablecloth, on which stood a plate of cold ham, bread and butter, cheese, a glass and a jug of milk.

When he had finished the food, the girl led him silently to a narrow passage between living-room and kitchen. She put blankets and a pillow over his arm and pointed to a ladder which led to a square opening in the ceiling.

"You'll find an old mattress up there in the attic," she explained. "I think you'll be fairly comfortable for the night."

Lying on the mattress, staring up at the stars though the tiny skylight window of the attic, the convict dropped off to sleep almost at once.

He awoke to find the morning sun streaming in through the skylight above his head. As he lay watching a spider which dangled from one of the rafters, he heard voices; the gruff voices of men, and the high, clear voice of Sam Jarvis's granddaughter.

"Seen anything of a stranger, miss?" one of the male voices asked.

"What sort of stranger?" he heard the girl reply.

"A pretty odd sort, miss. We're looking for an escaped convict."

"You're from Greyhurst, aren't you?" she responded. "That's almost nine miles away, isn't it? You're surely looking rather far afield for your man."

"A car was stolen from a house near the prison about the time of the escape," the warder replied. "We believe he took it to make his getaway."

"In that case, I should look for him a hundred miles from here," said the girl calmly. "If I were an escaped convict and had a car at my disposal, I shouldn't stop to pick daisies until I'd put the breadth of England between me and Greyhurst!"

"You're right, miss, neither should I!" laughed the man. "Well, I guess we'll get along. Good-morning, miss."

The convict could have shouted with relief as he heard heavy footsteps walking away from the cottage. In a few minutes he heard someone rapping with a stick on one of the lower rungs of the ladder. Descending, he found the girl waiting in the passage with a jug of hot water in her hand.

"Go in there," she said, nodding towards the living-room. "I've put out towels and shaving things and some clothes which may fit you. Grandfather isn't up yet. He can only rise for an hour or so in the middle of the day."

When he was dressed, he went into the kitchen and submitted himself for approval.

"Splendid!" she said. "They fit you beautifully. I thought they would. They were my brother's, and he was pretty much your build."

"Your brother is Charles Jarvis? Isn't he a driver for the National Transport Company?"

"He was. He was killed in a smash over a year ago. Burned to death at the wheel. That's why grandfather is so much in earnest about this invention."

The convict ate his breakfast in silence, stealing an occasional glance at the girl, who moved briskly about the kitchen in the execution of her household tasks. When he had finished, she brought a pile of books.

"I'm afraid you must hide in the attic most of the day, but perhaps you can find something among these which will help to pass the time."

As he bent over the books, a thin, piping voice from the next room called: "Mary!"

"I'm coming Grandfather," she cried.

"Who's in there with you?" asked Jarvis hoarsely.

The convict walked past the girl, opened the door of the room from which the voice had come and went in. Mary Jarvis followed at his heels.

Sam Jarvis stared. "It's—it's Mr. Grey!"

Stephen Grey nodded and for a moment their eyes met.

At last, Sam Jarvis put out a wrinkled hand. "Welcome back, sir," he said simply. "I'm glad to see you."

A tear glistened in Stephen Grey's eyes. He took the old

man's hand and wrung it warmly. "I ought to tell you," he said, drawing back a little, "that I haven't been pardoned or released. I escaped last night and ran into your granddaughter on the Great West Road. I was escaping in a stolen car—"

"I had to help him," said Mary eagerly. "You see that, Grandfather, don't you? I simply had to help him."

"I wouldn't have wanted you to do less, my dear." He turned to Grey. "I never thought ye were guilty of the crime they sent you to prison for."

"I was innocent," said Stephen sincerely. "I swear it."

"That's enough for me, sir. We'll hide ye here for a few days until it's safe for ye to make a break for another part of the country."

Mary went forward and put her arms about his. "You're a dear, grandfather," she said. "I knew you'd understand."

"This little girl has been a jewel to her grandfather," he said. "Soon she's going to have her reward. A few more months, Mr. Grey, and she'll live like a lady."

He patted Mary's shoulder. "Bring me the box, my child," he said.

Mary rose and crossed the room to a tallboy that stood in a corner. She lifted down a black japanned deedbox which stood on top of it and carried it back to the bed. Her grandfather opened it and spread a pile of papers on the counterpane. One of them, a blueprint, he flattened out with an air of pride.

"Take a look at this, Mr. Grey, sir—the invention that's going to put my little girl on clover for the rest of her life. I've slaved and sweated blood over it, but it's finished—and it's all for her!"

Stephen bent over the plans and examined them with interest.

"The greatest danger in a motorcar collision," said Jarvis eagerly, "is fire. With my invention, the fire danger is reduced to a minimum."

He explained the principal of his device, which was an automatic control of applying vacuum-principal brakes, switching off the ignition, and stopping the flow of petrol from tank to carburettor. The driver could apply it in the event of an imminent collision, or if the crash happened before the driver had time to touch the control, the force of impact would automatically apply the device.

"Have you applied for a patent?" Stephen asked.

"Not yet. I've only recently completed my model," Jarvis replied. "I want one of the big bus-building companies to take it up. The National would be ideal—it's the largest private enterprise on the road, but I don't trust Marcus farther than I can throw a piano. If I let him have the plans, I'd never see them again."

"I should approach the directors," said Stephen.

"Now you're talking! I did write to Sir John Mills, the managing director, but I believe Marcus intercepted the letter. At all events, it was Marcus who replied. I'll write again, though."

The old man stretched himself with a yawn.

"I'm sleepy! This is a bit early for me to wake up. I'm going back to sleep. And you, sir, you'd better lie low. We don't want anyone comin' to the door and seeing you and giving the show away."

Stephen climbed the ladder to the attic again, with a couple of books under his arm, and lay on the mattress, where the sunshine fell on the open page. About eleven o'clock he heard a sound which shattered the hush of the slumbering country lane. A car was approaching the cottage. Stephen slipped to the skylight window and peered down the sloping roof. A long, yellow two-seater was drawn up outside the garden gate. In it sat a large, burly man, dressed in a smart grey tweed suit, a salmon pink tie, a shade loud in colour, and brown shoes. His features were gross and puffy, and his eyes were almost hidden by the rolls of flesh which surrounded them. A strip of sticking-plaster decorated his forehead.

At the sound of his approach, Mary Jarvis came out of the cottage, leaving the door wide open behind her. In spite of the look of distaste she gave him, he raised his hat and smirked with oily politeness.

"Good-morning, Mary."

"I don't want to speak to you, Mr. Jarvis. Please go away at once."

"Mary you're being utterly brutal. I'm sorry about last night's affair. I'm ready to go down on my hands and knees in the dust and apologise to you. You can't imagine how disappointed I was when you didn't turn up at the office this morning. You don't understand me, Mary. You've got an idea into your head— Lord knows how—that I'm your enemy. The truth is that I'm desperately anxious to be your friend. Your grandfather's invention, for instance; with my influence, I could help you to put it on the market, and make a fortune out of it."

"I daresay you could—for yourself," retorted Mary coldly.

"That's unfair!" he protested. "If you'd try to understand—"

"Mr. Marcus!" Mary flashed. "I only wish you to leave me strictly alone, if you please."

"Very well," he snapped harshly. "I was going to allow you to keep your job, in spite of what happened last night—I might even have raised your salary—but now you're sacked. Sacked do you understand?"

"Your mistake, Mr. Marcus!" she said sweetly. "I've left!"

With an angry exclamation, Aubrey Marcus took a threatening step forward, then suddenly halted in his tracks, his eyes staring over her shoulder with an expression of horrified amazement.

"Grey!" he gasped.

Stephen Grey was standing in the grim passage just inside the door. He took a step forward, and the sunlight revealed his face, grim and haggard and terrifying, set in an expression of bitter hatred.

"You don't look pleased to see me," he said. "Although we were once such friends, and we haven't met for two years."

Marcus moistened his dry lips nervously. "You know we were, old chap."

"Even when I was sent to prison, you still believed in me, didn't you?" Stephen Grey went on remorselessly. "You wrote me a letter to that effect. I still have that—amusing epistle!"

"I—I never believed you were guilty."

"No, you knew I was innocent! No one knew it better than you! In prison I learned to value your friendship at its true worth. Thirty pieces of silver!... There isn't a coin of low enough value to buy your loyalty!"

The other man's forehead was bathed in perspiration and his face was livid with fear. He began to back away slowly, his eyes still focussed on Stephen's face. The convict advanced step by step until they were facing each other in the lane outside the cottage, and Marcus had his back to the door of his car, with one arm behind him. Suddenly the arm came up, and he was holding a large spanner. Clenching his teeth, he hurled it with terrific force at the convict.

Stephen ducked, and the spanner barely grazed his temple. He sprang forward and grappled with Marcus. Prison food and rigorous living had reduced Stephen to little more than a mere skeleton, while Marcus, if overweight, was in excellent health. Breaking loose, Marcus swung a vicious blow to the pit of Stephen's stomach. Stephen doubled up in agony; his face contorted with pain. Marcus followed up his advantage with a punch to the jaw and another to the side of the head which made Stephen rock on his feet. Dazed, he stumbled forward, his arms reaching out blindly. In trying to shake himself free, Marcus tripped and fell, dragging Stephen down on top of him. With a quick twist, Marcus manoeuvred himself on top. His fingers fastened on Stephen's throat. His fingers squeezed relentlessly, until they seemed to be cutting into Stephen's neck. Stephen struggled and kicked, but the fingers only tightened like the jaws of a steel trap. He was losing consciousness when a wild thrust of his knee found its target in the pit of Marcus's stomach. Summoning his last reserves of strength, Stephen heaved him off and lay panting for breath.

Marcus staggered to his feet and wavered for a moment above his opponent. He swung a kick at Stephen's head, but Stephen sprawled back out of reach and was on his feet before his enemy could collect himself to aim another blow. Stumbling forward, Stephen shot over a left hook to the chin and a right jab to the stomach, dodging out of the way as Marcus's arms swung wildly. He was in again in a flash and delivered a punch to his enemy's nose which brought blood in a gushing stream. While Marcus swayed, he followed up his advantage with a straight left to the point of the jaw. Marcus tottered and his arms dropped helplessly to his sides. With a low moan, he toppled forward on his face.

Mary clutched Stephen's arm and shook it to bring him to his senses. "You've got to get away, do you hear?" she said urgently. "When Marcus comes to, he'll tell the police that you were here. Your only chance is to go at once. Do you understand? Take to the moors," she urged. "At dark, work your way back to the place where you hid the car. If I can, I'll be there with food, some money, and a change of clothing. Hurry! Please! Please!"

In a little while Marcus stirred feebly and opened his eyes. He winced at the glare of the sun on his dazed eyeballs. With a muttered curse he sat up and blinked about him.

Sam Jarvis approached with a cudgel in his hand. "Get away from here!" he said fiercely. "Get into that car of yours and go, before I crack your ugly skull!"

"I'll go," Marcus retorted angrily. "But I'll be back—and I'll bring the police with me! Your convict friend will be behind bars where he belongs before nightfall."

He walked towards the yellow two-seater. Mary ran after him and caught his arm.

"You know he's innocent," she declared pleadingly. "Don't send him back to that awful place. Let him have his chance of escape."

"Here's a chance to show what your friendship for Grey is worth," he said, turning towards Mary and her grandfather. "I'll make a bargain with you; my silence—for the plans of the invention."

"Let him have it, Grandfather," Mary pleaded. "It's the only way we can save Stephen. I love him, Grandfather! I love him! I can't let him go back to prison! I just can't!"

The old man put a shaking arm about Mary's slender shoulders, and faced Marcus with eyes that blazed contempt.

"You give your word you won't betray him if I turn over my plans to you?"

Marcus nodded silently.

Jarvis went into the cottage, walking slowly as though every step wracked him with pain. He returned shortly and handed the black japanned deedbox to Marcus. "And now—clear out!" he snapped in a thin, harsh voice.

Marcus raised the lid and saw that the box contained the paper he wanted. With a smile of triumph, he walked towards his car. As he did so, running footsteps sounded on the rugged surface of the lane. Stephen came into sight, shouting something as he approached. Marcus dived to the driving seat and jabbed his foot at the self-starter. The engine sprang to life with a roar, and the yellow two-seater moved off up the lane, gaining speed rapidly. Marcus turned a frightened face as the car negotiated the first curve and looked back to see how far behind he had left his enemy. As he did the front nearside wheel struck a pothole and the steering wheel was wrenched from his grasp.

The car swerved and ploughed through a hedge; struck a gnarled old oak in the field beyond and overturned. Marcus was projected through the windscreen and sprawled in an ungainly heap in a welter of broken glass and splintered wood beside the damaged car.

Stephen and Mary hurried to the spot and found that he was badly cut about the head and shoulders and losing blood rapidly. It was obvious that he must be rushed to hospital at once if his life was to be saved.

Grey turned to the girl, his face grim and set. "Do what you can for him," he said quietly. "I'll run back to where I left the car last night and get it. I shan't be long."

"Stephen, you can't!" she pleaded. "It means prison if you do."

"It's a question of his life or my liberty," he replied grimly. "There isn't any choice."

Without another word, he hurried down the lane, leaving Mary looking after him with stark misery in her eyes. Within minutes he was back, driving the high-powered touring car in which he had made his escape the night before. As he hoisted his enemy into the back seat, Mary put a hand on his arm.

"Stephen—"

"What would you think of me if I escaped and left him to bleed to death?" he demanded.

As the car hurtled up the lane, Mary sat beside him, her eyes fixed with a vacant stare on the road ahead. "Stephen," she said in a small voice. "When—when you come—out—I'll be waiting—if you want me…"

A mile along the Great West Road they were halted by a policeman who stood in the centre of the road with his hand raised.

Stephen drew up and leaned out of the car. "I'm the man you want," he said quietly. "But there's an injured man in the car who'll bleed to death if he isn't taken to the hospital at once. Get in and come with us; I won't attempt to escape."

When they arrived at the hospital in Hurstleigh, the stolen car was leading a procession consisting of three police patrol cars and four motorcycles.

Stephen stepped out and walked to the rear of the car to meet the group of uniformed men who were hurrying toward him.

"I'm ready," he said simply.

Sitting on the hard wooden chair in his cell, Stephen looked up hopelessly at the tiny patch of blue, scored with iron bars, which was revealed by the narrow window, several feet above his head. The grim stone walls had closed in on him again and the hopelessness of his plight was intensified by his love for Mary Jarvis.

He had reached the zero peak of despair when a key grated in the lock, the heavy door swung open, and a warder appeared on the threshold.

"You're wanted," he said. "Come along."

In a daze, Stephen allowed himself to be conducted to the Governor's office. There were two men awaiting him there—the Governor of the prison and Sir John Mills, Managing Director of the National Transport Company.

"Sit down," said the Governor. "I have good news for you, Grey. In the belief that he was dying, Marcus has confessed that he is guilty of the crime for which you were sent here. Nothing can mitigate the bitterness of the undeserved term of imprisonment you have already undergone, but at least you will spared further hardship. There are certain necessary formalities to be complied with, of course, but it is my pleasant duty to tell you that you are at this moment a free man."

"Free!" Stephen repeated. "Free!"

There was a roaring, pounding, drumming noise in his ears and the walls of the room spun about him in an ever-accelerating whirl which made chaos of his thoughts. He was dimly aware of Sir John's kindly face as the elderly company director bent over him and shook his hand warmly.

"I think, Sir John," remarked the Governor shrewdly, "that what you have to say had better wait until the first shock of surprise is over. Someone is waiting outside whom I fancy will do him more good than a pair of old fogeys!"

With smiling glances at Stephen, the two men left the room. A moment later, the door opened again, and a newcomer entered.

Stephen looked up; through the mist that was clouding his eyes he saw the sweet face of Mary Jarvis. She was smiling through tears and her arms were invitingly outstretched.

The gates of prison closed behind him, and the shining gates of Heaven opened to receive him.

THE END

ACCIDENT

Peter . . . For the love of heaven. . . Come at once!

That was the frantic telephone message which had brought Peter Ramsay in desperate haste from the House of Commons where he had just delivered his maiden speech—to his fiancée's riverside studio on a dark winter night.

Daphne opened the door to him, her face deathly pale, and silently motioned him into the large room where she did her work. A trembling hand pointed to something sinister and still which lay prone on the Persian rug before the fire; something which sprawled awkwardly, like a fifth of November guy; something which had once been a living man!

Peter knelt beside the lifeless figure and raised the head to look at the face, which was buried in the deep pile of the rug. A feeling of nausea almost overwhelmed him and he let the head drop again quickly.

It was—had been—Gerald Marlay. Peter looked numbly at his fingers which were coated with something warm and sticky—blood that had oozed from a deep gash in Marlay's white forehead!

He stumbled to his feet and stared at Daphne, who was holding to a chair for support. "Daphne! Good Lord! How did this happen?"

"Peter!" she whispered hoarsely. "Don't look at me like that! You don't think that I—"

Daphne passed a shaking hand over her damp forehead, brushing aside the thick golden hair which hung in disorder about her pale face. Peter noticed with a thrill of horror that her smock was torn at the shoulder. It was stained with smears of paint of many colours —but there was one ugly smear across the front that was not paint.

Their eyes met and Peter shook his head.

"That's the last thought that would enter my head," he replied. "But, Daphne, what happened?"

The girl's face was contorted with horror. "Half an hour ago," she stammered. "I was touching up the painting I'm working on at present. My model had gone. I was alone when the doorbell rang. I answered it and found Gerald Marlay standing on the doorstep. He forced his way in and laughed at me when I told him to go. I hadn't seen him since he was mixed up in that awful suicide; you remember, the case of the servant girl who took poison. I told him then that I never wanted to see him again."

Peter nodded. Marlay's name had been mentioned at the inquest on a pretty little servant girl who had poisoned herself some months before. The coroner had uttered some ugly truths about Gerald Marlay which had cost the philanderer the few friends he had among decent people.

"He had seen the announcement of our engagement in one of the papers," continued Daphne shakily, "and he was furious. He must have been drunk, or he wouldn't have talked the way he did. He swore you wouldn't have me—that I was engaged to him.

"There—there was a—a sort of understanding between us at one time. Peter—you knew that—but it was over long ago. I told him that I despised and loathed him and he seemed to go mad. There was a struggle and I pushed him away as hard as I could.

"He tripped on something and struck his head on the corner of the mantelpiece. He lay there on the rug—so still—Oh, Peter, so terribly still! —and I could hear every beat of my heart while I waited for him to rise.

"But he didn't rise. A red stain on the rug beside his head kept widening and widening. I knelt beside him and touched his head, and then Peter I knew."

With a convulsive shudder, the girl covered her face with her hands.

"Don't, Daphne," whispered Peter. "You mustn't give way. Be brave, dear. We've got to phone the police and tell them. The thing's happened and we've got to see it through."

He had the telephone in his hand and was giving a number when Daphne snatched it away.

"Peter, we can't do that! We can't! Think of what it would mean—the scandal! People would say terrible things about me: they'd point me out in the street. I'd never be able to hold up my head again. And you—Peter, you'd be dragged into it. It would mean the end of your Parliamentary career…the end of everything you've struggled to accomplish."

She was right. A scandal now would ruin him. And if he summoned the police a scandal was inevitable. They were all in the public eye; the dead man, because of his unsavoury reputation; Daphne, as a rising woman artist; Peter, as a young member of Parliament with brilliant prospects.

The cheaper sensational papers would revel in the story; they would dwell on all the unsavoury details, which a gullible public would accept as a fair picture of the whole.

"If there was any way to hush this thing up, Daphne, I'd do it," said Peter, struggling to speak calmly. "Not for my own sake but for yours. But—"

He made a hopeless gesture. His eyes travelled beyond her to rest on the motionless form on the rug before the fire.

"If only there was some way to dispose of…that!" he whispered.

He paced up and down the room, revolving the whole sorry

problem in his mind. Suddenly he wheeled and looked at her with a light of hope in his eyes.

"Did anyone see him arriving?"

She shook her head. "I don't think so. There wasn't anyone about when I opened the door."

"Then there's just a chance. My car's outside. If I can get him" —he glanced distastefully at the limp form— "out to it. I'll smuggle him away somewhere. Say, Hampstead Heath. If he's found dead there, no one will ever connect his death with you or with this studio."

"But, Peter, it you were stopped—"

"I've got to risk that," he said firmly. "It's our only chance."

Daphne threw her arms about him sobbing inarticulately.

"No, I can't let you. I'd rather face the scandal. I couldn't let you risk being caught."

Peter gently disengaged the clinging arms. "The risk is very slight, Daphne," he lied. "Besides, we've got to chance it for the sake of our future happiness. We're to be married in a month. We can't let anything prevent that."

"You'll let me, go with you?" she pleaded. "You must! I can't let you do it alone."

"My car's a two-seater, Daphne," he reminded her.

He took her gently by the shoulders and pushed her towards the door. "Go outside and see if the coast is clear."

With a despairing look at her lover, Daphne went. When she returned, the body of Gerald Marlay was sprawled limply across Peter's shoulders.

"Clear?" muttered Peter.

She nodded, unable to speak.

Peter stumbled through the open door with his terrible burden and staggered with it to his car. Daphne followed and saw the body placed in a sitting position in the wide driving seat and propped up with cushions. Peter turned and motioned her away.

"Go inside, Daphne," he commanded.

"But, Peter—"

"Go inside!"

She obeyed him without another word.

With a feeling of revulsion, Peter tucked the dead man's collar up about his chin and drew his hat down over his eyes—and over the ugly wound in his forehead. He climbed in behind the steering wheel and pressed the self-starter. The car moved off into the night.

The drive through London with the dead body of Gerald Marlay sitting upright beside him was a nightmare to Peter Ramsay. He imagined the awful things which might happen; the body sinking sideways as the side door swung open (it was never very secure) and falling into the road; the horrified crowd that would collect; the inevitable policeman followed by his own certain arrest.

He imagined that the driver of every car that passed him was looking back, realising his awful secret. Momentarily he expected to be stopped by an inquisitive policeman.

The lighted windows of the shops…the street lamps, the oblong splashes of light from tramcars and buses…light seemed to be coming from everywhere, reaching its long fingers into his car, revealing the grim passenger who rode by his side…Surely the most casual passer-by could see that the man who rode by his side was dead!

In the end it was his own overwrought nerves which proved his undoing.

At a street corner, a hundred yards ahead of his car, a police-man suddenly stepped into the middle of the road. He put up a white-gloved hand, a signal to Peter to stop. Common-sense should have told Peter that the policeman was merely holding him up to let another car cross the intersecting thoroughfare. But common-sense deserted him. In a moment of panic, he trod hard on the accelerator. The car leapt forward. Too late he realised his mistake.

The high dark shape of a removal van lumbered across his path. Peter stood on the brakes but the effort was useless. His last conscious thought was that now the whole unsavoury mess would be exposed, then oblivion overwhelmed him as giant fingers plucked him from his seat and hurled him with stunning force against the windscreen.

*

The sickly odour of chloroform filled the little white room in which he regained consciousness. He was lying on a small iron cot, and his whole body seemed to be swathed in bandages. His eyes looked out of a head that was bound up like the head of a mummy.

The face of a woman, blurred and vague, swam into his vision. As his sight became clearer, he saw that she was clad in the prim uniform of a nurse. "How do you feel, sir?" she asked.

"Quite well," he croaked.

"That's fine! You aren't badly hurt, only some bruises and a few minor cuts. There's a lady waiting to see you Shall I show her in?"

"Please," he mumbled.

She opened the door and Daphne entered the room.

The sight of his fiancée brought memory in a flood. He had failed her, he realised. Probably by now an ugly tissue of lies was in all the papers, lies that would damn them both forever.

The nurse bent over him. Above her bead he saw Daphne putting a finger to her lips. 'Don't talk!' Her eyes warned him. 'Don't talk!'

"I'll leave you together for a few minutes," said the nurse. "But he mustn't be worried, Miss."

As the nurse left the room, Daphne knelt beside his bed. She held a newspaper clipping in front of his eyes.

He read the headlines over and over, scarcely comprehending their import.

M.P. HURT IN MOTOR SMASH

PASSENGER KILLED OUTRIGHT

"Don't you understand, Peter?" whispered Daphne, "Marlay's body was thrown out of the car at the time of the accident. No one suspected that he was already dead. They think he was killed in the collision!"

Peter closed his eyes, too relieved for words. They were safe! Scandal could not touch them now!

The nurse looked into the room again. "A policeman wishes to see you, sir," she said.

A policeman! Daphne and Peter looked at each other anxiously.

"Show. him in," replied Peter quietly.

The man in blue came into the room. He stood at the foot of Peter's bed, bareheaded, his fingers toying with the strap of his helmet.

"You want to see me?" whispered Peter hoarsely.

"Yes, sir. I am the constable who took charge at the time of your accident."

The policeman glanced over his shoulder at the door which had closed on the nurse, and then at Daphne.

"Your young lady, sir?"

"Yes. What is it?"

"About the man who was in the car with you, sir." The policeman's tone was peculiar and his eyes met Peter's searchingly. "I want to know how he died."

There was a moment of stunned silence.

"Why, of course—" Peter licked his lips. "—he—he was killed in the smash—"

"No, sir, he wasn't. I examined him shortly after it happened and there was only one wound on him—a deep gash in his forehead. And his hat, sir, was jammed down over that wound."

The colour drained out of Daphne's cheeks and she uttered a choking cry. She threw her arms about Peter, as though to protect him from the policeman's accusing eyes.

"Suppose you tell me how that man died?" said the constable quietly, still looking steadily at Peter.

In halting, stumbling sentences, Peter told the truth. The policeman listened gravely; his face utterly expressionless.

"I see," he said, when the narrative was ended. "Then it was an accident. I hoped it was something of the sort, for I didn't want to be forced to take action. You see, sir, I removed Mr. Marlay's hat before my mate saw the body. Even then, he half suspected the truth. He pointed out that the corpse was colder than it should have been and that it hadn't bled much.

"But my mate won't cause any trouble, sir. You see, I told him that just before the crash I had seen the man who was killed putting out his hand to signal which way the car was going. Well, a dead man couldn't do that, sir. could he? So, my mate is satisfied. And now that you've explained how Marlay died, I'm satisfied too.

"No one is likely to shed any tears about Mr. Gerald Marlay being killed in a motor accident. Some people are more likely to thank heaven he's dead. He made a lot of trouble while he was alive—I'll see he doesn't make any for you now that he's dead. There was a girl...you may remember the case; she took poison..."

He put on his helmet and adjusted the chin strap carefully.

"That girl was my sister," he said quietly. "Well, I think that's all, sir."

The door closed behind him and Daphne and Peter were left alone together.

THE END

OUT OF THE FOG

T he bottle was empty. Even by turning it upside down above the cracked glass, Staines failed to coax a single drop from its transparent black interior. He said 'Damn!' and dropped it with a clatter among the empties that crowded the camouflaged orange-box which served as a larder.

Staines needed a drink. His hands shook and there was a hunted look in his watery blue eyes. But his pockets were as empty as the bottle and of all the scores of men he knew in London, not one would invite him up to the polished bar and say: 'Well, old boy, what'll you have?' if he ventured into one of the cosy pubs up west which had once been his nightly haunts.

He glanced about him at the cracked plaster, the sloping ceiling, the torn wallpaper, and threadbare carpet of the drab room in which he had lived for months. The atmosphere was steeped in unsavoury odours. The frying-pan, which stood on the grease-spattered gas-ring, contained a half-cooked sausage lying in a bed of congealed fat, some slices of potato, and a shrivelled strip of bacon. Suddenly he could bear the room no longer. Snatching up a battered felt hat he crushed it on and went out.

It was early evening. The streets were shrouded in a grey blanket of fog through which moved dim shapes that hugged the walls. Vehicles crept past, their lights appearing through the gloom like dull, yellow eyes. Street lamps were invisible until he was within a few feet of them, when a pale-yellow glow overhead betrayed their presence.

The first breath Staines took into his lungs wracked his whole body with choking coughs and the handkerchief he put to his lips came away stained with red. When he was able to walk again, he turned up his jacket collar and plodded along doggedly.

The fog hung motionless, impenetrable, along the embankment, where his feet wandered with him. Beyond the parapet he could faintly see an oily swirl that was the Thames and hear the mournful hooting of the sluggish river traffic, but above the black water and above the wide embankment, the atmosphere was packed with fog as thick as cottonwool. The air tasted like singed fur and rasped through his raw lungs, shaking his body with another spasm of coughing. He held on to the parapet for support and spat the warm red flow that came into his mouth into the oily depths below.

As he straightened up someone blundered into him.

"Sorry to trouble you," said a pleasant voice, "but I've lost my way. Can you give me any idea how to get to Radley Gardens?"

The squarish outline of a greatcoat beneath the pale blur of the other's face was all that the fog rendered visible of the speaker.

"You're within a few hundred yards of Radley Gardens," replied Staines, who boasted he could find his way blindfolded about London.

"That's what I thought, but I hardly know the neighbourhood and in this fog it's all I can do to put one foot in front of the other!"

"I'll show you the way."

"That's very good of you, if it isn't taking you out of your way?"

"I wasn't going anywhere."

They moved off together. Staines began to feel happier about the drink for which his nerves were clamouring. Surely when they reached Radley Gardens the stranger couldn't do less than offer him a bracer—on a night like this!

As they walked along slowly the stranger talked cheerfully,

as some men do when they have unexpected companionship. He chatted about the weather, about the way business was looking up—for him at least—and about the extra special surprise he was taking home for his wife.

"A pearl necklace," he confided. "Not a fabulously expensive one—I can't aim as high as that yet—but a pretty little string that cost me sixty pounds. Madge will be crazy with delight—after she's finished scolding me for extravagance! But she deserves it. Our first few years of married life were a bit of a struggle, but Madge never crumbled. Lord knows how she made ends meet, but somehow, she did it. I'm taking her to a fancy-dress ball tonight, our first flutter for Lord knows how long. Thank goodness she'll have things a lot easier in future. Business is getting better every day and I can afford to do things properly. You don't know how glad I am for the sake of the kids—we've got two bonny youngsters, a girl and a boy—and for Madge. She's the best wife a man ever had!"

"Lucky devil!" grunted Staines. "I picked a dud!"

The other shot him a brief glance, then lapsed into silence.

"I had a kid once, too," Staines added. "But the poor little devil died. Her mother neglected her. I came from—er—a business trip to find my little girl buried and my wife skipped."

"It must have been a terrible blow," murmured the other.

"This is Radley Gardens," said Staines. "What's your number?"

The other groped his way up the front steps of one of the houses and struck a match. "This is my house. I'm very much obliged to you, Mr. —er—"

"Staines is the name."

"Mine's Nixon. It's a cold night, Mr. Staines, won't you come in and have a drink? Usually, we haven't anything in the house— my wife doesn't like it—but my brother is stopping with us at the moment and I can offer you a drop of really good whisky."

"That's very good of you."

Nixon bent down and inserted his key in the lock. The door swung open and the front steps were bathed in soft, golden light. There was a scamper of slippered feet, two shrill voices shouting 'Daddy!' and two rosy-cheeked children were all over Nixon.

Gerald Staines stood on the threshold staring at a quiet, smiling woman, who stood in the shadows at the rear of the hall. Not tall, not short, scarcely pretty, but with an expression that was almost beautiful on her face as she watched the broad-shouldered man and his golden-haired children.

Nixon moved toward her—dragging with him the children who were clinging playfully to his arms—and put his arms about her.

"You nearly lost me tonight sweetheart, but fortunately I met this gentleman, who guided me home through the fog." He turned, with an apologetic exclamation. "Do come in, Mr. Staines. Madge, this is Mr. Staines, who brought me home. I've asked him in for a drink."

As Staines came into the light, the quiet woman lost her smile and her eyes widened with horror. Nixon, who was shutting the front door, did not notice her agitation, nor hear the single word that her pale lips. whispered. The word: "Gerald!"

"I am charmed to meet you, Mrs. —er—Nixon," said Staines with a little bow. "Only too pleased to have been of some slight service to your—er—husband."

She did not speak. It seemed as though she had suddenly frozen into a woman of ice. She stood there looking at him. Her face the pale white of the moon mirrored in the still waters of a lake.

"Come in here, old man," said Nixon heartily, throwing open a door. "I shan't be a minute throwing off my coat and finding a corkscrew."

Gerald Staines entered the cosy room with its gay curtains, bright blue carpet, and cheerful fire. He stood with his back to the fire eyeing the comfortable surroundings appraisingly.

Nixon's wife came into the room and closed the door. She stood with her back to it, her arms outstretched, as though to protect her children and their father from the haggard man who watched her sardonically from the hearth.

"How did you find me?" she whispered hoarsely.

"You seem to have done rather well for yourself, Margaret."

"How did you find me?"

"I didn't. Your—er—husband brought me here. We met, as he explained, in the fog, and I simply volunteered to help a stranger to find his bearings. So, you left me for that big, grinning baboon!"

"That isn't true!" she flashed. "I hadn't met him when I left you!"

"But you've married him since. Bigamy, my dear Margaret, is a serious offence!"

"I thought you were dead."

"That's what they all say, my dear girl!"

"But it's true! Six years ago, I met one of your old friends and he told me that you'd fallen from a hotel window in New York and died in hospital. He even showed me clippings about the accident."

"Oh, the accident happened, all right. Considering the awful stuff they sell over there as gin, it's a wonder more people don't fall out of their hotel windows. But I didn't die. Sorry to disappoint you!"

Margaret made a weary gesture. "God forgive me! It is the greatest disappointment I have ever had!"

His eyes darkened and a savage scowl distorted his haggard face, but he controlled himself by an apparent effort.

"Got a cigarette?"

Margaret motioned to a silver box on the mantelpiece. He selected a cigarette and lit it.

"Death to me, these things are," he said, coughing at the first whiff of smoke. "But I've got to have something to steady my nerves."

At the questioning look in her eyes he laughed and drew out his handkerchief, shaking it open to reveal the crimson stain.

"Prison started it, and after I came out to find you gone and the kid dead, booze and this filthy climate finished the job. Now one lung's gone and the other isn't much better. I tried the States, but I couldn't make a living in Colorado, where the climate was healthy, and I was coughing up my lungs in New York, where the pickings were plentiful. So, I came home."

He glanced at the clock. "That husband of yours is taking his time about finding a corkscrew. In our little home, before I went to gaol, a blind man could have turned up half-a-dozen of 'em in as many seconds!"

Margaret closed her eyes as though to shut out an ugly picture. "Don't remind me of it! My life with you was one long misery. I stood it because I was your wife and because of poor little Betty. Even when you were sent to prison for embezzling money you had spent on drink—and other things—I waited for you. But when my little girl died, I shut you out of my life. You killed her! A small part of the money you squandered would have saved her life. I went away and started life afresh under a new name. Later I met Phil—a real man—a clean man. When I heard you were dead, I married him. We've been happy."

Her eyes, as she spoke of Philip Nixon, were soft and lustrous.

"Glad to hear it," murmured Staines dryly. "But remember, my dear Margaret, we have to pay for happiness. That term in gaol finished me with rich Aunt Jane. When she died all she left me was a wretched two hundred a year for life. Some people could live on that. I can't—not at the present price of whisky. At the moment I haven't a penny and my quarterly cheque isn't due for two weeks."

"If a few pounds would help—"

"No," he grinned. "A few pounds wouldn't help. The climate of Switzerland would, though—and a sufficient income to live there comfortably…I hope you understand?"

"Oh, I understand all right," said Margaret bitterly. "Blackmail."

"That's an ugly word. Let's say 'Paying for happiness.'"

"I've no money."

"Your—er—husband has."

"You mean you'll tell him?"

"I mean you can choose which of us tells him."

"He'll throw you into the street!"

"Oh, no he won't. There are the, children, you see. He wouldn't like them to be branded with the stigma of illegitimacy."

Her face flamed as though he had struck her a stinging blow.

The door opened and Nixon entered the room bearing a tray on which stood a decanter of whisky, a soda syphon, and two glasses.

"Sorry to keep you waiting, Mr. Staines."

Nixon's back was turned toward the white-faced woman and the scowling man, as he set the tray on the sideboard.

Gerald Staines listened with satisfaction to the gurgling of liquid and the hissing of soda-water.

Suddenly Nixon wheeled with the glass of amber liquid in his hand and walked across the room to where Staines was sitting. "Your drink, Mr. Staines," he said—and threw the contents full is the other's face!

For a moment the blackmailer was so taken aback that he could only gape at the empty glass in the other's hand.

"I happened to find the corkscrew some minutes ago," said Nixon icily. "I've been listening to all you've said—you swine!"

Gerald Staines rose, his face twisted with fury, his watery blue eyes blazing hatred. "Rough stuff won't get you anywhere," he snarled. "You've got to treat me decently, and you'd better realise that right away—that is, if your precious 'Madge' and the kids mean anything to you!"

Philip Nixon turned to the woman who had been the best wife in the world to him for five years. "Sit down, my dear," he said gently. "I'll settle this."

"Philip—" her voice broke.

"Don't worry. Everything is going to be all right. Well, Staines, what do you suggest?"

"That's more like it! Let's say four hundred a year. That's cheap, really for the best wife in the world!"

"For four hundred a year you'll leave us in peace?"

"That's it!"

"And if I refuse?"

"I'll broadcast my story!"

The door was slightly ajar. Philip crossed the room and threw it open. "Come in, constable."

A policeman entered the room with a notebook in his hand.

"Got it all down?" asked Nixon.

"Word for word, sir!"

Gerald Staines stood up and backed away, trembling in every limb. "You wouldn't dare give me in charge!" he whispered hoarsely. "Think what it would mean…I'd see the whole story came out—your children would be branded as—"

"I've considered all that—and the reverse side of the picture! If I yielded to your demands, I'd never have another moment's peace from you as long as you lived. There's your man, officer!"

Gerald Staines had been in prison and he knew the hell that

prison can be. What is more, to return there meant death! With a wild cry, he dodged the approaching man in blue and darted out of the room. The front door crashed back on its hinges as he plunged down the steps of the house into the street.

Two malignant yellow eyes loomed up out of the fog, and then something hit him in the back with terrific force and he knew no more.

The constable who had followed him came back into the room where Margaret and Philip were standing in horrified silence.

"He's dead," he said simply. "A car struck him and went over his body. I didn't show myself, of course, but I could hear the driver and another man talking in the fog. They think he blundered off the pavement. They haven't the slightest idea he came from this house—the lighted doorway wasn't visible from the street."

He removed his helmet and mopped his perspiring brow.

"Why!" exclaimed Margaret, "It's Harry!"

Philip Nixon put a hand on his brother's shoulder. "Yes. when I went for the corkscrew, I found Harry in his room dressing for the fancy-dress ball. Later, when I heard Staines threatening you, the police uniform gave me an idea. I thought we might be able to frighten him into leaving us alone."

Margaret sank down upon the couch and buried her face in her hands. Philip knelt beside her stroking her hair gently.

"Madge, when we were married all we could afford was a registrar's office wedding. Do you remember we promised each other that when business improved, we'd go through the ceremony again in church? That's what we're going to do, sweetheart, just as soon as it can be arranged...a Church wedding, bridesmaids, cake, and all..."

From the kitchen they heard the happy shouts of children besieging the flurried cook for goodies.

THE END

www.ingramcontent.com/pod-product-compliance
Lightning Source LLC
Chambersburg PA
CBHW071138180726
48291CB00007B/2230